# ISLAND SHIFTERS

## BOOK TWO

## AN OATH OF THE MAGE

### VALERIE ZAMBITO

ISBN-13: 978-0-615-59975-5
Cover Art by Lou Harper
http://louharper.com

#### OTHER TITLES BY VALERIE ZAMBITO

ISLAND SHIFTERS - AN OATH OF THE BLOOD (BOOK 1)
ISLAND SHIFTERS - AN OATH OF THE MAGE (BOOK 2)
ISLAND SHIFTERS - AN OATH OF THE CHILDREN (BOOK 3)
ISLAND SHIFTERS - AN OATH OF THE KINGS (BOOK 4)
ANGELS OF THE KNIGHTS - FALLON (BOOK 1)
ANGELS OF THE KNIGHTS - BLANE (BOOK 2)
ANGELS OF THE KNIGHTS - NIKKI (BOOK 3)

#### ISLAND SHIFTERS SERIES REVIEWS

*"FROM THIS BOOK'S FIRST PARAGRAPH, I WAS HOOKED UNTIL THE VERY END."*

*"I HAVE TO SAY IT HAS BEEN A VERY LONG TIME SINCE I READ A BOOK AND GOT GOOSE BUMPS!"*

*"I WAS SWEPT AWAY BY THE COLORFUL CHARACTERS AND BRISK PACING OF THE BOOK, ALMOST COMPELLED TO KEEP TURNING THE PAGES AS ZAMBITO'S ACTION-PACKED STORY CARRIED ME ALONG."*

*"WITHOUT A DOUBT, THIS IS, BY FAR, THE BEST BOOK I HAVE EVER READ IN MY ENTIRE LIFE. AS SOMEONE WHO HAS READ OVER 780 BOOKS IN THE LAST 20 YEARS, THAT'S SAYING SOMETHING."*

# MAP OF MASSA

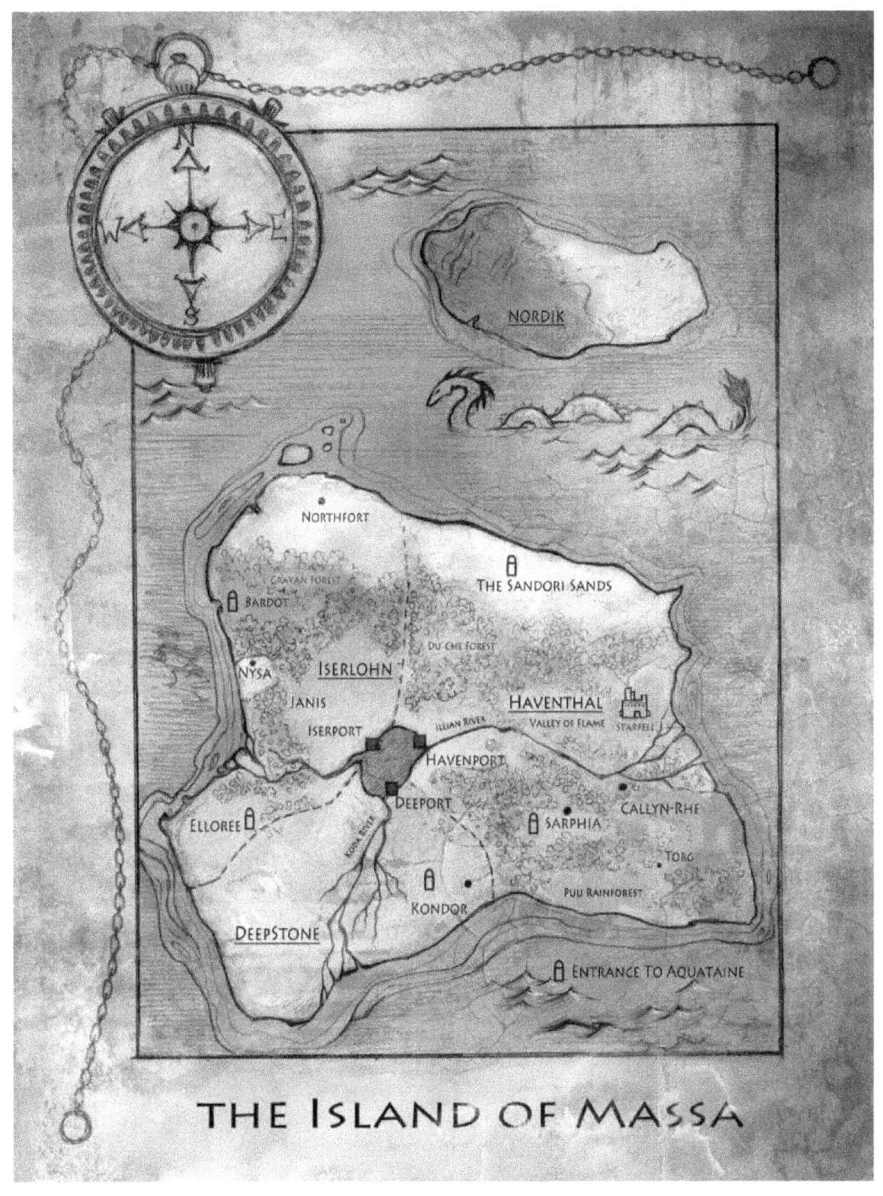

# TABLE OF CONTENTS

# PROLOGUE

The hooded figure stood well back in the shadows of a partially collapsed merchant's building ignoring the piteous screams and shouts that drifted to his place of concealment. Broad shouldered and muscular though he was, Iserport was not the place to be caught out alone these days. There were only two types of people who roamed the dark in Iserport.

Predator and prey.

Gangs and rioters littered the city streets hoping to relieve victims of their coin and valuables or worse, to use as a torturous form of mob entertainment. No, Iserport was definitely not safe and if he had a choice, he wouldn't be here. But, he didn't. Events long in the planning stages were coming to a head, and a mistake now could very well prove fatal to him and his co-conspirators. This meeting of the faction was critical to finalizing the last minute details of their assignments.

"Master Red?"

The voice caused him to gasp audibly. *Demon's hell,* he swore to himself. Showing any form of impotence with this group could prove as deadly as the mob in the streets.

It was Master Black.

"I'm here," he acknowledged, pushing his fury at himself aside.

"I am present as well," said a gruff voice from the dim recesses behind him.

He managed to steel his reaction this time. But, just barely.

Master Blue.

*How did both men enter without my knowledge?* At the top of his profession due to his proficiency for stealth, he was compensated to be aware of every detail concerning his surroundings at all times. So, what had he missed?  It was his nerves, he knew, that were scrambling his ability to concentrate. He needed to pull it together. Quickly.

"Follow me," commanded Master Black, and their leader picked his way carefully through the concrete rubble and debris of the vacant building. Master Black stopped in a dark corridor and held open an interior door that was on the verge of ripping off its hinges.

He ducked past into the dilapidated room and noticed the same table and four ladder-back chairs that were present when they had met on two previous occasions. Master Blue entered behind him and proceeded to light the single taper in a brass holder in the center of the table.

Taking a seat, he silently studied his companions in the flickering candlelight.

Master Black, the leader and mastermind behind their plot, was thin, but handsome, and already held a significant amount of power in Iserlohn.

A man of few words, Master Blue was several years older than Master Black but with a soldier's rugged countenance and constantly roaming eyes.

"Court is in session in ten days," began Master Black as he sat, apparently not deigning to wait for the tardy Master Orange. "Has the portrayer been well tutored?  He knows his part?"

"Yes, and he is very good," responded Master Blue, turning one of the chairs around and straddling it. "Trust me. They will believe every word he says."

"Good, his performance will remove the first card from Maximus' teetering house."

"Am I late?" questioned Master Orange as he stepped into the room. The last member of their group was the only man Master Red did not know by his real name. He had never seen him before these clandestine meetings began and knew nothing about him except that he was bald and had the strangest eyes. If the man ever blinked, he had never seen it. Master Black brought the fellow on board a few months ago, but did not elaborate regarding the reason or what he would be contributing to their plans.

Their leader grunted noncommittally to Master Orange's question and continued. "Master Blue, I trust you will ensure that the portrayer you hired does not live long after his performance?"

"I have a man in Nysa now."

Master Black nodded. "It will take at least three weeks for the army to reach Nysa. When do you plan to depart?"

"We leave at dawn tomorrow."

"Very good." Master Black swung his gaze to Master Orange. Their eyes met and in the gesture was an unmistakable acknowledgement of a silent understanding between the two that they did not share. Seemingly satisfied by the unspoken exchange with Master Orange, their leader looked his way. "Master Red, you know what you have to do." It was not a question. "Any last minute reservations? She is a woman after all."

He snorted. "None."

Master Black looked at each conspirator around the table. "Anything else?"

They all shook their heads, and Master Red watched them depart one by one.

When he was alone, he again thought of Master Orange and his lack of knowledge regarding this particular collaborator. A wise man knew that it was safer to know the motives of those you worked with. It is what kept you alive.

But, true motives could be tricky to ferret out. On the surface, the motive of the faction was to rid the island of a threat to their very existence. A royal family with the capacity to wield powerful magic was a powder keg waiting to explode, and they were all in agreement that House Everard must be eliminated at all costs.

However, he knew there were other motives just as compelling.

Master Black wanted supreme power.

Master Blue wanted money, the Crown's money.

And, his motive had always been clear. Revenge. Even more than he wanted to take his next breath, he wanted Kiernan Atlan dead.

But, what did Master Orange want?

# CHAPTER 1

## Pureblood

Five-year-old Kenley Atlan sat cross-legged on the floor of Grace Hall in her grandfather's royal palace and looked up curiously at the adults peering down at her. Her mother, glaring at her father with hands on her hips, looked angry.

"Beck, admit it, you must be mistaken. You are just seeing what you want to see. Enough of this now, Kenley needs to be seeing to her lessons with Captain…," Kenley watched her mother throw a nervous glance over her shoulder at Miss Belle who was waiting with an arched eyebrow for the remainder of her sentence, but she clamped her mouth shut without finishing. Her mother might have the upper hand with her father, but Miss Belle more often than not, had the upper hand with her mother.

Kenley brushed black curls away from her face. *This is getting interesting.*

Her father shook his head adamantly and picked up the leather ball on the floor next to her. "Kiernan, she can do it. Just watch." Squatting down in front of her, he held out the ball and said, "Kenley, darling, show Maman how we play catch."

Kenley paused, unsure. Her grandfather, King Maximus, paced anxiously by the hall doors muttering something about allowing little girls to be little girls. Uncle Airron leaned against the wall with an amused grin on his face, which he did most of the time. Uncle Rogan stood with his arms crossed at his chest and tapped his toe impatiently, which he also did most of the time. They weren't really her uncles, of course, since Airron

Falewir was an Elf and Rogan Radek a Dwarf, but she called them by the familial name all her life. Miss Belle still watched her mother intently, and Baya, her Draca Cat, lounged nearby licking her paws indifferently, ignoring the humans around her.

Then, Kenley shrugged her small shoulders and did as her father asked—the one thing that always caused him to laugh and throw her in the air until her belly tingled.

She flicked her wrist and sent the ball screaming toward his face.

The adults in the room gasped and shouted simultaneously. "An airshifter!"

She hoped that was a good thing.

****

Kiernan marched down the tapestry-hung corridor toward the suite of rooms she shared with Beck and Kenley when they were in residence at the Nysian royal palace.

"Come now, Kiernan. You knew this would happen," Beck pointed out as he easily kept pace beside her. The ever-present Royal Guard, only two since they were inside the palace walls, trailed unobserved behind them.

She shook her head of blonde wavy hair. "I know, but at five?"

"She is almost six," he reminded her. "Besides, look at her parents."

She turned her head to glare at him. *Why is he grinning so ridiculously?* Kenley was pureblood. There had never been any doubt that she would be a shifter, and a very powerful one at that, but she was just a baby yet. Most shifters didn't begin to develop their powers until their late teenage years.

Kiernan stopped in the middle of the hallway and put her arm out to stop him. "You are happy about this!"

"Of course, I am," he confessed with a chuckle and simply walked around her without pausing. She stared at him in disbelief and with a shake of her head, followed behind and caught up to him just as he reached their suite.

Her handmaid, Leah, hovered anxiously outside of the room with a handful of dresses flung over one arm.

Kiernan waved her away. "No."

"But, Your Grace! The royal seamstress spent hours making these beautiful gowns! You are to choose one for Court this morning."

"I already have more than enough perfectly suitable gowns to wear, Leah. I told the seamstress as much yesterday."

The handmaid's eyes widened in shock. "But, Your Grace, at least let me help you dress!"

"I can and will dress myself. Thank you, Leah. You may go."

"Your Grace…"

"Goodbye, Leah," interjected Beck and swiftly ushered Kiernan inside. When the door closed, he said, "I thought we were supposed to allow the servants to do their jobs."

"Normally, we do, but I have other—" She yelped when he swept her off her feet and carried her through the sitting room to their large canopied bed. Laying her down gently, he laid his large frame alongside hers and caressed her swollen belly.

"Are you finished gloating about our daughter?" she asked peevishly.

"I do not gloat, Kiernan. If you think about it calmly, you will remember that you were not much older than Kenley when you first discovered mindshifting. And, she has already bonded with Baya, so you knew it was just a matter of time."

She remembered fondly her own bond with her Draca Cat, Bajan, at the age of six. Bajan had been dead for years now, but the pain still cut like a knife whenever she thought about him. "I just worry."

"Well, try not to. It's not good for our son," he said and pressed his lips to her abdomen.

"A son, is it?"

"I told you before, I am very rarely wrong."

"So, you keep telling me," she laughed, dragging his face to hers and kissing him deeply, feeling like the luckiest woman alive. The world had changed so drastically in the last six years that sometimes she had to pinch herself to believe it was real. *Was it really just six years ago that we were confined to exile? That shifters were outlawed from living anywhere in Massa except the land of Pyraan?* The Demon War changed everything for her and Beck, and it truly was a new world. A world where magic users lived free, and Kiernan was returned to the throne for which she was born. Both paled in comparison, however, to her marriage and child. Beck and Kenley. Her husband. Her daughter. Her life.

"Hmm…let's forget about Court. We can stay right here and the nobles can fight among themselves without us," she murmured contentedly.

"If only we could. You know how much I despise the politics of Iserlohn."

She raised her eyebrows. "And, this coming from the Prince of the land?"

"Prince by marriage only."

She pursed her lips in a pout. "If you feel that strongly, maybe you should leave me and go live a quieter life elsewhere."

He grabbed her with a growl. "Over my dead body."

She laughed and wrapped her arms around him. "That is what I thought. Now, let me up. I have to get dressed." As Prince and Princess of Iserlohn, their absence would be tantamount to throwing fire on a stack of hay with the current climate surrounding her family. Before soup was served, a dozen rumors would have leaked outside of the palace doors regarding the probable reason for the missing royals.

Beck let go of her, and she stood from the bed and pulled her dress over her head and let it drop to the floor as she walked to the mahogany wardrobe. "Did Airron take Kenley to Captain…," she paused and had to stop herself from looking over her shoulder for Miss Belle. The insufferable but dear woman was opposed to Kenley learning how to handle a sword with Captain Franck, but this was one area where Kiernan would not relent. No daughter of hers was going to spend her time sipping tea and learning embroidery. Not when she should be learning how to defend herself and her realm. She glanced back at Beck and finished her sentence, "…to Captain Franck?"

Beck nodded and followed her. "Yes, she is there. Where is my black silk coat?" he asked, rummaging through the wardrobe over her head. As an earthshifter, he towered over her much smaller stature. Of course, all earthshifters exhibited an abundantly muscular physique and a powerful strength, but none alive today was as strong as her husband. "Did I leave it at home?" *Home.* Much to the King's dismay, home for them was the city of Bardot two leagues north of the city of Nysa. Beck adamantly refused to live at the palace. After a lifetime of exile, living behind walls was unimaginable to him.

Kiernan pulled out a scarlet and black silk gown, the House colors of Everard, and stepped into it. "Three coats from the left."

Beck found the coat embroidered on the collar and cuffs with King Maximus' Golden Lions and slipped it on over his broad shoulders.

Kiernan whistled appreciatively. "You look very handsome, Prince Beck."

He bowed graciously. "As do you, Princess Kiernan."

Thanking him with another kiss, she quickly ran a brush through her long hair. When she was satisfied with the result, she exited the room with her husband and turned her thoughts to the troubling rumors about this evening's council brought to her by the her personal guard, Captain Kirby Nash. It seemed that one of her father's liegemen, Lord Davad Etin, intended to make trouble of some kind. That the Lord was allowing gossip to spread freely could only have one meaning—he had considerable backing for his schemes. And, they *were* schemes. He had always been the most cunning and ambitious of the nobles, but with civil unrest brewing in the section of lands he controlled, he was becoming desperate to lay the blame at the feet of another.

*My father?* She shook her head. *Not on my watch.*

Attuned as always to her emotions, Beck gave her arm a brief squeeze. Highworld, but she was fortunate to have him.

Together, they descended to the first floor of the palace and when they arrived at the open doors of Grace Hall, she was surprised to find a line of citizens awaiting an audience with her father. For some reason, and totally against custom, he was seeing petitioners at the beginning of Court. All knelt to one knee or curtsied as they approached.

"Please rise," she commanded and, with the help of the Sabers, a path opened up for them before the doors.

Kiernan felt tense as she entered the hall and made the walk between towering black marble pillars to the front. For once, the colorful fresco of the city painted on the concave ceiling above did nothing to calm her. She would not feel at ease again until she knew exactly what Lord Davad Etin was about.

Her father, sitting on his throne atop a raised dais with three wide steps, looked resplendent in a scarlet robe with black trim, his dark eyes showing not a hint of the concern that plagued her.

The nobles occupied the spaces to the left and right of him. Lord Etin, Lord Winslow and the young Lady Conry sat to one side and Lord Hamilton, Lord Gregaros and Lady Knapp to the other. A clearer line of House loyalties could not have been made.

Kiernan and Beck took their places in the two empty seats to the immediate right of her father, and Captain Kirby Nash slid into position behind her chair and alongside her father's personal guard, Captain Darin Morel.

A man stood in front of the dais wearing a threadbare tunic and wringing his hat in his hands nervously.

"You may continue," her father told him kindly.

"It is a disgrace, my King! An honest man just cannot make a living in Iserport. There is no work! Buildings are abandoned and left in disrepair and the roads are impassable. Rioters roam freely and terrorize the folks that are left. Most of us don't even have enough food for our tables!"

An agitated murmur rippled through the crowd at the open doors of the hall.

The King's eyes, hard as obsidian, turned to Lord Etin, the overlord of Iserport. "Davad? Would you care to respond? I was under the impression that improvements had been made and legitimate business was thriving again in Iserport."

"Bah!" spit the petitioner.

Lord Etin met her father's eyes squarely. "Your Grace, I assure you—"

The man spit again. "Bah, I say. Speaking my mind is gonna cost me my head, I realize that, but it's worth the price if I can leave a better life for my wife and children!"

Lord Etin snorted out a laugh and held out his hands in question. "Your Grace, how long are you going to let this farce continue?"

Her father raised his eyebrows. "Farce? This is neither the first nor the fifth complaint I have heard of the conditions in Iserport. Sources tell me that your lands are poised for civil war. What say you, Lord Etin?"

Kiernan smiled slyly. So, her father was not so unaware after all.

The devious Lord lifted one corner of his mouth. "I planned to have this conversation at Court, Your Grace. Are you sure you wish to have it now in front of so many...witnesses?"

"I have nothing to hide," her father replied at once. "Answer the question."

Lord Etin rose from his seat and walked down the dais steps to the petitioner who was still mangling his hat. Placing a hand conspiratorially on the man's shoulder, Lord Etin turned back to the Court, but said loud enough so that the citizens waiting their turn at the hall doors could hear.

"This man is correct. Life is deplorable in Iserport. I have made countless claims to the Crown for support and my requests have all gone unheeded!"

Kiernan stood. "Lies!"

Lord Etin shook his head. "No! Not lies, Princess Kiernan, and that is why I have called this a farce. The King is very well aware of the conditions in Iserport, because I have requested aid on several occasions and he has denied me." He turned back to the petitioner and put his arm around his shoulders. "If this brave man can risk all to tell of the situation in Iserport, I can do no less!"

"Lord Etin…," Kiernan warned.

"No, Princess! Let everyone hear how the King has forsaken Iserport. How he refuses to provide succor to the people who need it most—the women and the children!"

The whispers from the crowd grew tinged with anger.

"Father!" she whispered urgently. "Do something!"

The King did not turn his gaze from the belligerent Lord as he stood from his throne and all eyes in the room turned toward him. He was not a very tall man, but the compact, muscular body exuded power. He wore his black hair shoulder length with long sideburns, and his black eyes gave the impression that they could penetrate stone. "Bring him in," he said softly to Captain Morel. The lithe Scarlet Saber moved down the stairs to a side door and a moment later escorted a young man into the hall.

She heard Lord Etin's sharp intake of breath. "What is this?" he demanded. "What are you doing here, Kenith?"

The young man's face, almost a mirror image of Lord Etin, was pale and tormented. "It is all over, Davad."

Kiernan recognized him as Davad Etin's younger brother.

Unattractive red blotches appeared on Lord Etin's face as he tried to approach Kenith.

Captain Nash came off the dais and blocked his way.

"Kenith, whatever you are about, shut your mouth and do not say another word! You do not know what you are saying!"

Kenith hung his head. "I overheard you, Davad. I know all about your plans."

"I am warning you!"

"I have already confessed all to the King." The younger Etin paused. "Even your plans to overthrow his regime."

A roar of surprise erupted from the gathered citizens and echoed throughout the room.

"Shut up!" Lord Etin screamed furiously and unsheathed his sword, lunging at Kenith. Captain Morel stepped forward and slashed his saber down, deflecting the blade and knocking it from Etin's hand before it could complete its deadly thrust. "You are my brother! What have you done?"

"I spoke the truth, Davad. I could not let you ruin Iserport any further. Nor could I allow your intended coup to succeed."

Kiernan looked over at her father's passive face, but it did not fool her. He had carefully orchestrated this event playing out, of that she was certain.

"Take him to a cell," Maximus said softly.

The other members of the Court had been silent up to this point, but the oldest of her father's vassals—close to ninety years and once a good friend—now stood. "Your Grace, I am sure there is a misunderstanding here. You cannot send a Lord to the cells."

"I can and I will, Lord Winslow," her father snapped, his feelings now etched clearly onto his features. *He is hurt.* In the recent division of power in the Court, Lord Winslow sided with Lord Etin, and her father could not understand how the levelheaded and intelligent Lord had abandoned all of his principles, and their friendship, to align himself with Davad Etin. "Unless there is more you know about this situation, Abram, that you would like to share?"

The older man's eyes were filled with remorse as he sat down again. "No, no."

"You will regret this, King Maximus!" screamed Davad Etin as the Saber Captains wrestled him toward the door. "You have no idea what I am capable of! You stand on that throne so pompous next to your filthy shifter daughter. It will not last! Your reign is done, Maximus! Mark my words!"

Kiernan felt a tremor in the floor and put a restraining hand on Beck's arm.

"Enough!" roared the King. "Get him out of my sight!" He sat and turned back to his Court. "Now, where were we? Next!"

# CHAPTER 2

## Bardot

When Beck entered the vast interior of the royal stables, he was disappointed to find his black stallion, Chasin, and Kiernan's blue roan mare, Milan, already saddled and waiting. After six years, it was still difficult for him to get used to people seeing to his every need. Was it really so hard for the servants to understand that he preferred to saddle his own horse? And, draw his own bath? And, fluff his own pillows! He was a man, for Highworld's sake, not a child.

Despite her own actions to the contrary earlier, Kiernan reminded him often that the servants were simply performing their duties and he offended them when he turned them away. Clearly, his modest upbringing in a small community had not—and could not—have prepared him for the life of a Prince. Four houses from his home city of Parsis could have fit easily in the stables where he now stood.

Fortunately, he only had to deal with the excessive cosseting when in the city of Nysa. The first decree he issued as Prince in his new home of Bardot was the abolishment of all acts of deference. Although, in truth the decree was probably not necessary—not when a good portion of Bardot's citizenry was made up of former sorceresses. Former, because once the three Kings of Massa sanctioned the use of magic, many of the sorceresses in Elloree abandoned their craft to hone their shifting abilities instead. Since shifting was innate and sorcery learned, it should not have been surprising, but Beck knew that Gemini Starr, the High Priestess of the coven, was saddened by the change. It had been her life calling for many years to care for and train female magic users in the art of witchcraft and now the need for her services was diminishing.

And, the sorceresses weren't the only magic users to call Bardot their home.

As it turned out, the land of Massa wasn't so chaste of magic after all. Since the abolishment of exile after the war, hundreds of shifters came out of hiding to seek training and more arrived every day. To accommodate the influx of magic users, Beck founded the Bardot Academy, a school similar to the one where he studied as a youth. In addition to the sorceresses, close to a thousand students of all races were now enrolled.

When Beck's parents died, he was uncertain whether he would ever feel rooted in Iserlohn like he had been in Pyraan, but his life in Bardot gave him exactly that. Nysa, on the other hand, had the opposite effect. The political maneuverings and intrigue were enough to make his head spin most days. King Maximus and Kiernan were experts in the dance, but he favored the simpler life he had carved out for himself teaching at the Academy.

Despite the spectacle of Court that morning, they were due back in Bardot that evening to travel to Kondor for Rogan's wedding to Janin Stonedge. The two Dwarves met when Janin helped Rogan escape imprisonment during the war and after all these years and two children later, Rogan finally asked her to marry him.

Beck accepted Chasin's reins from the royal groom and nodded his thanks. The sound of easy laughter drifted through the open stable doors, and he turned to see Rogan, Airron and Kirby Nash enter. The Scarlet Saber would accompany them on the ride to Bardot, but much to the Captain's discontent, his charges would be taking the waterways of Aquataine to Kondor where he could not travel. To this day, the Elders of Aquataine refused to allow any non-shifter access to their world and only magic users could open the grates. A troop of Sabers left more than a week ago on horseback to meet up with them in Kondor, but the royals would not have protection for two days while traveling underground.

Beck had to smile at Kirby's doggedness. He and Kiernan, Rogan and Airron were the most powerful shifters alive, but Kirby Nash had his duty, and by the Highworld he planned to see to it for all he was worth.

The Saber's real concern was Kiernan's temporary inability to shift. While with child, female shifters lost the ability to perform magic but regained their powers once the baby was born. Still, Kirby should know that Kiernan was a blademaster of incredible skill. She would be no easy meat for a person with ill intentions.

"Looks like we're all set! Is my horse saddled yet?" Airron asked. The Elf was smiling as usual, his violet eyes alive with vitality. He had no qualms at all of accepting the life of a royal and adapted as if he were born to it when he discovered that he was third in line to the Haventhal Crown. "We have to get fireball to his little flame before his feet get cold."

Rogan snorted. "No cold feet here, my Elven friend. Besides, Janin would douse my flame permanently if I failed to show up."

Airron barked out a laugh. "You will never find *me* in that trap."

"Maybe you just haven't met the right one yet?" Beck suggested.

"Oh, I have met several right ones, and I would like to keep it that way."

"Daddy!" Kenley ran into the stables and he caught her and tossed her into the air. With black hair like him and luminescent green eyes like her mother, she was a perfect blend of the two of them. She was also a remarkably bright and inquisitive child and the light of his world.

"Beck! You spoil her so," admonished Kiernan from the open doorway.

He smiled. "Of course, I do. Isn't that my job?"

Kiernan mumbled something incoherent while Kenley's snow white Draca Cat, Baya, slunk in and rubbed up against his legs. The same age as Kenley, the cat was still young as far as Dracas go and would not reach maturity until around ten years. By that time, Baya's head would be up to his chest. The half cat, half dragon swished her spiked tail eagerly just as anxious as he to leave the city.

Beck helped Kiernan mount Milan and then lifted Kenley into the saddle on Chasin and swung up behind her.

A nervous hush fell over the working grooms. King Maximus walked into the stables with Gemini Starr on his arm. A fierce combatant in the Demon War, the sorceress had been like a second mother to both him and Kiernan over the years and a loyal companion and advisor to Maximus. Beck dismounted and embraced her. "What are you doing here? I would have visited had I known you were in the city."

"I arrived only this morning to give this old sourpuss my counsel," she said with a sidelong glance at Maximus. "We hear the rumors in Elloree the same as you, Beck."

"Bah!" said the King. "Another counselor, just what I need."

Gemini ignored him. "I am also here to visit Diamond, so I will ride with you to Bardot if you do not mind."

"Of course not," he replied and quickly called for another horse to be saddled.

When Beck remounted, Maximus approached him. "Take good care of my girls," he said, staring brazenly at Gemini. "All three of them."

The sorceress sniffed loudly.

"I will." Beck leaned down to put his hand on the King's shoulder and whisper in his ear. "You take care as well, Maximus. You may have lopped the head off the serpent today, but I would not count the snake dead yet."

The King frowned. "That is why I decided to cancel my trip to Kondor. I will remain here in the city in the event a new head emerges."

Beck nodded. "We'll be back in less than a week."

"I will be waiting."

Amid several more goodbyes and promises to be careful, Beck prodded Chasin forward and led the party of eight out of the stables. A profusion of cheers and genuflecting greeted them as soon as they turned onto Dannery Row, the road that cut through the heart of Nysa and would take them to the outer gates.

*I cannot get out of here fast enough!*

He craved open space away from the noise and commotion of the city. There, his elemental magic would greet him affectionately, and the power of the earth would course through his body making him whole and content.

The horses' hooves clattered on the paving stones as they passed first the busy merchant's district now teeming with shoppers, and then the stately homes of the nobles. Beck recognized Lady Lillian Knapp's manor house by the immaculate hedges and profusion of flower gardens out front. Soldiers with the Shadow Panther emblazoned on their tunics slammed fists to chests as the procession went by.

In Beck's impatience, it seemed to take forever to pick their way through the bustling city and longer still when they had to wait at the gates to allow through a troop of Cavalry in the brown and black of House Conry.

It didn't escape Beck's notice that an unusually large number of soldiers were pouring into the city, but he wasn't overly concerned. He would be more so if not for the fact that Lord Davad Etin was currently spending time in the royal dungeons. Still, he decided to ask Kirby to look into it.

At last, the party made its way through the gates and out into the public marketplace, the accompanying Sabers cutting a wide swath for them through the crowds. A suffocating cornucopia of noise, smells and colors, it was even more congested here and again Beck had to swallow back his annoyance while they weaved their way through the vendor stalls, pedestrians pushing carts, entertainers and animals.

When the open grassland between Nysa and Bardot finally stretched out before him, Beck sighed a breath of relief.

Kenley turned her head to look at him. "Are you happy now, Daddy?"

He could not help but smile. "I am, Princess. How could I not be with you next to me?"

She giggled, but then he detected a frown in her voice when she said, "I don't think Maman is happy."

"Why, Ken?"

"She doesn't like my magic."

"Of course, she does!" he said and put a comforting hand on her shoulder. "She is just worried for you since we don't know that much about airshifting right now."

"I can do really fun things with it, Daddy! I want to show you all I can do."

The excitement in her voice reminded him of the day he discovered his own magic. "After Uncle Rogan's wedding, we are going to come back here and see what you can do. Just think, Kenley. You are the very first airshifter on the island!"

She seemed happy with his words and sat up a bit straighter in the saddle.

When an unexpected drizzle began to fall from the sky, Beck pulled the hood of Kenley's cloak over her head. He couldn't see from his position behind her, but his daughter's eyes had turned black.

\*\*\*\*

*Baya!*

*I am right here, Princess.*

She looked over the side of her Daddy's horse and saw the white cat loping gracefully alongside them. *Will you go into the Grayan to feed?*

*Yes, soon. I am enjoying the outing right now.*

*Even in the rain?*

*Yes, even in the rain.*

*I could get rid of it, you know. Blow all of this rain right away from us.*

*No! Absolutely, not. Remember what happened the last time?*

*What? That little funnel of air?*

*Little? It was a tornado of considerable size and you broke out two windows in the palace.*

Kenley giggled. *Miss Belle is still trying to figure out what happened.*

*You must be careful when you use your magic, Princess.*

*I know. It is hard to control sometimes.*

*Sometimes?*

*Fine, all the time. I just hope that soon I can learn how to use it properly.*

*For all of our sakes, I hope so, too.*

# CHAPTER 3

## Another Star Fades

Unlike the pageantry of their arrivals or departures into Nysa, a few waves and shouted greetings were all the citizens of Bardot offered.

Home to hundreds of earthshifters to cultivate and nurture the grounds, Bardot offered magnificent views in every direction. Colorful landscaped terraces surrounded a public park with gigantic shade trees and rock gardens. Stone walkways in a variety of patterns bordered a central city square with a highly wrought, three-tiered fountain of scalloped basins and carved benches.

Cobblestone roadways led to the royal palace directly north of the square and west to the most prominent building in the small city—the Bardot Academy.

Diamond, one of the Gem Sect Leaders, intercepted their party. "Welcome back." The beautiful blonde sorceress lifted her arms to help Kenley down.

"You don't know how good it feels to be back, Diamond," Beck admitted honestly.

"Oh, I think I do," she replied knowingly.

He turned to Kiernan. "I am going to the Academy for a few minutes. Why don't you see if you can get some rest before we leave?"

His wife arched her back and offered him a tired grin. "I think I'll do that."

Beck waved and turned Chasin onto the western boulevard and as he rode alone, he suddenly realized what was out of place. His personal guard, Roman Traynor, wasn't by his side. The Saber was part of the team that left a week ago to meet up with them in Kondor. Although still not entirely comfortable with the constant shadowing, Beck liked to think that he and Roman had become friends since the Saber's appointment. As friendly as their statuses allowed anyway. Protocol was very strictly enforced in Iserlohn and, if not always by the nobles, by the people themselves. To their way of thinking, the rigid hierarchy was in place to provide for their well-being and protection, and any breakdown in those traditional roles left them feeling vulnerable and afraid. That is why it was so devastating that Lord Etin misplaced the people's trust the way he did.

As Beck made his way along the street, it made him smile to see earthshifters using their magic openly to assist in the beautification of the city. Large, muscled men moved enormous boulders as if they were pebbles while others waved their hands over the dirt to open up furrows for planting.

Beck involuntarily ducked when an airstream passed by overhead, and a bodyshifter came out of the sky and shifted out of his hawk form on the run and dashed into a building built for this purpose to cover his nakedness. He emerged a moment later dressed and with several rolled parchments clutched in his hand to deliver to their intended recipients. The bodyshifters had become indispensible in recent years in relaying messages between folks from all over Iserlohn, and he could easily see their services expanding to the other lands in the future.

Inside the open doors of a forge, a fireshifter assisted one of the blacksmiths in keeping his hearth hot with summoned fire.

Magic.

Wherever one looked.

Bardot's enchanting way of life left Beck feeling as though all things were possible.

In the training field, a block before the Academy, Beck noticed three young earthshifters practicing their craft, their over-developed chests gleaming with sweat. When they saw him, they waved him over. "Prince Beck!"

He rode over to the trio whose names escaped him. "Working hard, boys?" Beck asked, leaning from the saddle.

"Yes, Your Grace," said the dark-haired boy in the middle. "We were just running through some defensive moves, but need someone to practice on. Would you care to give it a go?"

Beck noticed the young man elbow the friend next to him. *Hmm...is there a hint of a challenge here?* Beck shook his head. "Wish I could, fellows, but I really can't. Another time?"

The shifter in the middle nodded, but as soon as he turned Chasin around, Beck heard him say under his breath, "I think his royal duties are making him soft."

"Or maybe he's just getting too old for his sort of thing," another whisperer suggested.

Beck stopped.

*Too old?* The young men were only a few years younger than him!

He turned back to the trio and dismounted, leading Chasin to the fence surrounding the field to tie the reins to a post. "You know, maybe I do have a few moments after all." He vaulted the railing. "What are you boys working on?"

"We're just thinking up the best way to disable a bad guy, but it really wouldn't take much for shifters like us," one of the boys declared smugly.

"Just one bad guy? Against the three of you?"

"Well, yeah."

"Why don't we say you are the three bad guys and I am the one good guy?"

One of the boys laughed derisively. "That wouldn't be fair."

"For you or for me?"

"You can't fight three shifters at once!"

"Sure I can. I once fought a hundred sorceresses at the same time." It was more like twenty and he didn't even come close to winning that one, but he didn't tell the boys that. He was trying to make a point after all. "So, you agree that you are the bad guys?"

"If you're sure," the middle boy stated, the tone in his voice suggesting that Beck better think twice about it.

Beck walked a few paces away and then turned to face them. "Give me your best shot."

He had hardly finished the last word when a good-sized ball of dirt erupted from the earth in front of the middle boy and whirled toward his face. Beck overrode the summons with a flick of his wrist and sent the ball crashing harmlessly to the side. Undaunted, the boy shifted an earthen suit of armor and a cloud of dust misted the air as the dirt and stones on the ground rolled up and over his body until he had a thick protective layer covering him.

He rushed toward Beck.

With no time for armor, Beck reached down, summoned a fist of stone from the earth, and cuffed the boy as soon as he neared, sending him sprawling. With a wave of Beck's hand, the tree behind another boy groaned as it reached down and sucked the youngster up into its boughs, holding his struggling body fast and silencing his shouts in a leafy cocoon. The last boy standing screamed out when the earth pulled at his boots, and he started to sink into the ground.

"Keep yelling," Beck told the boy as he walked away. "Someone will hear you and dig you out!" He jumped over the fence and remounted Chasin. "Don't forget, gentlemen! The good guys always win!"

\*\*\*\*

When Beck arrived at the Academy, no one approached to take his horse and this pleased him immensely. He took a few moments to rub down Chasin and provide him with feed and then left the stables and headed for the entrance to the Academy.

Larger and more imposing than the royal palace he shared with Kiernan, the building boasted an extensive mélange of fanciful stonework and brick. Tall and graceful twin towers graced the east and west ends of the Academy, and the pennants mounted on the peaks with the imprint of House Everard's Golden Lions flapped in the wind.

Students of all ages hurried to and from classes, and he smiled at them as he made his way to his study on the second floor. When he arrived at his office, he closed the door quickly behind him to forestall any interruptions, anxious to spend some time before his trip studying The Protetor, the last recording of Mage wisdoms. Bequeathed to him by his very great grandfather on his deathbed, it was Galen Starr's intention that Beck study the book to become a Mage. Today, no other wizard existed on the island and, due to the devastation caused by Adrian Ravener six years ago and the Mage War before that, most thought this to be a good thing. Including his wife. In fact, she became unreasonably angry any time he brought it up, so he had learned not to broach the subject with her.

Beck felt differently. He knew that there was much to be learned in sorcery and was eager to explore its secrets. The Gems, phenomenal sorceresses though they were, were limited in their powers to the energy harnessed from their gemstones. A Mage's powers had no limits.

Beck read through the last chapter several times before finally giving up. He shut the book with a frown.

"Your wife would not be pleased to find you reading that."

Beck looked up. Gemini Starr stood in his doorway with a smile on her face.

He set the book down and walked around his desk. "Gemini. I didn't hear you come in."

"Obviously," she said dryly.

She strode past him to the desk and picked up The Protetor. "Can you really read anything in this book?"

He nodded. The book was bespelled so only his eyes could see the contents.

"Like I said, your wife would not be pleased. Nor would most people on this island. The time of the Mage is past, Beck."

"And, how do you feel, Gemini? You know what can be accomplished with a Mage's knowledge."

"You sound suspiciously like your great grandfather."

"Is that so bad? He was a great man."

"Yes, and you saw where that got him."

Beck decided not to pursue the matter further and plucked the book from her fingers. "There is nothing more I can do in any case. The last instruction is a cryptic passage that I have no ability to decipher, so you will have your wish. It is done, for now."

"It's for the best, Beck."

"So, I keep hearing. Now, I'm sure you didn't come here to talk about Mage business."

"No, I came to tell you that I have decided to go back to Maximus this evening after my visit here. I don't like the thought of him without a close advisor at hand. He may need me."

"I'm sure he does," Beck said with a wink and then ducked her swat. "Kidding aside, I know I will sleep much better knowing you are there. Are you sure you have the time?"

She nodded. "Sapphire is seeing to the administration of the coven in my absence."

Beck looked at the sky outside through the window. "And, I must be leaving myself. Make yourself at home," he said, gesturing around the room. "Would you like an escort back to Nysa?"

She reached up to pat his face tenderly. "No, I will be fine. Be careful on your trip, Beck."

"I will." He turned and went to the door.

"B…Beck?"

Her small gasp behind him caused him to spin back. "What is it?" he asked, suddenly concerned. Her face was lined with a fear that wasn't there a few seconds ago, and she gripped the desk so hard her knuckles were white.

"I…I am not sure. I just had the strangest feeling overcome me." He started to approach, but she waved him away with an embarrassed chuckle. "It is gone now. Please accept my apology, Beck. Just an old woman's superstitious mind is all. Go on or you will be late."

"Are you sure?"

"Yes, yes. I am fine. Honestly."

Beck nodded but was still reluctant to leave her. "Are you…"

"Beck, go!"

He held his hands up in surrender and walked out of his office, but a disquieting feeling that he should be doing something more followed closely on his heels.

\*\*\*\*

When Beck left, Gemini regained her composure. Whatever premonition caused her to react in terror disappeared before she had time to examine it more closely. And, this was not the first time.

Still uneasy, she went to the window to peer down at the busy streets of Bardot. Oh, how she loved this magical city. Unheard of only a few years ago, here magic shifting was practiced out in the open where it belonged.

She told Beck that the time of the Mage was past, but maybe the same could be said for the sorceress. Every day, more of her precious Gems were leaving sorcery to study shifting. It wouldn't be long before their numbers dwindled to almost nothing.

She really should put more thought into moving the rest of the coven from Elloree here to Bardot so that the Gems would still be unified no matter which course of study they chose. At her urging, Diamond relocated here a few years ago to watch over the Gems enrolled at the Academy.

A move would also allow her to be closer to Beck, Kiernan, Kenley, and, of course, Maximus. They needed her. And, if she was honest with herself, she needed them as well. They were her family now.

Despite all of the reasons for moving to Bardot, one urged her more than all of the others. Every sorcerous sense in her body warned her that danger was near, that an ominous threat hovered over those she loved most. Whatever evil was on the horizon, she wanted to be in a position to protect her family and she couldn't do that from Elloree.

Out of habit, she reached behind her head and brought forward the thick, gray plait of her hair. Whenever she was troubled, it helped calm her nerves to stroke her braid—the sign of her sisterhood.

Lost in her thoughts, she didn't hear the soft footsteps until they were upon her. She grunted from a vicious, sharp impact to her back. "What..?"

A strong arm whipped out and gripped her around the neck. "King Maximus will not need your assistance in Nysa after all, High Priestess," a sinister voice whispered in her ear.

Instinctively, she twisted her body to get a look at her assailant. "You!"

Gemini snarled, but the spell she had ready to cast fell flat on her tongue. A paralyzing heaviness flowed through her body that began in her lower back, traveled up to lodge in her chest and then filled her head.

Darkness seeped in at the edges of her vision, but she clawed in desperation at the flicker of life still burning within. *Dear Highworld, no! There is so much more I have yet to do! Maximus and the children need me!*

No longer able to stand on her own two feet, she slid down the wall beneath the window in Beck's office and was dead before her body hit the floor.

# CHAPTER 4

## A Pregnant Pause

The dank dungeons of the royal palace, located two stories below the ground, reeked with the smell of urine and unwashed bodies. In the beginning, Davad had to press a handkerchief to his nose just to keep the bile from his throat, but he had grown used to the putrid, silent air. The only sounds in the oppressive gloom were the skittering of tiny feet in and out of the cell and the mournful sob of one of the other prisoners.

Suddenly feeling claustrophobic, Davad shot up out of his cot and banged on the cell door. "Guards! Where is my meal? I requested food hours ago!"

There was no answer from the guards, only the contemptuous laughs from his neighbors.

*Idiots.*

He really wasn't the least bit hungry, but felt like he needed to do something or he would go crazy. He returned to his cot and sat with his head in his hands. It was still unconceivable to him that his own flesh and blood—his brother—had been responsible for derailing his plans. He had not even been aware that Kenith had been anywhere near his surreptitious conversations. He could hardly imagine that his brother betrayed him out of a singular concern for the people of Iserlohn, but then again maybe he did. He always did take after their mother with that soft heart of his. Regardless, after years of suffering under the rule of Maximus Everard, Davad was ready to make his move, and he would not be thwarted by his little brother or this cell. The Court was split and his army was at that very moment on the march toward Nysa.

He heard the door to the guardroom one story above clang open and footsteps descended the short set of steps to the cells.

He stood imperiously. "About time…"

But, it wasn't a guard. It was Lord Abram Winslow, and he was alone.

The ancient and angry face stared at him through the bars of the cell. "How did you let this happen, Davad? You assured me that matters were well in hand."

Davad smiled disarmingly. "Minor setback, Abram. I can assure you—"

"Minor setback! You are accused of treason against the Crown!"

Davad glowered at him. "I am well aware of the charge, Abram. The important discussion point is what you are going to do to get me out of here!"

The old man shook his head. "There is nothing I can do, Davad. There are guards and Sabers everywhere."

"You must."

"It is impossible."

"Only impossible if you care nothing for the life of your grandson, Abram."

The Lord's lined face flushed so red that Davad thought he might fall over dead onto the stone floor.

"Don't worry," Davad said hastily, "he is unharmed. As promised, the boy will be returned to you just as soon as I am King."

Abram's head hung low. "Don't hurt him, Davad. I have done everything you have asked these past months. For Highworld's sake, please don't hurt him."

Davad cocked his head. "Well, now, his well-being is entirely in your hands now, isn't it, Abram?"

"I will see what I can do," he said in a resigned whisper. "It cannot be accomplished without bloodshed."

Davad smiled. "Naturally. Now, run along. Commander Hugo Bassus and my army will be here in two weeks. I fully expect to be out of this dungeon by then."

The Lord gave him a long withering look and then turned on his heel and walked away. Davad went back to his cot, feeling more confident. Abram would get him out of here soon, he was sure of it. He seemed to be very fond of that grandson of his. In the meantime, there was nothing else for it but to be patient.

The guardroom door opened a second time and another set of footsteps moved down the stairs and approached. A very large guard stopped in front of his cell door.

Surprised gasps came from the other prisoners and furious whispering filled the air.

"What is it?" Davad demanded.

The guard remained silent as he inserted a key into the door of his cell.

"Am I to be freed then? Already?" Davad stood and dusted off his jacket, anxious to leave the foul-smelling cell.

"Turn around," the guard commanded with a leer.

The confusion must have showed on his face because the guard reached out and grasped a fistful of his jacket at the shoulder to spin him around.

"Put your hands against the wall."

"What is this? Let go of me this instant!" He tried to turn, but the man, easily twice his size, leaned his full weight into his back.

The mutterings of the prisoners grew louder.

When the guard reached around and unfastened Davad's trousers, the cold realization hit him.

"Stop! Guards!"

The guard's fist lashed out and struck him in the side of the head. "Be quiet."

The force was so powerful that it scrambled his senses and he almost fell to the ground. "The King would never approve of this," he said groggily as his trousers were yanked down to his ankles. "You will be executed when he finds out."

The guard laughed. "The King will not find out, my Lord. I do not expect that you will ever tell anyone about this. Now, bend over."

White hot pain shot through him at the brutal impalement of the guard. As the assault continued, something inside of Davad's mind snapped. He tried to formulate a more effective protest, but he couldn't string the words together to do so. With the grunts of the guard filling his ear, it was not only his mind that was lost in that moment—it was also a piece of his soul.

****

Kiernan was busy packing the last of her clothes when a knock sounded on her door. Captain Kirby Nash poked his head into the suite and announced that Diamond had returned.

"She may come in, Kirby, thank you," Kiernan yelled from the bedroom.

A moment later, the blonde sorceress appeared. "Are you finished?"

"Almost."

Diamond looked at her critically with a tilt of her head. "What's wrong?"

"What do you mean?"

"I know when something is bothering you, Kiernan. What is it?"

Kiernan sighed and sat down on the bed. "How do you know me so well?"

"Because I am a sorceress of exceptional talent in Divination, and," she walked over and sat next to Kiernan, "I am also your friend. Now, spill it."

"You forgot humble."

"No, never that," she admitted with a laugh.

"So tell me, am I having a boy or a girl?"

The sorceress shook her blonde braid. "Just like the countless other times you have asked, I am not telling."

"What good is it to have a friend who can tell the future, if she won't share any of it you?"

"I guess my winning personality will have to suffice."

Kiernan smiled, but Diamond didn't join her, still waiting for an explanation. "Oh, all right!" She took a deep breath and looked her friend in the eye. "I'm just very worried about my father and the discontent of the people of Iserlohn. It all has an orchestrated feel to it." Diamond gestured for more. "And, if you must know, I am worried about *her*."

The sorceress' eyebrows rose in confusion. "Kiernan, we have not seen or heard anything from *her* in six years, and I have seen nothing in my stone. For some reason, it is frustratingly silent when it comes to that black witch."

"I know and something just feels wrong. Call it women's intuition if nothing else."

"If it makes you feel any better, I will redouble my efforts to seek *her* out. We do have a number of Gems still on the hunt for *her*."

Kiernan snorted. "Do you think it's just the pregnancy talking?"

"No. I trust your instincts. Are you sure you don't want me to travel to Kondor with you?"

Kiernan shook her head. "You have your own work to do here. You cannot very well follow me around."

"If you are sure…"

"I am."

Diamond rose from the bed, but hesitated. "By the way, you don't plan to visit any remote, tribal villages on the way to Kondor, do you?"

Now, it was Kiernan's turn to raise her eyebrows. "No. Are there any on the island?"

Diamond shrugged it off. "It's probably nothing. It is just that a tribal village keeps appearing in my stone and it has the death shroud over it. But, it could mean anything."

"Is this the same vision you had before of Beck? The journey that would result in his death?" She asked the question calmly, but inside her heart raced as if she had been sprinting.

"Don't read anything more into it, Kiernan. Until, I know more, it is senseless to worry. These images can resolve themselves in the most benign and unexpected ways."

Kiernan nodded reluctantly. Any vision that concerned Beck and a death shroud was not easy to cast aside.

The door flew open then and Kenley ran into the room.

"I am ready, Maman!"

"No tribal villages!" reminded Diamond as she left the bedroom.

Kiernan picked Kenley up with a groan. Although she wasn't due for another two months, she felt abnormally large and uncomfortable. "That's my girl, Ken."

"I can't wait to go on the slide, Maman!"

Kiernan smiled and remembered the first time she and Beck slid into the underground waterworld of Aquataine. They were rushing off to the heat of battle and it was the only way to travel there in time. It was also one of the last times she was with her dearly beloved Bajan who died protecting her. According to ancestral lore, a Kenley was never to be without their Draca Cat, but she never bonded with another after Bajan. The Sovereign of the Dracas offered another bondmate, but she refused. It would have felt like a betrayal to such a unique and pure friendship. The void was filled somewhat by Bajan's offspring, Baya, but Kiernan had to admit that the adventurous and impulsive young Draca was nothing like her sire.

A scrabbling noise caught her attention, and the object of her thoughts sprinted into the room and crashed into a side table when she was unable to stop in time.

Her daughter's eyes turned black, and Kiernan listened in on their conversation.

*Highworld, Baya! What is the matter?*

*Princess, we must find your father right away.*

*Why? What has happened?*

*I was just in the Grayan Forest, and I need to show him what I saw.*

*Tell me! What did you see?*

*A murder.*

\*\*\*\*

Kiernan knuckled her lower back as she followed behind Beck, Rogan, Airron, and Captain Nash through the dense wooded area of the Grayan Forest east of the city. Her son had chosen a very inconvenient time to be so active. *Her son?* She smiled to herself. Beck even had her believing now that it was a boy, but she would be content either way.

Beck looked back at her worriedly, but she waved him off. He wanted her to stay behind, but she refused. If a murder occurred in her dominion, she would do everything in her power to bring the culprit to justice. For that to happen, she had to see the crime first hand.

A dozen Scarlet Sabers were fanned out behind them, but she could neither see nor hear them. In contrast, her small party sounded deafeningly loud to her ears. Especially, Rogan, who strode ahead seemingly oblivious—or more likely, just not caring—about the noise he made.

That uneasy feeling was back in the pit of her stomach, but she pushed it down and away from her, attributing it once again to her pregnancy.

She heard Baya whine and then the ground under her feet began to tremble as Beck instinctively summoned his magic. Beside him, the air around Airron shimmered and Rogan called fire to his palms.

Beck pointed. "I see something. Over there."

The men moved cautiously now, not knowing what they would find. Stepping into a small moonlit clearing, Kiernan stopped suddenly and looked up.

A body hung from one of the trees. The rope secured to the noose creaked ominously in the still air as the corpse rotated below.

"Oh, Highworld."

It was the man from Court that morning who made the complaint about the living conditions in Iserport.

"Get him down from there," ordered Beck, and a Saber materialized out of the darkened woods and scampered up the tree. The soldier used his saber to cut through the rope on the tree branch and the body fell to the ground with a sickening thud.

"Who could have done this?" asked Rogan.

"One of Lord Etin's cohorts, no doubt," replied Kiernan sourly. Even in a cell, the man caused problems. She had been right to keep Kenley at home so she wasn't here to witness this gruesome sight.

"All the man did was come to Nysa looking for a better life for his family and he is killed for it," Beck remarked ruefully. Turning to the Sabers, he instructed that the body be transported to Nysa and the man's wife contacted.

As they made their way back to their horses, Kiernan remembered that the man had prophesized his own death that very morning. He obviously knew what Davad Etin was capable of. Did Etin's reach really go beyond his cell or was she only blaming him because it was easy to do so? If it was Etin, how many others were working with him? How many *friends* were now *foes*? It was impossible to fight an enemy that slinked in the shadows instead of coming for her directly.

*Cowards.*

The thoughts were disturbing and she regretted even more that her father was remaining behind.

As if reading her thoughts, Rogan informed them that he would understand if they decided not to make the trip to Kondor that evening.

Kiernan shook her head. "No. This is too important of a day for you, Rogan, and we wouldn't miss it for the world."

"Besides," interjected Beck, "I spoke to Gemini earlier, and she has decided not to go back to Elloree until we return. Trust me, harm will not get a glance at the King with the High Priestess by his side."

# CHAPTER 5

## Baya's Gift

Kiernan held Kenley's hand tight as they stood side by side on the platform built just inside the Bardot grate to Aquataine. "Are you ready, darling?"

"Oh, yes, Maman!"

This new entrance to the underground world of Massa's watershifters had been constructed a few years ago so that the shifters that lived in Bardot could utilize the waterways. Aquataine was quickly becoming an invaluable travel resource for the shifters of Massa and, like the bodyshifters, a valuable source of information. Since the watershifters could travel from place to place so quickly, they were the first to know and pass on the events happening around the island.

"Kiernan, are you sure you should be doing this?" asked Beck from behind her.

"Beck! Stop fussing so! I'm not due for months yet." She shook her head at him in frustration and then looked into the shining eyes of her daughter. With a mutual nod, they jumped, and loud giggles escaped from them both as they soared down the slide and spilled out into a warm blue lagoon.

As had been previously arranged, their watershifter escort, Digby, waited for them on the white beach. As the self-proclaimed official transporter for the royal family, Digby moved his family to this new Aquataine village of Barbary as soon as the grate was built.

Kenley popped her head up through the water and, although she was a good swimmer, Kiernan swam directly to her side and helped her from the lagoon.

Digby immediately dropped to one knee.

She smiled. "Please rise, Digby. It is good to see you again."

"Good morning, Your Graces," greeted the lanky shifter as he unfolded himself from the ground, his pale, unclothed body glimmering with droplets of water.

Despite being evening in Bardot, it was early morning in Aquataine. Because the only underground natural light source came from the nocturnal glow worms, there was a reversal in day and night from the Surface World.

Behind them, additional splashes sounded the arrival of Beck, Rogan, Airron, and Baya.

Kiernan noticed that Digby looked somber, and it was a look totally out of place for the cheerful watershifter. "Digby, is everything all right?"

He lifted red-rimmed eyes to look at her. "No, Your Grace, it…it is my wife. She came down with pneumonia a few months ago. The healers have been trying to help her, but tell me now there is nothing more to be done. I can hardly stand to say the words, Your Grace…but, she is dying. My wife is dying." The watershifter put his head in his hands and began to weep quietly.

She rushed over to him. "Digby! I'm so very sorry. You should be with her. Go to her now!"

He shook his head adamantly. "I have my duty, Your Grace."

"Yes! To your wife first and foremost. I command you to return home. We will find another to transport us to Kondor."

An urgent tug on Kiernan's arm caused her to look down at Kenley. "Maman! Baya can save Digby's wife. I know she can."

Kiernan paused. Yes, it was possible that the Draca could heal Digby's wife with the Healing Breath. The Sovereign of the Draca Cats, Moombai, healed her own terrible injuries when she traveled to Callyn-Rhe years ago. Although the Healing Breath of the Draca could not reverse illness related to the natural aging process or congenital diseases—the inescapable road to death could be eluded by no one—it could heal almost all contracted ailments and injuries.

Kiernan looked to Beck who was emerging from the lagoon and then back to her daughter. "You are right, Kenley, we should give it a try. Has Baya learned to do the Healing Breath?"

Her daughter nodded enthusiastically. "Oh, yes. Moombai himself trained her last year during her visit back to Callyn-Rhe. She already healed me of a fever I had a few months ago."

Kiernan shook her head in wonder. Thank the Highworld for Baya and the bond they shared. It gave her such immense peace of mind knowing that her daughter had the Draca as her protector.

She looked over at Digby who was glancing at them expectantly.

"Do you really think…?"

"There is only one way to find out. Lead the way."

Kiernan quickly explained to the others about Digby's wife and Kenley's suggestion, and the watershifter hurriedly ushered them over the beach and into another cavern where several rafts were moored to crystallized stalagmites that jutted from the ground. They boarded one of the small crafts, and Digby dove into the water to propel the raft forward from the rear.

"How far?" shouted Beck.

"Just up ahead." Digby pointed with one webbed hand. "There. The limestone house on stilts."

Kiernan noticed Kenley's eyes turn black and heard her relay to the Draca Cat what was needed.

When the raft pulled up to the dock in front of Digby's house, Baya leapt to shore and up the stairs of the house. A young girl with red hair opened the door and her eyes widened in fright when she saw Baya, spiked tail swishing with excitement.

Digby hurried up the stairs. "Don't be frightened, Alia! It's just Princess Kenley's Draca Cat, Baya."

The girl put her arms out to her father, nonetheless, anxious for the safety of his embrace.

"Where is your wife, Digby?" asked Kiernan.

"She is in the back room, Your Grace."

"May we?"

"Yes, please."

She nodded and then followed Kenley and Baya through the small, neat house. Kenley knocked on the only closed door along a short corridor and was granted permission to enter from a coarse voice inside.

Digby's wife looked painfully frail as she lay on the bed in the dark room, the blankets pulled up to her chin. Digby entered behind them, knelt by the bed and explained to his wife, who he addressed as Liliana, why they were there. The woman's watery eyes brightened at the prospect of a cure, and she waved Baya toward her bed weakly.

"Come."

The Draca Cat obeyed and padded over to the sick woman. Without hesitation, Baya leaned over Liliana and exhaled a vaporous breath. Sinuous, silky strands of energy coiled around the two heads joined mouth to muzzle. The room crackled with powerful, ancient magic and the hair on Kiernan's arms lifted straight up.

After a moment, Baya lifted her snowy head and stepped back.

Liliana's eyes remained closed and she didn't stir.

*It didn't work*, thought Kiernan. If anything, Liliana looked closer to death. When Kiernan noticed a small tear make its track down the woman's face, she wanted to cry out in helplessness. She could never imagine being faced with the prospect of death while a young child still lived. To leave a child behind, vulnerable and unprotected by a mother's love was heartbreaking to contemplate. A new empathy for what her own mother must have suffered welled up inside her.

Liliana let out a soft moan suddenly and reached for her husband.

"I am so sorry, Liliana," Digby cried into her shoulder. "I had so hoped that it would work."

A gurgled laugh erupted from Liliana, and Digby pulled back to look at her. "I think it did, my husband. I am just terrified to test it out."

"You feel better?"

She nodded enthusiastically. "Yes!"

"Well, try to get out of bed," he encouraged her.

Everybody in the room stepped back as Liliana threw the blanket off her body and swung her feet to the ground. Her laughter mixed with her tears as she stood.

Little Alia ran to her mother and wrapped her arms around her leg.

"Alia! Be careful with Maman," cautioned Digby.

But, Liliana shook her head. "No, Digby. I never want her to let go."

Digby turned to Baya. "I cannot thank you enough. If there is ever anything you need now or in the future, you have only to name it. You cannot know what you have given back to me and Alia."

The Draca Cat nodded her head regally, and her eyes turned black.

After a few seconds, Kenley spoke up. "She said a honeycake would be lovely."

The quiet laughter that rang out so close on the heels of death lifted the spirits of all in the room.

****

After producing the promised cake to Baya, Digby left the house in a rush to retrieve the boat they would use for their passage to Kondor. Just moments after his wife was cured, he appeared around a bend in the waterway with one of the newer transports that had been constructed over the past few years to accommodate the heavier traffic in Aquataine now that all of the shifters had been given leave to utilize the underground metropolis for travel. The boat was large enough to offer spacious sleeping quarters below deck so that passengers could rest in comfort during their travel. Two watershifters were needed to propel this particular model, but because of the distance, three would go so that one could always be resting while the other two shifted.

Beck looked down at the watershifter. "Are you sure you wouldn't rather stay here with Liliana?  She just—"

Digby immediately shook his head. "No, Your Grace. It's the least I can do after all you have done. Liliana is already sending for her sister to come stay with her, but she says she feels perfectly fine. Also, *nobody* escorts the royal party except yours truly!"

"As you wish," Beck conceded and boarded the spacious boat behind the others. With a journey of two days ahead of them, Beck was grateful that Kiernan would be able to travel in comfort. He could easily see that the pregnancy was starting to take its toll on her.

He spent the first day of the journey on the top deck with Rogan and Airron. Airron didn't waste the opportunity to rib Rogan at every chance about his upcoming marriage. Beck couldn't remember the Elf ever being so averse to marriage before and wondered what was driving the sentiment.

Rogan crossed his arms at his chest. "What about you, Elf? Not yet ready for matrimony?"

Airron's purple eyes grew wide in shock. "Not me! I would like to keep my neck for a few years yet, thank you very much."

"Your neck?"

Airron massaged his throat as if it were in danger of the headman's axe. "Yes, you know the saying. Once you get married, the man becomes the head of the house. But," he said, holding up a finger, "the woman is the neck, and she turns that head *any* which way she wants."

Rogan looked over at Beck. "How many times do I have to tell you that he is not right?"

He simply shrugged and the evening continued in much the same way with Beck mostly silent while his two friends continued to engage in harmless banter. It was late when he climbed down the small ladder to the lower deck and entered the cabin he shared with Kiernan and Kenley. They were cuddled together, slumbering on the narrow bunk built into the hull of the boat. He smiled, pulled the blanket up over their shoulders, and then laid down on the bunk on the opposite side.

He was sound asleep in seconds.

The next morning, he awoke to dark. It confused him for a moment until he remembered that it was nighttime in Aquataine. He left Kiernan and Kenley and walked onto the upper deck. The watershifters were still in the water propelling the boat forward and he was alone. He glanced up at the glow worms on the cavern ceiling emitting their green radiance. The cavern where they now traveled was very narrow, and he could reach out and touch the limestone walls if he leaned over the rails far enough.

Soon, the others joined him, and they slid into the easy conversation of old friends. Just like that, they were teenagers again and sitting around a campfire near the Grayan Forest outside of Pyraan, sharing stories and laughs. Although they lived in separate lands these days, their bond of friendship was as strong as ever, and they made it point to visit with each as often as possible.

Second in line—at the moment—to the Deepstone Crown, Rogan lived in Kondor at the royal palace with Janin and his two children, Reilly, four years of age and Jala, three. Rogan's cousin, Erik Rojin, was now King, his father, King Rik, having been killed in a hunting accident a few years back.

Erik was only eighteen, but should he marry and have children, they would become heir to the throne.

Airron lived in Sarphia and was third in line to the Haventhal throne. King Jerund J'El sat the throne now and Airron's cousin, Prince Thorn J'El, was second.

It was somewhat surprising that Kiernan, Rogan and Airron were all of royal blood when their pureblood status spoke to the fact that as descendants of the original *Savitars*, they were pure in magic, not royalty.

The second day passed as uneventful as the first, and Beck was relieved when the boat finally began to slow for he knew that they must be approaching Kondor.

"Almost at the grate!" Digby confirmed and within moments, they pulled into the small Aquatainian village of Fontaine. Shouts of greeting drifted to them from the shore and waterway. All villagers who could, knelt to the ground.

Beck helped Kiernan and Kenley disembark while Baya leapt off the deck in an impressive leap and landed in the sand with an enthusiastic shake of her white coat.

"Thank you, Digby. Can I talk you into leaving now and going home to be with your wife?" Beck asked.

The watershifter shook his head. "I will go home as soon as I escort you back to Bardot, Your Grace."

Beck nodded reluctantly, knowing he would not win the argument against Digby's unfailing loyalty. Stepping off the boat, he led his little party to the stairs cut into the limestone walls of the cavern that led the way to the Surface World just outside of King Erik's castle in Kondor. It was a considerable walk to the top, so Beck waited for Kiernan and scooped her up in his arms. She yelled at him to put her down muttering that she was quite capable of walking a few steps, but he ignored her and soon she gave in and snuggled into his shoulder.

He set her down when they reached the summit and opened the grate.

"They're here!" came an immediate shout from outside.

Beck ducked through first and was greeted by his guard, Roman Traynor. The Saber was tall, almost as tall as he was, and well-built with an olive complexion and short cropped black hair and black eyes. Beck thought he resembled an eagle, always alert, always wary. The two men traded grips. "Good to see you, Captain. Any problems?"

Roman shook his head. "None, Your Grace. We are safe."

While Beck waited for the others to exit, he scanned the area carefully. If it was as safe as Roman indicated, why did it not feel that way to him? He couldn't explain it adequately, only that there seemed to be a malevolent pall hanging in the air, and he couldn't shake the eerie feeling that eyes were boring holes into his body. And, the most remarkable feature about those eyes?

They were full of hate.

# CHAPTER 6

## The Wedding

"Janin, you look stunning," breathed Kiernan, looking over her friend's shoulder at the reflection in the mirror. Rogan's bride wore an ivory, floor-length gown with wide sleeves and laced bodice. A wide, maroon ribbon cinched her at the waist in an elegant bow. Around her temples, she wore a silver circlet with a drop stone sapphire that hung in the middle of her forehead. A matching velvet hooded cape was worn over the dress and would remain in place during the ceremony until her new husband removed it for her, claiming her as his wife. Before that happened, though, Janin would pluck a hair from Rogan's beard to prove he was worthy.

Kiernan shook her head. As Janin's bridal matron, she was still reeling from her expeditious tutelage in Dwarven customs. After the ceremony, there would be a bizarre attempt to steal the groom's boots by the male guests, Janin's father would be doused in oil and feathers, and the dancing and drinking would not end until the following morning.

Kiernan hoped she would at least be able to make a good show of it for her two dear friends, but was still exhausted from the days of traveling. "So, are you ready to be Rogan's wife?"

Janin spun around and the shining light in the Dwarf's eyes said it all. "The only thing that could make this day any more perfect would be if Dillon was here to share it with us."

She reached for Janin's hands. "I never knew Dillon, but Rogan has told me often how much he meant to you."

Janin straightened with a sigh. "For Highworld's sake, enough of this melancholy! This is my wedding day!"

Kiernan laughed. It was so like Janin. A soldier for many years, Rogan's bride had a very pragmatic view of the way of life.

A loud knock on the door to Janin's chambers signaled that it was time. "Kali Janin! All is ready!"

The servant's use of the honorific address was premature. Officially, the feminine Dwarven title for a royal in waiting—Kali—was not to be used until after the ceremony. Rogan had already been dubbed Kal Rogan after the Demon War and his ancestry was made known.

Janin exhaled an anxious breath and went to the door to open it. Immediately, three servants rushed in and six hands flowed over their soon-to-be new Kali. Her chestnut hair was molded into shape, her dress smoothed, the hood of her cloak raised, and a bouquet of flowers thrust into her hands.

The poignant lilt of the wedding music drifted through the open doors of the room. One of the servants turned to Kiernan, looked her up and down with a critical eye, and then nodded. "You are first, Princess."

Kiernan patted her swollen abdomen to ease her nerves and went through the door. As soon as she came into view on the second floor balcony, she caught Beck's eye below and smiled at him. He stood next to Rogan and Airron beyond the wide open doors of the enormous and lavishly decorated Dwarven great hall.

She drew murmurs of approval for her floor length silk, black and scarlet gown and nodded her head graciously.

Many of the prominent members of society from all three lands were in attendance. Kiernan noticed Thorn J'El, the Prince of Elves, and Gladewatcher, Loren Faolin, a close friend of Airron's from Haventhal who often traveled with Airron during his visits to Iserlohn.

It was unfortunate that her father couldn't be there, but a number of Iserlohn nobles were present, and Roman Traynor, Beck's personal guard, stood in the back of the room with the rest of the Sabers looking splendid in his crisp black uniform and scarlet slash. Several Gems from Elloree stood among the esteemed congregation and, as always, they made Kiernan feel frumpy and dull in their glamorous presence.

Dwarven nobles and gentry gathered in the hundreds, and General Klay Arsten and his elite Iron Fists surrounded King Erik Rojin, the only one seated. The pride of Deepstone stood proud and alert in their magnificent dress tunics of blue and maroon.

At the bottom of the stairs, Kenley, Reilly and Jala looked like little angels wearing all white, waiting to escort her and Janin to their places at the makeshift altar.

The baby kicked vigorously halfway down the steps, but she managed to keep the sharp pain from her face. Kenley reached for her hand as she descended and led her toward the great hall. They had only taken a few steps when another appreciative gasp filled the room.

Janin had appeared at the top of the balcony.

"Highworld, woman, you look beautiful!" Rogan exclaimed loudly.

He ignored the ladies in the room who scowled at his lack of etiquette, and the men tried to hide their grins. Janin, however, laughed aloud as she glided down the stairs to the waiting hands of her children. Reilly and Jala escorted her to their father and, in a touching moment, kissed Janin's hand before placing it in Rogan's hand.

The music stopped then and all was hushed.

The Dwarven cleric smiled at the couple. "Kal Rogan, we are here to witness your marriage to this woman, Janin Stonedge. Do you find her worthy?"

Rogan reached out and gently pushed back the hood from Janin's face. "I do."

"Janin Stonedge, Kal Rogan has found you worthy. Do you find him the same?"

Kiernan held her breath as Janin's fingers searched through Rogan's short brown beard for a small hair. Finding one that suited her, she yanked it out. Rogan didn't flinch.

"I do."

Kiernan let the breath go. If Rogan *had* flinched, Janin would have found him unworthy and left him at the altar.

The cleric spoke eloquently and at length regarding the covenant of marriage and the blessings of their union. Then, his expression turned solemn as he turned to Rogan. "A Kal is greatly revered by his people. Do you find them worthy to protect and defend for as long as you shall live?"

Rogan faced the congregation and bowed from the waist. "I do."

The cleric turned to Janin. "A Kali is greatly honored by her people. Do you find them worthy enough to love and nurture for as long as you shall live?"

Janin steepled her hands under her chin and bowed to her guests. "I do."

"Kal Rogan, please remove the cloak and declare your right to this woman."

Janin turned around so Rogan could remove the velvet cape.

The cleric smiled. "It is with great honor that I present to Deepstone and all honored guests, Kal Rogan and Kali Janin!"

The crowd rose to their feet with great applause. Kiernan hurriedly kissed Rogan and Janin and then stepped back to give the new bride and groom room to receive their guests. Beck and Kenley came to stand beside her.

Kiernan sighed and mentally prepared for the long evening ahead. She would need every ounce of energy she possessed to get through the night. Especially, since her unborn son seemed intent on kicking up a celebration of his own.

****

The screeching rasp of the guardroom door opening drifted down the stairs of the dungeon, and Davad Etin recoiled. Every heavy footstep that followed felt like a sadistic physical blow to his mind and body. When his large assailant came into view outside of his cell, he scrambled back on his cot and curled into a protective ball.

"You have a visitor," the guard told him gruffly.

Davad hissed and sat up, the relief flooding through him. *Is it Abram?* It had been several days since he last saw him. *Please let it be Abram.*

But, it wasn't Abram, it was the Lady Ava Conry.

The eighteen-year-old came into her Ladyship when her mother, Isabella Conry, died at the Valley of Flame fighting alongside King Maximus. Isabella's son also perished in the war and that left Ava in position for the seat on Court.

What a windfall that had been for him. Isabella Conry would never have turned against Maximus, but Ava had no such loyal tendencies toward the King. Having Abram and Ava in his front pocket was what tipped the scales in his favor and started his plans in motion. Where he had gained

Abram's support through blackmail, he had gained Ava's through sex. At thirty-six, he was twice her age, but Ava Conry was no innocent. She was a parasitic opportunist and knew exactly how to achieve her goals, and when she used her considerable feminine assets to her advantage, few men were able to resist.

Of course, he didn't fool himself that she loved him any more than he loved her. He just happened to be the biggest catch of the moment. From him, she wanted the most treasured prize of all. She wanted to be Queen of Iserlohn.

He hoped she didn't notice his initial panic and berated himself for his frailty. The perverted guard was contorting his wits into mush, and he knew for his own sanity he needed out. Soon.

Collecting himself, he rose from the bed and walked to the cell door. The voluptuous blonde turned to purse her red lips at his abuser. "You may leave us."

The guard smiled at her like an imbecile. "Just remember our deal," he told her with a quick squeeze of her breast.

Fury surged through Davad's chest and red flashed before his vision. *This sick, low-life guard thinks he can touch a noblewoman of Iserlohn! How dare he!*

The disgusting pig then turned and left them alone in violation of every regulation he had been entrusted to enforce. It didn't matter. The guard would die. The moment Davad was released from this cell and not one single second later.

Ava waited until the guard was out of sight before reaching her hands through the cell bars toward him. "I've missed you," she purred.

"You let a filthy pig like that touch you?" he screamed at her.

"I did it for you, Davad. Otherwise, he never would have left us alone to talk."

With effort, Davad let go of his anger and approached her outstretched embrace. There was no one better at this game than he. "I was starting to think that you had abandoned me," he confessed honestly.

Ava shook her blonde curls petulantly. "Now, Davad, how could I do that? I tied my fate to you long ago. I couldn't walk away now even if I wanted to."

"When am I getting out of here?" he asked, hoping she didn't hear the tinge of desperation in his voice.

"Soon, I hope. Abram is working quite diligently on your release."

"What about you? It appears as though you hold sway with the guard. Surely, you can convince him to release me."

Ava laughed. "Why, Davad, you do have a high regard for my talents! I was able to get the man to leave us alone with the promise of a fondle or two, but he would never risk doing anything as blatant as releasing you against the King's orders."

Davad kicked the iron bars and turned away from her. "I still cannot believe Kenith did this." After thinking it over the past few days, he came to realize that this was all Maximus' doing. The King must have grown suspicious and somehow convinced his spineless brother into spying on him. But, the King couldn't know all that he planned—not when he had effectively cut off all lines of communication from Iserport. He doubted very much that Maximus was aware that an army was marched toward Nysa at this very moment. Especially, with people in the palace still providing those blind spots Davad needed to keep the Iserlohn royals in the dark.

He shook his head. It had been pathetically easy to dupe these people, and in his view, that was precisely why they should not be in power. Then again, was Maximus really as in the dark as he supposed? It was obvious now that he had some knowledge of what was going on when he sought out Kenith and arranged that little spectacle at Court. He would need to get out of this cell to know for sure but unfortunately, his fate was in the hands of others.

He turned back to Ava with a snarl. "If you wish to be Queen of Iserlohn, either get that old man to move a little faster or lay on your back for that guard. Today!"

# CHAPTER 7

## Missing

Outside in the festooned courtyard and surrounded by the flickering glow of torchlight, Beck sat back in his chair and tapped his foot in time to the lively music of a stringed dulcimer, trying very hard not to laugh as he watched a bootless Rogan attempt a clumsy reel with his new wife.

In true Dwarven fashion, the party was still going strong. Although it must have been after midnight, the celebration was in no danger of ending any time soon.

He glanced down at Kenley, asleep in his arms.

He loved her so very much. Her childish beauty and curious innocence never failed to tug at his heart. Black ringlets clung to her heated cheek so Beck gently tucked the unruly tresses back behind her ear with a smile. She had worn herself out playing with Reilly and Jala. Just four and three years of age, neither of the Dwarven children had displayed shifting talents as of yet. As direct descendants of a *Savitar*, there was no doubt that they would be magic users, it just remained to be seen when.

Kiernan had gone to bed hours ago but Beck stayed, enjoying his seat at the periphery of the festivity. Not surprising, Airron was still in high spirits and actively engaged in dancing with any woman he could get his hands on.

Beck yawned. It was now time for him to get some rest as well. He enjoyed many hours in honor of his friend's wedding, but his tired body signaled that it was time to go.

"Your Grace."

Roman Traynor materialized at his side so quietly that Beck almost jumped. He had long ago instructed Roman never to kneel to him and was pleased that the Saber obliged. Although, he was the only Saber Captain that did.

"Still up, Captain?" he asked.

Roman laughed, and it was nice to see gaiety on the Saber's normally severe countenance. "If you are up, I am up, Your Grace."

"Well, I apologize for that then. We are at the home of a friend, Roman, why don't you get some sleep?"

"You?"

"Headed there now."

Roman looked around and his narrowed gaze didn't miss one detail of the ongoing party. "There are six Sabers stationed here at the palace."

Beck's eyebrows rose. "Six? I haven't seen a single Saber tonight."

"Your point, Your Grace?"

It was Beck's turn to laugh. He knew that it was unlikely anyone had seen a black and scarlet tunic this night as skilled as the guards were at disappearing into the background. "Never mind. Go to bed, Roman. We are in friendly territory."

The Saber nodded. "Very well. I will name a replacement and be at your door by sunrise."

"That is fine."

Roman walked off, and Beck looked down to make sure that Kenley had not awakened. When he glanced back up, a movement to the side captured his attention. He thought he saw a shadow moving among the grove of boulders that surrounded the courtyard of the palace. Alert, he shifted Kenley's weight and continued to peer into the dark recesses. He almost called Roman back, but seeing no further activity, he finally decided that it was probably just reflected shadows from the revelers dancing or an elusive Scarlet Saber making his rounds.

Airron picked that moment to rush over and plop down in a chair next to him.

"Bloody great party, isn't it, Beck?"

"Airron!" he whispered harshly and nodded his head down toward Kenley. "Ssh!"

Airron shrugged his shoulders and his pointed ears shrank back. "Oops."

Beck shook his head affectionately at his lifelong friend. Since the war, Airron had made quite a name for himself as a premier Gladewatcher, the elite Calvary regiment of the Haventhal Army and King Jerund J'El's personal warriors.

Airron leaned back in his chair and sighed, his voice hushed now. "Ah, what a life, my friend! A cup that overflows with wine and plenty of pretty girls to kiss. Who could ask for more?"

It felt almost as though Airron was trying to convince himself of his great life as a bachelor rather than Beck. "Is there anything you would like to talk about, Airron? You seem on edge lately."

The purple eyes blazed and the pretense disappeared in a flash as the chair thumped back down to the ground. "You think? You would be on edge, too, Beck, if…"

"If what?"

"There you are!" A redheaded woman sauntered over and ran her fingers through Airron's silver hair. "Ready for another go, darling? You promised."

Airron stood with a flourish and took the woman's hand in his to bring it to his lips. "It would be my pleasure, fair maiden." He took a few steps and then tossed a look back at Beck. "We'll talk in the morning."

Beck watched the duo disappear into the gyrating mob. *I will be here for you, my friend. Tomorrow, you can tell me all about your problems.* He stood, and Kenley stretched in his arms. "Time for bed, little one."

Shadowy motion to the left caught his attention once again. "What?..."

He would never remember this later, but he remained frozen in place for several long moments, his stare fixed on a trio of large boulders.

Finally, he sat back down on his chair.

"Kenley, wake up."

\*\*\*\*

Kenley came awake with a start. "Daddy?"

"Yes, Kenley. You must wake up now. Please go into the palace and go to sleep. Maman is there and you can crawl into bed beside her."

"What about you, Daddy? I want you to take me there."

Her father shook his head. "I must do something else right now, Kenley. It is important."

"But, Daddy…"

"Do as I say!" he hissed sternly. Kenley almost started to cry. Her father had never been unkind to her before. Not even when he caught her stealing cookies from the kitchens instead of working on her studies.

She nodded to him sadly and watched him walk away into the night beyond the torchlight. A tear slipped down her face. Something felt wrong, but she didn't know what.

*Baya!*

Within seconds, the Draca Cat appeared at her side.

*Where were you?*

*Sleeping. The same as you.* The cat opened her mouth in a large yawn as proof.

*Daddy woke me up and left me here by myself. He walked into those boulders over there,* she said, pointing.

*Would you like me to follow him?*

*Yes.*

*I will go.*

*I'm going, too.*

*As you wish.*

*Hurry.*

Baya put her nose down to the ground and stepped in front of her. *I have his scent. Follow me.*

Kenley put her hand on Baya's back and walked beside her, careful to be very quiet like Captain Franck taught her to be when tracking an animal.

Not far into the warren of rocks, she caught a glimpse of her Daddy up ahead. He was walking normally and then abruptly he stopped and turned to a voice that spoke to him. *He is meeting someone!* She couldn't see who it was, but Baya had the same idea as her and turned in the other direction to come around the boulders from the other side.

"Well, that was easy enough," said a female voice.

Kenley and Baya crept low to the ground and then peered through a crevice in between the rocks. A woman was there, but Kenley had never seen her before. Despite the heat, she wore a heavy cloak with the hood up over her head.

"Mistress," her Daddy said and lowered the woman's hood. Kenley watched as he put both hands on the stranger's face and begin to kiss her the same way he always kissed her Maman.

**\*\*\*\***

Diamond sat at her desk in her office at the Bardot Academy and listened to her fellow Sect Leaders gathered at the large table in front of her fireplace argue. The sorceresses traveled to Bardot immediately upon learning of Gemini's death and had not agreed on much since.

It was still hard for her to believe that Gemini was dead. Murdered. Right here under all of their noses, but especially hers. As the Divination Leader, she should have foreseen this monstrous act, but instead had been caught completely unawares. It was almost as though blinders had been placed over her eyes, veiling her abilities. Of all the times for her magic to fail her, it had to happen when Gemini was murdered? She was not a fool. She didn't believe it was coincidence and neither did any of the Sect Leaders, and that is what caused them to argue so passionately.

As High Priestess, Gemini was ruler of the coven, but she was also their friend and a mother figure for many of them. With the loss of their beloved leader, Diamond worried what would become of the coven now. Who would be raised to take her place? *Maybe no one*, she thought regretfully. The island had rid itself of the last Mage six years ago and now the only High Priestess was gone.

The door to her office slammed open and Sapphire, the Spell Casting Sect Leader, stormed in. Her eyes were red and puffy, but her expression was angry. Gemini had been her mother.

"You were right, Diamond. A spell had been cast over all of the diamonds used by you and your entire Sect. The traces were faint, but I can confirm without a doubt that they were there. The counterspell has been delivered and the stones are now clear." She paused, and Diamond could tell there was more. She gestured impatiently for her to continue. "Once cleared, the stones revealed devastating news. An army is headed for Nysa's gates, Diamond, and according to your Gems, it is most likely happening at this very moment. "

The arguments began anew.

"I say we step out to meet this force!" demanded the new Combat Sect Leader, Citrine. Unlike her redheaded predecessor, she was dark-skinned with dark-hair, although she happened to be just as fiery in temperament.

The Sect Leader for Runes, Ruby, shook her head. "No! For whatever reason an army may be on the march, it is up to King Maximus and his soldiers to deal with. The sorceresses and shifters should have no part in this. It is the law. It is Prince Beck's law."

Ruby was right, of course, thought Diamond. Practitioners of magic were to remain neutral in any political discord of the lands. Unless magic was being used for harm, they could not intervene in the upcoming conflict, if indeed that is what it turned out to be.

She wished Kiernan and Beck would hurry back. She sent Seana, once a member of her Sect but now a student of fireshifting, to Kondor to inform the four *Savitars* of Gemini's murder. She loathed having to dispatch such devastating news during Rogan's celebration, but what else was she to do? And, now this new evidence from Sapphire pointed to the fact that magic was indeed in play when a spell had been cast to intentionally confuse and deceive her. Citrine's suggestion may very well be justified after all. Diamond never thought she would have to worry about this fact, but a chilling truth blossomed in her mind.

The sorceresses were never marked with the athame after the Demon War.

They were not bound by a blood oath.

It now appeared as though that may have been a fatal oversight.

# CHAPTER 8

## News From Home

Kiernan opened her eyes and it felt like she had never gone to sleep, although she could tell by the faint pink light through her chamber window that she had. It was sunrise.

The baby kicked and she groaned in discomfort. *This child must have ten arms and legs*, she mused to herself as she sat up. Kenley was snuggled up in the blankets beside her and Baya was lying on the rug, but Beck wasn't in the room. The bed was large enough to hold all three of them, but he probably didn't want to wake her and Kenley when he returned from the celebration last night and slept in the sitting room.

A faint musical chant sounded outside the palace. Curious, she got out of bed and picked up her cloak to throw over her nightdress. Padding quietly to the window, she smiled when she saw the Elves performing their Morning Song to Elán. She knew it to be a ritual that all Elves in Massa performed at sunrise—a tender and moving prayer to their woodland deity. It always threatened to bring tears to Kiernan's eyes whenever she heard it, as it was so pure and stirring in tone and lyrics.

With a lighter heart, she turned from the window and walked into the sitting room. "Beck?" she whispered, looking around the large room that contained a couch, two chairs that faced a fireplace and a serving table that—she could now see and smell—held their morning breakfast.

He wasn't there.

She went back into the bedroom and slipped into a dress and soft leather sandals that laced to her knees. Returning once again to the sitting room, she crossed quickly to the outer chamber doors and opened them, surprised to see Roman Traynor outside along with Saber Anton LaFrae who Kirby Nash had assigned as her guard in his absence.

"Roman, why are you here and not with Beck?"

The dark Saber, instantly alert, brushed past her into the room. "He's not in here?"

"No. I was on my way to look for him."

Roman turned to Anton. "Gather up the Sabers. I want every inch of this palace searched for Prince Beck."

Kiernan was surprised by the Captain's ardent response. "Roman, is that really necessary? I'm sure he's here somewhere. If I know my husband, he is probably downstairs stealing sweets from the kitchen."

Roman didn't respond as he walked out of the room and stormed down the wide stone corridor. Kiernan had to run to keep up with his long, angry strides. At the top of the stairs, she saw Rogan and Airron, who must have just returned from his mornin prayers, standing at the front doors. They were talking to someone else and, although the voices weren't raised, their tones sounded anxious.

She continued down the stairs behind Roman, and Rogan turned and nodded to them in relief. "Good, you are awake." He stepped aside, and Kiernan now saw that it was Seana they were talking to, one of the sorceresses from the Academy. *What is she doing in Kondor?*

"What is it? What has happened, Seana?" she demanded.

Seana bowed her head in greeting. "Your Grace." That was as much as she would ever receive from a sorceress. "Terrible news, I am afraid. Diamond sent me."

Kiernan immediately thought it had something to do with her father and braced herself for whatever Seana had to say.

"There is no easy way to prepare for news like this, Your Grace, so I will say it straight out. Gemini Starr is dead."

Kiernan felt the blood rush to her head and reached out to grab Roman's arm. "What? Gemini? That can't be."

"On the day you left for Kondor, she was found dead from a stab wound in Prince Beck's office."

Kiernan shook her head in disbelief. "But, who…?"

Seana shrugged. "We are unsure, but that is not all."

Kiernan scrubbed a tear from her eye. "Go on."

"As I was traveling through Aquataine, one of the watershifters informed me that an army is on the march toward Nysa, although Diamond said nothing of this to me. It is possible that even she does not yet know."

"An army?" Kiernan looked at Rogan and Airron. "Why would the Dwarves or Elves be marching against Nysa?"

Seana shook her head. "Not Dwarves or Elves, Your Grace. Mostly, soldiers of House Etin, but there are also legionnaires from House Everard and even an angry mob of Iserport citizens."

So, the civil unrest that had been simmering had boiled over, but the grievances, it seemed, were directed at House Everard. But, if that was the case, then why were there soldiers involved? Were they along simply to keep the peace during the protest of the people or was this something more? As Kiernan tried to process her thoughts, Airron asked, "Where is Beck?"

"He…he was not in our room, so Roman and I were just coming to look for him."

Rogan turned to Roman. "When you find him, bring him to the great hall." He turned back to Kiernan and Airron. "I will meet you there in a few moments with Erik. As my King, it is my duty to let him know of this at once."

She nodded glumly. Her intuition had never let her down, and she had known for some time now that the intrigues of the Court were becoming more malignant. From Lord Davad Etin's machinations to the murdered man in the forest and now to this news of Gemini. As if that were not enough, for the second time in her life, an army was on the move against those she loved. An army of her own people apparently. To make matters worse, she could not shift to save her own life due to her pregnancy.

Regardless, she would find a way to save her land.

Find a way to stop whoever was responsible for these events.

And, find a way to find her husband.

\*\*\*\*

When Davad heard the shouts and cries coming from the guardroom, his heart thudded in his chest. He knew in that instant that either Abram or Ava had come through with their promise to get him out of this dungeon. Most likely Abram. The Lord had predicted that Davad's release would not come without bloodshed and evidently, he had been correct.

Davad rose from his cot, anxious to confirm that this was indeed a rescue.

He didn't have to wait long. A soldier in the gray and white tunic of House Winslow appeared at his cell with a victorious grin on his young face. He inserted a key into the lock. "My Lord, if you will come with me. Your release comes at the compliments of Lord Winslow." The soldier threw the cell door open wide.

"About bloody time. What have you to report?"

"The Houses of Winslow and Conry hold Nysa. The gates are secured," he said, handing Davad his sword belt.

Davad was impressed. He had not hoped to gain the city until after his army arrived. He took the belt and strapped it around his waist. "Maximus?"

"He is being detained in his chambers under heavy guard. Lord Hamilton and Lady Knapp are also being held separately in their estates, their soldiers all secured. But, Gregaros is missing. He could not be located here in the city or in his home city of York. Curiously, not one soldier from House Gregaros has been seen in Nysa."

"Casualties?"

"Quite a few. Mostly the Scarlet Sabers of the Royal Guard. Maximus' Lions reluctantly laid down their arms when they realized they were outnumbered."

"Very good. Well done, soldier. Now, for the moment I have been looking forward to for a very long time. Take me to our prisoner."

The soldier nodded and proceeded up the stairs to the guardroom. Davad noticed several guards sprawled dead on the floor, including his brutish aggressor. He stepped over to the man's body and kicked him in the head with a forceful blow. Immensely satisfied with that small victory, he ignored the look from Winslow's man and gestured for him to lead the way out.

Emerging onto the main floor of the palace, he was pleased to see the corridors teeming with the colors of House Winslow and House Conry and even some of his Flying Eagles who had traveled to the city with him to attend Court.

Winslow's second, Commander Raj Mendel, noticed him and jogged over to fall into step beside him. "Good to see you, my Lord."

He nodded. "Commander."

"Commander Bassus sends his regards. He should arrive with your army in eight to nine days."

"Good. Walk with me."

The Commander simply nodded without asking questions.

"Do you know what happened to the three Saber Captains?" questioned Davad.

"Roman Traynor is in Kondor, Kirby Nash, we believe, is still in Bardot, and Darin Morel is dead, killed during the siege."

"Bo Franck?"

"Confined with King Maximus."

Davad looked over at Abram's man. "Where is Lord Winslow?"

"Seeing to the security of the city. He should be along any time."

"Very well. I shall see him then. Oh, one other thing. After our visit with King Maximus, you will see to another task right away."

"It will be as you command, my Lord."

"I want you to bring me my brother's head."

Narrowed eyes darted his way. "I will personally see to it, my Lord."

Battle calls for the Savage Badgers or the Crouching Wolves rang through the palace. The skirmish was over, but the bloodlust still hung in the air like a tangible entity. Scarlet clad bodies and servants in livery lay unmoving on the floor at every turn. Maximus' cherished tapestries, pulled from the walls, lay in slashed heaps. Soldiers picked through broken vases, furniture, and porcelain dishes for anything of value still salvageable.

"What did you say?" Davad asked Mendel as he started up the stairs to the upper levels.

"Excuse me, my Lord. I did not say anything."

Davad twitched his head sharply. That was the second time he had thought he heard voices whispering close to his ear, invasive and filled with malicious undertones. The first time was in his cell, alone. "Never mind," he snapped.

On the third floor of the palace, soldiers lined both sides of the corridor in front of King Maximus' chambers. As they approached, Commander

Mendel ordered the guards to stand down, and he threw open the doors to the King's suite.

Davad strode through and scanned the interior. There were several people in the room with Maximus, who currently had his back turned to the door gazing out of a window as if it were any other day. Bo Franck, the scarred Captain of House Everard's army, a Saber, and three female servants, one of which was Belle, Maximus' long-time house manager.

Davad smiled. "Maximus! I would ask how your day is going, but it is clearly not going very well."

Maximus' dark eyes turned to him, and Davad suddenly felt the urge to kneel, but he resisted.

"I know you are not a fool, Davad, so stop acting like one."

He laughed. "A fool! I have control of the city and you are imprisoned! Who is the fool here?"

"And, how long do you think this will last? House Everard has twice the size of any standing army, and I still have the House support of Gregaros, Knapp, and Hamilton. You have two allied Houses, Davad."

"Your House support and their legionnaires are in custody, Maximus. You are finished."

"The people of Iserlohn will never accept an unlawful attempt to overthrow a legitimate reign, Davad. Surely, you realize that."

Davad nodded. "You are right, Maximus. The people would never accept this if it were not absolutely necessary."

The King's eyebrows rose in question.

"The people would never accept the illegitimate ousting of a *sane* King," he replied. "They will, however, praise me for my actions once they learn of all of your crimes. In fact, the talk has already begun. They now know that it was you who drove Iserlohn's largest port city to ruin, the children and women starving to death under your watchful eye. Lord Winslow will testify to your erratic behavior during Court, and Lady Conry will recount how you repeatedly raped her. Oh, yes, you have been a very naughty King."

"You disgust me!"

"And, you disgust me, Maximus! You and your vile shifter family!"

"That is what this is about, isn't it? You have always resented the fact that my family can wield magic."

"Of course, I do!  As should any decent citizen of this land!  You were much too powerful, Maximus, but the fact is, your family will be of no help to you now. You see, I have planned this moment very meticulously. Your daughter cannot shift at the moment and your son in marriage, well, let's just say that we will not be seeing him around any time soon."

Dark eyes blazed with anger. "What have you done?"

Davad leveled his gaze squarely at his nemesis. "Not for you to worry about. Not where you are going in any case."  He slowly unsheathed his sword. "At the cost to your lives," he said to the others in the room, but did not take his eyes off Maximus, "stand back and do not interfere."

# CHAPTER 9

## A Child's Tale

For the first time since Rogan returned to the royal seat of Deepstone to live in the King's palace, the magnificence of the great hall escaped him. On any other day, he marveled at the unparalleled skill of the intricate masonry carvings and Dwarven runes that encircled the room and the stone walls polished to a high sheen. The ceiling, easily a hundred feet high or more, was supported by square sandstone pillars and arches mottled with veins of swirling color. A crystallized marble floor sparkled richly in the light of several braziers placed strategically throughout the hall.

At this moment, he didn't see any of it. It had been quite a long time since he had lost his temper, but he was getting very close now. An army was headed to Nysa, and his mild-mannered King refused to send military aid to King Maximus. Many people he called friends could potentially die if he didn't find a way to convince Erik to change his mind.

He took a deep breath and tried again.

"You were very young during the Demon War, my King, but have you forgotten so soon what isolation did to this island? The Kings vowed at the end of that war to unify the lands and now is our chance to fulfill that oath. King Maximus is in need of our assistance."

The young monarch shook his head. "This is not an invasion of outside forces, cousin. This is a civil war, and one for which the Dwarves have no interest or business taking part in."

"My King! You must listen to reason!"

"Kal Rogan…," growled General Klay Arsten in warning. The leader of the Iron Fists, planted directly behind his King, gave him a look that indicated he would tolerate no disrespect. His brown beard, parted into two plaits was decorated with a large array of gems. A glistening shirt of chainmail covered his chest and hung to his knees.

Rogan ignored him. This was too important. "But, Beck Atlan is now missing!"

"Are you somehow convinced the two events are related?" King Erik inquired.

Rogan nodded. "Sure as I am standing here, and so does his wife, the Princess of Iserlohn."

As if on cue, Kiernan and Airron entered the great hall. Sympathy for Kiernan washed over him. He would never say it to her directly, but she looked ill from the dark circles under her eyes and the way she hunched over her belly as if in pain when she walked. Airron held her arm at the elbow and steered her toward them.

"Any news?" he quickly asked her.

She shook her head. "No." She reached out to hug him. "I'm worried, Rogan."

He held her tight and whispered in her ear. "You have my word, Kiernan, we will find Beck. I promise you that."

King Erik rose from his seat and approached. "Princess, let me assure you that everything that can be done is being done. All available soldiers and the Iron Fists are actively searching for your husband."

She nodded. "I know. Thank you, Erik."

Rogan put a protective arm around her waist. "I was just discussing with my King the need for action from Deepstone."

Arsten once again growled, but didn't say anything intelligible.

"Kal Rogan speaks truthfully, Princess. We have discussed this matter, and I very much regret to tell you that my hands are tied here. I cannot commit military support to the civil disputes of other lands."

Rogan grunted and threw his hands up in the air in frustration. Surprisingly, Kiernan put a hand out to restrain him. "King Erik is right, Rogan. I have been involved in the politics of Massa far longer than you, and I understand and support his decision. This is Iserlohn's problem and for Iserlohn to handle."

"Princess!" The shout drew their eyes to the doors of the great hall. Roman Traynor, his eagle eyes furious, stomped toward them ahead of two of his Scarlet Sabers, a third being dragged between them.

"Roman?" Kiernan asked.

"This is Saber Lino Brega, Your Grace. He saw Prince Beck last night before he disappeared."

The Saber hung his head in regret and sported a bloodied gash on his cheek.

"Go on," ordered Roman. "Tell the Princess what you told us."

The Saber fell to one knee. "I...I saw Prince Beck last night, Your Grace. But, I had no idea that Captain Tray—"

Roman Traynor's hand swept out and backhanded the man with tremendous force. "Idiot! Just tell her what you saw!"

The soldier shook his head and when he looked up, a deep cut in his lip bled onto his chin. "I saw Prince Beck leave the party last night. I...I was patrolling the outside perimeter and watched him approach a woman who was standing among the boulders."

"Why did you not report this, Brega?" demanded Roman Traynor.

The soldier shook his head miserably. "Forgive me, Your Grace. I thought he was simply meeting with...with a mistress. That is what he called her. My duty was to the perimeter, not to—"

Again, Roman hit the man and he fell over on his side to the marble floor.

"Roman!" screamed Kiernan. "Enough!"

"I saw him, too, Maman." All eyes turned to the little girl standing just outside of their circle. Kiernan rushed to her, and Rogan inwardly cringed that she had just witnessed Roman's unusual brutality.

"What, darling? What did you see?"

Kenley was crying now, the tears streaming down her pink cheeks. "I saw Daddy."

Kiernan knelt in front of Kenley and grabbed her shoulders. "This is important. Where did you see him? What was he doing?"

"He left me alone at the party, Maman. He told me to go to bed, but I didn't want to go by myself, so I followed him."

"Where, Kenley? Where did you follow him?" she urged.

"Into the boulders, Maman. The Saber was telling the truth. He met a lady there."

"And, what happened?"

The little girl paused. "He kissed her."

Rogan heard Kiernan moan and gestured for Airron to take her away. The Elf immediately lifted Kiernan from her position kneeling in front of Kenley and, in her anguish, she offered no resistance.

Rogan took her place in front of the little girl. "Do you remember what this lady looked like, Kenley?"

"Yes." Her bright green eyes rapidly blinked back the pool of tears settling in their depths like puddles. "She had a cloak on, but I could see that she had black hair. She also had something strange on her face."

"Strange? What do you mean?"

"Well, there were three long scars on one cheek."

\*\*\*\*

There is a place deep in the soul where people carry their innermost fears. For the fortunate, these fears never materialize. They surface every once in awhile, but get pushed back down and tucked into place and never amount to much.

For the not so fortunate, they come in the form of Avalon Ravener.

Kiernan had always known that this day would come. From the little she knew about the sorceress, it had been easy to predict that she would never let things lie. She would need to settle the score, just like she did with Titus. There had been no reason for her to enter Nysa and kill the young Cyman all those years ago, but she did.

And, now she had Beck.

*What does she want with him? Will she physically harm him? Does she hope to receive a ransom?* Kiernan winced and reached out to grab her bedpost. It was impossible to stop the mental images that played across her mind like a sick and tortuous display. Titus told them about the depraved desires of this woman, and now her husband could well be the focus of them. Both Rogan and Airron vowed to search until Beck was found, but Kiernan had her doubts. Avalon had many years to plan this abduction, and she was a sorceress and bodyshifter of incredible skill. If she didn't want to be found, she most likely would not be.

Kiernan could not remember ever feeling so helpless before. Even when she spent those weeks with the Gems in Elloree and was kept behind a locked door, she always knew that she had options still available to her. This time, she had none.

Thinking of the Gems naturally caused her to think of Gemini. The sorceress who had been like a second mother to her would know what to do. She would know exactly how to track the woman who she had known over three hundred years ago.

The errant thought hit her then. *Is that why Gemini is now dead? Because she would have had the best chance at tracking down and destroying Avalon?* It seemed likely now. Because of Avalon, two of the most important people in her life were gone—one permanently and the other's future still undecided.

The realization caused her heart to flutter until she felt like it would burst from her chest and take flight. Taking deep breaths to calm herself, she sat on the edge of the bed with her head between her legs. She stayed that way for a long time, until her panic eased and she could breathe evenly again.

When she felt she finally had the strength to stand, she rose to her feet and finished packing the rest of her clothes. She decided to leave Beck's bag here, just in case he returned, and that seemingly harmless decision almost triggered another panic attack. *I'm abandoning my husband along with his clothes.*

A knock sounded on her door, and she walked into the sitting room on shaky legs. The panic would have to wait. She had a daughter to think about, and a father who could be in mortal danger if she didn't return to him.

Saber Anton LaFrae opened the door and announced Rogan, Janin and Airron.

Janin immediately rushed to her and held her in a tight embrace. "I am very sorry, Kiernan."

Kiernan simply nodded. She didn't trust herself to speak fearing it would come out incoherent.

Airron approached and took her hands as soon as Janin released her. "Kiernan, we *will* find him. Do you hear me?"

She nodded again and cleared her throat. "I...I have to return to Nysa to help my father. I can't abandon my realm and the people I am responsible to protect." She paused. "Beck would understand."

"I know he would, Kiernan," Airron quickly assured her. "You are making the only decision you can. King Erik still refuses to send aid to Iserlohn, so Rogan and I discussed our options and have decided to split up. I will stay here and search for Beck. My animal forms will help me to scent and track him better than the soldiers can, and Rogan and Janin will seek aid for Nysa and your father."

Kiernan shook her head. "But, how? Where?"

Rogan smiled slyly. "If I can't raise the Deepstone Army, I will raise one of my own." Before she could question him further, he held up a hand. "Don't ask."

She looked at the two Dwarves. "But you two have just been married."

Janin snorted. "I have been married to this man for six years. We just happened to make it official yesterday." She looked directly in Kiernan's eyes. "There is nothing we would not do to help your family or to help find Beck."

Her comment touched Kiernan's heart. "Thank you, Janin." She looked at her best friends. "I thank all of you."

A loud commotion sounded in the hallway. Kiernan hurried toward the door, but it slammed opened before she arrived.

"I said let me in!"

A beautiful Elven woman stormed into the room, her violet eyes furious. Her gaze landed on Airron and pinned him in place. "There you are! You will not get away from me so easy again, you lout!"

Kiernan waved away the angry Sabers at the door and looked at Airron. "What in the Highworld is going on here?"

Airron burst out in laughter.

"Airron! Who is this woman? Why are you laughing like that?"

"I am only laughing because otherwise I will be crying."

Rogan glared at him. "What did you do now?"

Airron shook his mane of white hair and then held out his arm toward the woman. "Kiernan, Rogan, Janin. Let me introduce you to the Lady Melania Shael. My wife."

**\*\*\*\***

Davad Etin stopped short in his intention to run his sword through King Maximus' heart when Bo Franck, the Saber, and the servants stepped up together to form a line in front of their King. Even the stout palace steward, Belle, who looked ready to take him on single-handedly.

Raj Mendel spoke over his shoulder. "My Lord?"

Davad shook his head. "Stand back, Commander. I will handle this."

The soldier moved to the door.

"So, you are going to allow these people to be cut down in your defense, Maximus? Are you that much of a coward?"

Maximus calmly pushed through to the front of the line. "Oh, they have no fear of being cut down, Davad, because you are just about to leave."

Davad tilted his head. "Oh, I am? You do not give the orders any longer, Maximus. Are you that arrogant that you can't see what is happening? Or, are you really as crazy as I have suggested?"

Maximus ignored his comments. "Before we part company, Davad, think on this. The people of Iserlohn will never accept your lies. They will never accept you. Find it in yourself to give up your schemes now so that more innocent people are not killed."

"I have no intention of giving anything up, you fool! And, for the record, the innocent do not die under my rule—only those that stand in my way. My *schemes* are really quite simple. You will be dead momentarily, and I will be sitting on the Iserlohn throne by the end of next week. I will have no problem rallying the support of the other Houses once they face the reality of their limited choices. You have lost, Maximus! I have won!"

Maximus snorted. "I should have known you wouldn't listen to reason. A King protects and serves his people, Davad, he doesn't walk across their backs to obtain a higher position. I implore you one last time to have mercy on them."

"Enough of this! Stand back!" he once again ordered the line of people.

"As I said, you will now be leaving us. Goodbye, Davad, and think on what I said." Maximus turned to the side and gave a terse nod. Suddenly, one of the servants, a blonde woman, thrust her arm out and pointed.

"*Reversi!*"

Davad's body involuntarily wrenched upright and his sword fell from his fingers. The door slammed open, and he turned to the cry of surprise from Raj Mendel behind him as the man backed out of the room with unnatural, jerky movements.

Davad issued his own shout as he began to jerk backward. He felt like a marionette powerless to fight against an unseen puppeteer. His arms flailed wildly as his feet took step after step toward the back of the room. With a final yelp, he was yanked through the doors and slammed into the wall on the opposite side of the hall.

The soldiers in the corridor, finally realizing something was amiss, rushed to enter the room, but the doors crashed shut. As soon as they did, Davad felt the invisible strings over his body dissipate, and he convulsed once in a repulsed shudder. *That blonde woman cast a spell at me! She's no servant, but a bloody sorceress!*

He stood up from the floor and strode through the knot of soldiers. "Move!" He reached for the door handle, but it was locked. He knew then that they would never get that door open. His instincts told him that it was magically sealed and no amount of force would open it.

"Stay here!" he ordered Commander Mendel. "If anybody so much as takes a peek out of this door, strike them dead!"

With that, he retreated back down the corridor. *Oh, this is not the end of it, Maximus. You may have found a temporary hole to hide in, but you will be ferreted out and disposed of. I promise you that.*

"And, find me a new sword!" he shouted over his shoulder.

# CHAPTER 10

## Sinister Motives

*Beck Atlan is mine.* Avalon Ravener could hardly believe that her plan had worked so flawlessly. She pressed her body against his chest and wrapped her arms around his waist.

His large hands framed her face as he gazed down at her with unadulterated love in his eyes. With pressure from his thumbs, he tilted her head to the side and slowly lowered his lips to hers. He moaned softly against her mouth.

Avalon allowed the kiss for a moment and tried to enjoy it but, unable to do so, she pulled back.

*"Ejektelo!"*

Her spell sent the earthshifter soaring through the cavern to crash hard against the stone wall with a grunt.

This was the third time she had to use the repel spell on her captive. For some reason, the glamour spell worked very strongly with him. She guessed it was due to the fact that he was a shifter because she had never seen this type of reaction when used on the Cyman men who did not have the gift of magic.

She laughed inwardly when she realized that he must have acted this same way when she cast the glamour spell on him years ago in Iserport. *What a scene he must have made with those two prostitutes!* She only wished she had been there to witness the spectacle.

"Mistress, please!" Beck pleaded, getting to his feet. "Did I do something wrong? Do I not make you happy?"

She turned her back on him. "You will make me happy by staying right where you are."

"Yes, Mistress. Then, you will give me another kiss?"

"Maybe," she muttered noncommittally over her shoulder. Unfortunately, the glamour was necessary until she could secure the earthshifter properly. Once he did not pose a physical threat to her, she would remove the spell so she could question him regarding the reason for his kidnapping.

The Protetor.

She only learned of the existence of the book from one of her informants this past year. With that book, she would have access to all of the secret arts of the Mage and, most importantly, the formula for the LifeFire Tonic. In the six years that she had been unable to take the life-giving elixir, she had aged considerably. More every day, she felt the attrition of her three hundred and twenty five years. Her hair was starting to gray at the temples and her face had become hollow and gaunt, the fine lines of age spider-webbing across her face.

Oh, yes, she needed that tonic, but she also needed something else from Beck Altan.

His body.

Her plans required access to the palace that only a royal family member could provide. She originally thought to use Kiernan Atlan—she was the weaker of the two—but, once she discovered that Beck was in possession of The Protetor, she decided that he would fulfill both purposes quite nicely.

She moved to the stone table cut into the cavern wall and studied the maps strewn across its surface. They were still a considerable distance from her hideaway in Farout Falls where she had been living in isolation with her small group of twelve Cyman followers. Why the Cymans who deserted during the war willingly followed, she was unsure, but it did help that this particular band was unaware that most of their brethren had traveled back to Nordik. She made sure these outcasts had little access to information and stayed well hidden. In truth, they had formed an unlikely family of sorts and depended on each other for survival.

A shadow fell across the cave entrance and a Cyman soldier ducked into the spacious cavern. "What is it, Cyrus?"

"The place is crawlin' with soldiers, Mistress. We will 'ave to git movin' to The Falls much sooner than we thought."

She figured as much. The disappearance of a Prince was sure to trigger a very significant manhunt.

"Very well."

She looked over at her prisoner. He leered at her ridiculously, and she shuddered. He was far too pretty for her taste. After living with Cyman men for hundreds of years, the smaller and weaker men of Massa seemed like pitiful creatures to her. Almost feminine. Oh, Beck Atlan was larger than most Massans, but still paltry compared to her Cymans.

She thought about her last lover, Titus. She had wished often over the years that it had not been necessary to kill him, but it had. She had not taken another lover since then. She wondered why? It wasn't as if she had ever been in love with the boy. Or had she? She shook her head. Whatever the case, that was then and this was now. The bottom line was that Beck Atlan needed to die and not just to gain The Protetor or because she needed his body. He needed to die so that a new King could be raised in Iserlohn.

**\*\*\*\***

"Your wife?" questioned Rogan incredulously. "Very funny, Airron. Now, tell us what is really going on. We don't have time for your usual games right now."

Airron's smile melted from his face when he turned to address the Elven woman. "Melania. I would like to have a few words with my friends in private. Will you please excuse us for a few moments?"

The silver-haired beauty lifted her chin and crossed her arms at her chest. "No."

"Melania, you don't understand—"

"It is *you*," she declared, uncrossing her arms and gliding over to him in a flash on her light feet, "who does not understand. You are my husband now, Airron Falewir, and you must start behaving as such. You cannot just disappear without telling me!"

"I left a note!"

"A note! We must have these discussions together, my husband. As your wife, I should be traveling with you wherever you go."

Airron ran a hand through his hair in frustration. "Look, I'm sorry, Melania. It appears that I need more instruction in being a proper husband."

"As well as a proper Elf!"

He nodded in acknowledgement. "Yes, you're right. But, right now, I must talk to my friends." He paused. "Princess Kiernan's husband, Beck, has disappeared and we're trying to find him."

Melania swung her head toward Kiernan, color blossoming in her cheeks. Evidently, her noble upbringing overrode her anger, and she bent her body into an elegant curtsy. "My apologies, Your Grace. I hope you do not judge all Elven woman by my behavior just now. Please forgive the untimely intrusion."

Kiernan gave her a gracious nod. "I appreciate your words, Lady Melania, and I assure you that I have nothing but respect for all of the Elven women of Haventhal. Besides, I can fully appreciate how marriage to Airron could bring about this type of reaction."

Janin snorted when she tried to hold back a laugh.

Rogan just turned his back on the conversation.

Airron's smile was tight. "Now that everyone has had their fun, I will ask you again, Melania, to please wait for me downstairs. I will join you in just a few moments. Loren is here if you wish to seek him out for company."

When Rogan turned back, he saw the Elven woman nod her head once and then leave the room.

Airron breathed out a sigh of relief and dropped into one of the stuffed chairs by the fireplace as soon as the door closed behind his wife.

"Married? Really, Airron?" Rogan started in immediately. "You didn't think that detail important enough to share with your best friends?"

Airron's trademark grin was nowhere to be found. "I guess I've been in denial." He stood abruptly. "And, it's all King Jerund's fault! He insisted that it was time I took a wife. For weeks and weeks, he badgered me about it and then one evening a few weeks ago, the old goat tricked me into attending one of his many fêtes which, by the way, I had been quite successfully avoiding, and it turned out to be my wedding!" He started pacing. "What could I have done? All of Elven high society was in attendance. Melania was already standing at the altar looking so lovely. Gorgeous, in fact."

"Have you consummated—" Rogan began, but Airron quickly interrupted.

"What? Highworld, no! Not that I don't want to," he promptly clarified. "She is very beautiful, of course, but how can you be intimate with a woman that nags at you all the time? For two weeks, she has been trying to mold me into the perfect Elf! Well, I am not perfect and that is perfectly fine with me!"

The women seemed to be at loss for words so Rogan approached his friend and patted him on the back. "Everything will turn out for the best, Airron, but right now we have important decisions to make."

Airron nodded.

"As Airron was saying before his *wife* appeared, we need to split up."

"Just find Beck," Kiernan pleaded, looking at Airron. "Please just find my husband."

"My word on it," the Elf replied. "I just need a few minutes first to send Melania back to Haventhal where she belongs."

Kiernan shook her head. "She doesn't seem the type who will go easily."

"No, she won't. She is a spoiled noble brat and is far too used to getting her way all the time. Well, those beautiful violet eyes do not work on me! No way! She will do as I say or my name is not Airron Falewir!"

\*\*\*\*

"So, she's going with you?" Loren asked, his thin eyebrows arched in disbelief.

Airron strode angrily along the marble foyer and exited through the palace doors. "It appears that way."

As always in Kondor, or anywhere in Deepstone for that matter, the sound of chisels and hammers striking stone permeated the air. Dwarven masons tended to the multitude of stonework in the city around the clock, and the pride they took in their workmanship was legendary throughout Massa.

"Where are you going?" asked Loren.

"To the stables to saddle the horses! I planned to track Beck on my own four legs as a Gangi dog, which by the way, are the best trackers on the island, but no. Now, I have to travel by horse with my *wife!*"

"Would you like me to go with you and help out?" his friend asked cautiously.

Airron quickly shook his head. "Thank you, but, no. The more people along, the more the scents will be confused."

"As you wish," Loren said, and for some reason he sounded relieved. "I will bid you farewell then. I need to return to my duty with the Gladewatchers."

Airron stopped and stuck out his arm to trade grips with Loren. "I'll see you soon, then. Explain to King Jerund what has happened and that I will be detained for a period of time."

Loren nodded and turned to depart, but then stopped and looked back at him. "I think you should give Melania a chance, Airron. If you dig under the surface a bit, I think you will find something quite unexpected."

A high shriek cut through the air. "Airron Falewir! Have you not saddled those horses yet? What is the matter with you?"

"You were saying?" Airron asked Loren.

The Elf bowed and backed away hastily. "I was saying that I must be on my way. Good luck to you, my friend." And, with that, he was gone.

Airron sighed and watched his wife approach. *Is there any credibility to what Loren said?* He had been busy avoiding Melania, but maybe he should have been putting more effort into getting to know her better. She was beautiful. A blind elf would be hard pressed to miss that fact. She wore a high-necked, sleeveless emerald dress that swirled around her hips. Her arms were tanned and muscular and her lips…

"Hello! Are you going to just stand there staring all day?" she asked.

Airron started. "Er, what? No! No, you're right. We must get moving."

She nodded her head in approval and walked past him toward the stables. A Dwarven groom was just bringing their horses around when they arrived. The Dwarf handed the reins of a powerfully built, sable Haventi to him and a black and white Pinto to Melania. Airron was pleasantly surprised to see such high caliber horses in Deepstone. If there was anything an Elf of Haventhal knew, it was horses.

An accomplished equestrian—that much he did know about her—Melania swept up into the saddle gracefully without assistance.

"Earlier I tracked Beck's scent moving in a westerly direction toward the Koda River," he informed her. "We should ride that way for few leagues, and then I will bodyshift again to get a fresh trail."

She simply nodded.

He suddenly thought of something. "You have never seen me shift. Will it bother you to see me transform into an animal?"

"I knew what I was getting into when I married you."

*What does that mean?* He decided not to pursue, and they started their journey through the Land of Stone sharing little conversation. Two hours later, they shared a cold meal of bread and cheese from their saddles, along with Airron's promise of fresh rabbit and leeks over a fire when they stopped for the evening. Knowing he wouldn't find wood along the desolate landscape, a bundle of logs sat behind him on the saddle.

He looked out over the horizon. The road they traveled cut through the red sandstone terrain like the winding body of a serpent and seemed to go on forever with no end in sight. Enormous buttes in a variety of shapes and sizes and colors lined both sides of the road in dramatic twisting patterns. The black holes of what must have been hundreds of caves and caverns dotted the stone bluffs.

Airron much preferred the lush hills and forests of Haventhal, but had to admit that Deepstone offered a picturesque beauty both alluring and mysterious. He could now understand some of the Dwarves unyielding obsession with preserving the luster of the stone.

The countryside this far outside of the city was eerily deserted, although he knew that they would encounter villages and people closer to the life-giving Koda.

He stopped the Haventi. "I better make sure we are still on Beck's trail."

Melanie halted her horse and alighted to the ground with ease, brushing the dust from her emerald dress and then securing a knife belt around her middle. "Is there any shade or water in this Highworld-forsaken land?"

Airron handed her one of the two water bags attached to his saddle. "You can rest over by those boulders," he said, pointing to a flat formation of rocks. "That should afford you some comfort from the heat. I won't be long."

Accepting the bag without further comment, she walked the Pinto off the road.

Airron reached out with his mind and tried to create a mental connection with his horse using the technique King Jerund showed him, but it didn't work. After all these years, he was still unable to perform the Elven magic that should have been innate to him. Frustrated, he called out to Melania. "Can you tell this bloody animal to stay put?"

Almost immediately, the Haventi let out a contented whisker, so she must have done as he asked.

He undressed behind the horse, and then the air glistened as his body contorted downward into a Gangi dog.

The dog took off at a run and put his snout to the ground, swinging his head back and forth along the road. The scent of the human he tracked was very well known to him, and he would be able to pick it out even with the overpowering smell of the horses nearby.

Many scents saturated the ground and the air. Humans, animals, and something else. Something not quite human, but he couldn't identify the source. Dismissing the puzzle, he ventured further down the road and it wasn't long before he found the scent he sought—the trail of the human.

The Gangi, busy with his work, did not register the new dangerous smell that suddenly coated the air. Simultaneous with the rabid aroma that drifted to his nose came the terrified shriek of the Elven woman.

# CHAPTER 11

## Half An Army is Better Than None

The hackles on the Gangi dog lifted in a wild desire to kill, and he tore back down the stone road toward the scent of the rabid mountain lion.

As soon as he skidded around a small bend, he saw the Elven woman crouched behind a boulder with a large knife gripped in her outstretched fist. The lion paced directly in front of the rock and issued a menacing roar in an attempt to intimidate his prey. The Elven girl made a sudden movement and the lion reacted, clenching his hind legs and leaping into the air to scale the boulder.

The Gangi jumped at the same time and transformed into one of the deadly black wolves that lived in the Grayan Forest. The two animals collided in midair and the wolf clamped his jaws onto the neck of the unsuspecting cat. The combatants tumbled to the ground in a fury of growls and muscled ferocity. The wolf bit down with razor-sharp fangs and ripped away a portion of flesh, delicious hot blood spewing from the wound. The lion yelped in pain and tried to rake the wolf with his claws, but the wolf was too big, too maddened in his need to protect.

The wolf knew there was something wrong with this particular foe. The lion carried a sickness and had to be destroyed.

Suddenly, the Elven girl was at his side, and she plunged her knife into the chest of the mountain lion. His quarry trembled violently, took a last dying breath and then was still.

The wolf got to his feet, angry that the kill had been taken from him. He snorted once, shook out his black coat and padded away.

The air flickered and Airron bodyshifted into his Elven form, grateful he could think like a human again. He didn't want to be consumed with unfulfilled bloodlust any longer. The hunger and thirst for dominion so natural to the wolf coalesced into razor-sharp physical pain for him. Though he always maintained complete control of the actions of the form he assumed, the instincts and perspective always came directly from the animal.

He took a deep breath to calm his simmering emotions and dressed quickly, anxious to see how Melania was faring. The first thing he noticed when he reached her side was how pale her face appeared.

"Well, that's not something you see every day," she observed. "If ever."

"Did I scare you?"

She hesitated, but then shook her head. "No, not really. I'm just grateful to you that you saved my life. *Sinsai*." Thank you.

Airron tilted his head in question. "Why didn't you just command the beast to turn away?"

"I tried, but it didn't work. He was rabid. Diseased in the mind. That's why I killed him. I never would have done so had he not been so dangerous to leave in his present condition. It goes against my nature to harm an animal."

"I sensed the disease in him as well."

"Can we continue on?" she asked suddenly. "The faster you find your friend, the faster I can get out of this blasted heat and we can return to our lives in Haventhal."

Her comment raised questions in his mind. "It seems strange that we are married, when we hardly know each other. Will you be moving into my residence in Sarphia? We really haven't had much of a chance to make these decisions since the...the ceremony."

"Of course, I will live with you. But, Airron, I tell you now that I will not tolerate any man who makes a mess of his home. You will take care of your own things as I refuse to cater to you. And, you will dress properly as befitting your station as a royal-in-waiting. That tunic you are wearing is far too plain, so I will personally see to your wardrobe." She paused but she wasn't finished yet. The hands had found the hips. "Lastly, Airron

Falewir, and on this I will not bend. There will be no carousing with other women! Do you hear me?"

"What does that mean exactly?"

"Was I not perfectly clear?"

"You wish for me to stop seeing other women, yet we have never shared a marriage bed," he pointed out bluntly.

The tips of her ears peeking up through her silver hair turned bright red. "No, we have not. Yet."

"And, when will...?"

"When I am good and ready! That is when!" She grabbed the reins of her Pinto and led, no, dragged, the poor animal back onto the road. Obviously, the conversation was over.

With a shake of his head, Airron had to wonder if Beck and Rogan found marriage this difficult.

****

"I wouldn't be overly concerned, Davad," remarked Abram. "Maximus will have to come out to drink and eat at some point. Stubborn he may be, but I do not think that he will choose to starve to death."

Davad nodded in agreement. The King couldn't hold out for very long. "You're right, Abram. We will be waiting when he does."

Seated at a table in the library of the royal palace, Ava Conry glared up from an intense study of her fingernails. "Until then?"

Davad ignored her and strode to the library door to reassure himself that the two Eagles he ordered posted outside were still there. The room had two exits, and he insisted that both be defended exclusively by legionnaires of his House. His paranoia of an assassin's arrow increased ever day.

After spotting the soldiers, Davad turned from the door and began to pace. With his mind racing so frantically, it helped to sort through the jumble of his thoughts if he was moving. Ever since he was released from the cells, he had been finding it difficult to think straight. *Am I ill? The Highworld knows I didn't eat very much.* With a mental shrug, he turned his concentration to the conversation before him.

"Hugo Bassus is still several days from Nysa. Our main concern until he arrives is Lord Gregaros. He is a former Scarlet Saber and it disturbs me greatly that he is missing. Where is he? What is he planning?"

The only other person in the room, Commander Raj Mendel, spoke up. "He is most likely in Bardot awaiting Princess Kiernan's return with Captain Nash. We could send a unit there to engage the White Tigers."

Davad quickly shook his head. "To invade Bardot would only invite the magic users to get involved. We don't want to give them any reason to enter this fight."

"It may be that Gregaros is simply sitting it out and waiting for a victor to emerge," Mendel offered.

"That would be ideal, but I don't think we can count on that. What we need is information."

"So, send a man in a Lion tunic to Bardot to see if Gregaros is there," Abram suggested. "Soldiers talk. If he listens in at the right places, he will be able to uncover what Gregaros is up to."

Davad stopped his frenzied pacing, Abram's sensible words soothing his anxiety. He glared at Ava. "Well, at least Abram is contributing some common sense to this enterprise. Well done, Abram. Commander, arrange for a man to go into Bardot immediately."

"As you command, my Lord."

"Are the town criers delivering the messages we discussed?" Davad asked.

Commander Mendel nodded. "By now every person in Nysa will have learned of the King's misdeeds and his cowardly refusal to come out and defend his city."

Davad returned to the table and sat again, calm for the first time all day. "And, what about you, Lady Conry? Do you have any useful ideas to share with the group or are you going to sit there like a lump?"

Ava Conry glowered at him and stood, all eyes on the large breasts that threatened to tumble from her dress. "Allow me to share this, Davad Etin. I'm sick to death of your tiresome plotting and posturing. Lord Winslow may have the patience to sit here and hold your hand all day, but I certainly do not!" Her lip raised in a snarl. "Hear me well. There is only one question I am concerned about. When in the Highworld am I going to be Queen?"

\*\*\*\*

Rogan propped himself up on his elbow and gazed down at his sleeping wife, feeling fortunate to have her and the children in his life. Growing up an orphan, he had always dreamt of a family to call his own and now that dream had become a reality. It made him shudder to think back on all those years in exile feeling unloved and abandoned by the people who were supposed to care for him the most—his parents. He found out later that all he had believed to be true had been a misconception and that his parents had in fact given their very lives protecting him, and the knowledge allowed him to open his heart to Janin.

She must have felt his weighty stare because she came awake with a small smile.

"Good morning, Kal Rogan," she murmured.

He reached out to remove a twig from her hair. After leaving Kondor two days ago, they traveled at a quick pace through Deepstone and had just now crossed over the border into Haventhal.

"Good morning, Kali," he replied lovingly. "I must admit that I had envisioned our first few evenings of marital bliss many times since the day I asked you to marry me, but I can honestly say that they never included us spending them out in the elements, lying on the ground and sharing a bedroll."

She turned into his body and wrapped her arms around his waist. "If you will remember, my husband, this is not the first time we have skulked together through the woods of Haventhal."

He smirked at the reminder. "Yes, trouble was chasing us then and appears to have found us again."

She sat up and ran her fingers through her long hair. "Now, tell me, where do we find this army of yours?"

Rogan stood and poked through his bag for a quick bite of cheese and fruit before they set out again. "Oh, it has already found *us*."

Janin jumped to her feet and scanned the wooded area surrounding their small campsite. "What? Where?"

Rogan handed her a pear, but she ignored it and buckled on her sword belt.

He shrugged and took a bite of the fruit. "We're surrounded."

The rustle of many feet moving through the trees broke the early morning silence of the forest. Rogan noticed Janin reach for the short sword on her hip, so he took hold of her wrist and stopped her. "No."

She directed an icy glare his way, but she did remove her hand. Albeit slowly.

"Hello, rude Dwarf," said a high-pitched voice from the woods and a pint-sized warrior came into view surrounded by a band of armed fighters. With blonde curls bouncing around his angelic face, Rogan recognized Vinni Vee, the Tribe Leader and Cloud Reader of the Halfies.

During the Demon War, the Balor Mountains where the Halfies made their home were lost. Since then, the two thousand or so Halfies on the island roamed from one location to the next searching for a suitable place to live. It was really quite a nuisance to Massans everywhere because of their bad behavior, but it was an inborn trait they couldn't alter any more than the color of their eyes. Trouble making was as innate as breathing to the Halfie race.

Rogan recognized that it was also what made them a formidable force in the Demon War. Despite their small size—most Halfie males stood around four feet tall—the damage they inflicted on the invading Cyman Army was considerable. Although, they were unable to kill the enemy with their tactics, they were able to render terrible debilitating injuries, and there were many a Cyman today who walked with a limp caused by the Halfies in battle.

Rogan vowed to try and find a permanent home for the Halfies when this new threat was behind him. The imps deserved to have a home to call their own, and it would eliminate the terrible mischief they caused across the island.

Now, though, he needed their help. Rogan feigned indignation. "Rude? Come now, Vinni! I wasn't rude to you. Well, maybe just a little bit, but if you will recall, I was under a great deal of pressure the last time we met."

"True," Vinni replied, "but, I still do not like you very much."

"That hurts, Vinni."

"So will my spear up your—"

"Come on! I need your help here! I wouldn't have come all this way looking for you if it wasn't important."

"Your problems are no concern of mine." Vinni stuck out his tongue and moved to stick him with his spear.

Janin was faster.

The scrape of metal grated in the air when she lunged forward and used her short sword to swipe at Vinni's weapon before it reached him. Her action caused the Halfie tribe to murmur in discontent and stomp their spears to the ground in a show of aggression.

*Demon's breath! This woman never listens to me!* He had a heartbeat to wonder if Beck or Airron found marriage this difficult, when the Halfies advanced, circling the two of them with inimitable hostility in their eyes.

"Back-to-back!" shouted Rogan, and for once, his wife complied right away. "Be careful! They will try to slice the tendons in your hamstring if they can get close enough."

Several warriors thrust their spears at them, but Janin blocked every one, turning his body with hers in tandem to defend from all sides.

"Vinni!" Rogan shouted. "I am *Savitar,* and you know what I am capable of. Stop now before someone gets hurt."

"Only you will get hurt in this, rude Dwarf," Vinni cackled.

Rogan growled in pain when one of the spears slipped through Janin's defenses and pierced his thigh.

"Summon your fire, Rogan!" Janin demanded.

Rogan shook his head. He had to try to end this without violence. "Vinni, it's not for me that I ask your help! It's for Beck and Kiernan. They need you."

The Tribe Leader stopped and held his hand up to halt the menacing Halfies. "Ill fortune has befallen the nice *Savitars*?" he asked in the sudden silence. "You lie, rude Dwarf. I have seen nothing in the clouds."

"I speak the truth. *Savitar* Beck is missing and *Savitar* Kiernan fights for the lives of her people in Iserlohn."

"A fight?" An excited buzz rippled through the Halfie tribe. "Why did you not say so in the first place, rude Dwarf! A Halfie *never* backs down from a fight!"

And, with that, Rogan outlined his plans to harry the rogue Iserlohn army.

# CHAPTER 12

## Gone

Kiernan expected the Aquatainian village of Barbary to be deserted at this time of night, but the town was ablaze in light. It looked as though the entire village was awake and either walking the sandy beaches or gathered in small groups of animated conversation, their nude androgynous bodies glistening in the glow of their lanterns.

When Digby guided the boat to the village dock, several people pointed out their arrival nervously. Kiernan peered down at the watershifter in the lagoon. "What's happening, Digby? The villagers look anxious."

Digby put both hands on the flat end of the rear of the boat and hoisted himself onto the deck. "I'm guessing that word has already spread that war is imminent, Your Grace. I will go talk to them to see if anything else has occurred while we were gone."

He jumped off the front of the boat, and Seana, Kenley and Baya appeared from the lower deck with their bags in hand.

Kiernan smiled at Kenley, grateful that the voyage home allowed her time alone with her daughter to discuss in terms that she could understand, what had befallen Beck. She explained to her that the scarred lady Kenley saw with her father had placed him under a spell and that was the only reason that he had spoken to her so harshly. Kenley's face lit up when Kiernan told her that Uncle Airron was tracking him and would do his very best to bring her father back home to them very soon. Thankfully, Kenley seemed to cope very well with the explanations. It seemed as though once she had a reason for Beck's treatment of her, it put her mind at ease.

"If I had known the lady was bad, I would have done something to help Daddy," Kenley whispered as they lay side by side in the bunk of their cabin that first night. It startled Kiernan at first because she had almost forgotten that her daughter's powers had developed. She wondered just how strong her magic was.

"What would you have done, sweetheart?" she asked.

"Well, sometimes my magic is hard to handle...," Baya interrupted with a coughing snort and her daughter glared at the cat, but continued, "...but I could have swept her up into a wind funnel."

The unemotional way Kenley described an act of violence told her that sooner rather than later, they would need to find a way to help Kenley harness her powers so that she did not pose a danger to herself or others. Oh, how much easier it would be if she had Beck to discuss this with, but wishful thinking wasn't going to bring him back, so she swallowed back her concerns and forced a smile on her face for her daughter. "Until you are marked with the athame, Kenley, I don't want you to use your magic. Do you understand me?"

"Yes."

Kiernan did not get very much sleep after that conversation last night. Now, Kenley walked toward her and lifted her bag proudly. "I'm all packed, Maman, just like you asked me."

"Good girl." Kiernan took her by the hand and together they disembarked onto the shore of Barbary. The ceiling wasn't as high here in this newest village of Aquataine and, not for the first time, it felt to Kiernan as though she were stepping into the jaws of a huge beast with the stalagmites on the ground and stalactites on the roof threatening to clamp down on her at any moment.

Digby joined them again. "Your Grace! Terrible news! Word has it that Nysa has been seized in an uprising of some of the nobles, and the King has been imprisoned. The watershifters here in Barbary are very loyal to you and your family and are concerned for your safety."

Kiernan was stunned. *My father imprisoned? But, who...? It has to be Abram Winslow and Ava Conry.* She had known for months that the pair had thrown their lot in with Davad Etin, but up until now their tactics to undermine the rule of House Everard had always been more circuitous in nature. This open and treasonous declaration of war against a rightful King was unexpected. Obviously, they must also be in league with the army marching from Iserport.

Kiernan shook her head in disgust. Clearly, she had underestimated the extent and magnitude of these scheming nobles. She had believed that there would be time to prepare the defenses of the city before the army descended, but she now knew that was impossible. The enemy had already arrived and was holding her father and her people hostage. The knowledge enraged her.

"Let's go, Digby."

"Over here," he said and led them down the beach. They still had another raft to board that would take them into the smaller cavern beyond where the larger boat could not travel.

The villagers knelt as they passed, and she stopped before one of the larger congregations to address them. "Please rise," she said in a raised voice so that most could hear her. "Digby informed me of your worries, and I am touched and grateful for your concern and loyalty. But, know this, my dear friends! I will not rest until my father and the people of Nysa are free from these aggressors! A Princess is entrusted with the welfare of her people, and I will not misplace that trust! Mark my words! I *will* take back my city!"

The watershifters lifted their hands in the air and shouted their approval.

"May the Highworld be with you, Princess Kiernan!"

"Barbary stands with the Princess!"

The shouts continued while they boarded the raft and did not let up until they disappeared around a bend in the waterway.

It was only then that Kiernan let down her guard. She walked to the rail and took a deep breath. *Oh, Beck, hurry home to me. I find myself reaching for your hand and keep coming up empty. I never realized how much I depended on your presence until faced with your absence. I just have to trust in Airron to bring you home. He will find you, my love, but you have to hang on. Hang on for me.*

She scrubbed away a tear and leaned over the rail to speak to Digby. "You have not seen your wife in days. Go to her now, but be ready. I am not sure what I will find in the Surface World and may need your services again very soon."

"As you command, Your Grace, so it shall be," Digby said with obvious pride.

She nodded gratefully and as soon as he pulled up to the small dock, she followed the others off the raft and toward the stairs. *I wonder what I'll find in Bardot? I can't imagine the coward nobles had the guts to march there.*

Halfway into the long climb, she noticed that the exertion winded her more than it should have, and she wondered if everything was all right with the baby. Just as she had the thought, a sharp pain laced through her abdomen and she had to lean against the cave wall to catch her breath.

Seana came up behind her. "Are you all right, Your Grace?"

"Yes…yes, thank you, Seana, I will be fine."

"All of the Sect Leaders are in Bardot. You should see Helenite as soon as you can. She will be able to give you something to ease your discomfort."

"I think I will do that."

When the pain subsided, she pushed away from the wall, climbed the remaining stairs, and went through the open grate. Kiernan blinked in surprise. Her sleepy, quaint city bustled with activity. Most of the commotion came from the multitude of soldiers swarming the city streets. Beyond the streets and into the plains east of the city, a sea of tents and campfires extended as far as the eye could see.

Sabers, Lions, and Tigers.

*What in the Highworld is going on? Why are the arms of House Everard and House Gregaros here in Bardot instead of in the besieged Nysa?* It may be that Gage was unaware of the hostilities, but no, that wouldn't explain why so many soldiers were in Bardot.

The two Sabers guarding the entrance knelt upon seeing her, left fists on the ground. "Please rise," she told them.

"Come this way, Your Grace. Captain Nash has asked that you be escorted to him upon your arrival."

She nodded and as they moved toward the city square, she noticed a knot of Sabers standing around a newly constructed wooden structure. One of those Sabers turned out to be Kirby Nash and as soon as he saw her, he hurried forward and knelt. "Your Grace."

"Please rise. Kirby, what is going on here?" She took Kenley by the hand and continued toward the square, the Saber walking beside her.

"The Houses of Etin, Winslow, and Conry are attempting a coup. Etin's legionnaires are on the march toward Nysa, and Winslow's Wolves and Conry's Badgers hold the city gates. Hamilton and Knapp are locked in their estates, and their soldiers and the Lions caught up in the trap are imprisoned in the grain warehouses, stripped of clothing and weaponry and under very heavy guard with orders to shoot to kill any escapees. There is no way to get in or out of Nysa."

"My father?"

"Barricaded in his suite of rooms. Fortunately, one of the Gems was with the King when they confined him to his chambers, and she magically sealed the doors."

"If there is no way in or out, Captain, how is it that you have all of this information?"

They had arrived at the square, and Kiernan now saw the man bound to the structure, his hands pulled tight above his head and secured to the overhead truss of the contraption.

She quickly blocked her daughter's view. "Seana, would you please bring Kenley to the palace? I will be along shortly."

"Of course, Your Grace." Seana took Kenley's hand and directed her away from the offending sight.

Kirby pointed to the man and answered her question. "That's how. It's one of Winslow's men sent here on a reconnaissance mission. According to the traitorous Wolf, Lord Etin is trying to figure out where Gregaros is. But, it was actually Prince Beck that tipped us off about the influx of soldiers. King Maximus and Gage already had an idea that an uprising may be imminent, so after Beck's timely observation, they ordered many of the soldiers of House Everard and House Gregaros here to Bardot before the seizure of the city. Unfortunately, it's Hugo Bassus who leads Etin's army and he brought over almost all of the Lions stationed in Iserport to House Etin."

"What?" Hugo Bassus was her father's man in Iserport. Second in command to Bo Franck, the captain had been serving the Everard family for thirty years or more. *Had* being the operative word. *So, it is Bassus who has been helping Etin stir up civil discord in Iserport. A man who I thought a friend.*

"Why do you have him on public display?" he said, pointing to the tied man.

"As a warning of what will happen to other spies who attempt to come into Bardot with the intention of gathering information for Etin."

Kiernan nodded. She didn't like it, but knew that sometimes in war these tactics were necessary. "Do not kill him."

He bowed his head. "As you command, Your Grace."

"Have you seen Diamond?"

He shook his head. "After Gemini's murder, all of the Gem Sect Leaders arrived and have been meeting behind closed doors ever since."

She had assumed as much. The sorceresses would be enraged at the loss of their High Priestess and friend. "Find Lord Gregaros and meet me at the palace. We must decide how we go about prying my father and the citizens of Nysa from Etin's greedy fingers."

Kirby looked around as if he had just noticed something. "Where is Prince Beck, Your Grace?"

"Gone," she said simply and walked away. If she stopped to explain further, it would be the end of her.

\*\*\*\*

Airron stood on the sandstone butte and stared out at the landscape before him. A sudden strong westerly wind swept his silver hair out behind him and whipped his clothes around his body, but he hardly noticed.

He had found Beck.

After days of traveling through the harsh landscape that was Deepstone, the trail ended here. His narrowed violet eyes scanned the one cave among the hundreds that he now knew held his friend. It had a distinctive swirling of red and tan color right above the black opening.

There was no movement coming from the cave, which caused him to wonder if Avalon had armed support. Was she capable of capturing and holding Beck on her own? He doubted it and knew he had to be prepared for a fight.

A flash of green caught his eye below and he watched Melania walk toward the inviting water source they found earlier that day in between the boulders. A fresh waterfall splashed down from a crevice between two rocks and formed a small, but deep turquoise pool of liquid.

Melania had been much more reserved and less demanding since his uncouth comment a few days ago. She awoke at sunrise and performed her daily prayers by herself away from their camp.

He would apologize when the time was right, but decided to let her stew for a little while longer. In order for their marriage to work, she had to understand that he was his own person and she could not mold him into someone he was not. Yes, he would agree to pick up after himself. He would even wear the gaudy tunic she was sure to choose for him. But, he would not live in a loveless marriage. He wanted what Beck and Kiernan had. What Rogan and Janin now had.

Melania bent to the pool of water and began to fill their two water bags. When they were full, she gathered water in the palm of her hand and splashed it on the back of her neck. Suddenly, her head picked up and she looked furtively back toward the path she came on, oblivious to the fact that he stood on the rock far above her.

As graceful as a dancer, she stood and her hands reached back to the clasp of her high-necked, halter dress.

Airron's breathing increased and a stab of desire pierced through him. He knew he should turn away. It is what any decent person would do. But, he found that he couldn't take his eyes from the vision before him.

His wife.

She looked back once more and then unfastened the dress, letting it fall to her waist. She unbuckled her knife belt and the dress came the rest of the way off. Naked, she stepped out of the emerald silk piled around her feet and slipped into the pool of water.

At this point, Airron did step back out of sight and took deep breaths to dispel his stimulated thoughts. He had enjoyed many women in his life, but couldn't remember one affecting him this intensely before. Silently, he made his way off the butte and back to their small camp.

While he waited for his wife to return, he busied himself caring for the horses while he mentally prepared himself for the confrontation with Avalon just ahead. He was securing his pack to the saddle of the Haventi when Melania, fully dressed now but silver hair hanging damply down her back, appeared around the rock formation.

She looked at him suspiciously. "Where were you?"

"I needed to get a good view of the cave with human eyes before I left." He decided not to lie. "From above."

Her face turned pink, and she bent to gather her belongings. "I hope you found what you were looking for."

"Oh, I did. The view is really quite stunning from that angle. Quite frankly, I have never seen anything like it."

She stood up in a flash of anger. "Airron Falewir!"

He held up his hand. "Obviously, I didn't know that you would be there, Melania, but I will still offer you an apology if that is what you need."

She swallowed visibly. "How much did you see?"

"All of you."

She groaned and turned her back on him. He put his hands on her shoulders. "You have nothing to be embarrassed about. As your husband, you will just have to trust me on that one." She made a little whimpering sound but didn't respond. "Look, I'll apologize again when I get back, but right now Beck needs my help."

"Just go," she whispered and turned to face him.

"All right, but be ready to leave. I don't know what I will find or who will be after me when I find it."

"Be careful," she offered softly.

He looked at her questioningly.

"What?" she asked.

"I need to bodyshift now."

She waved her arm. "Oh, go ahead. I'm used to it by now."

He cleared his throat. "Then, you should also be aware that I must disrobe first."

"Right!" she said and averted her gaze, dropping into a squat to rummage through her pack. Although, what she could possibly be looking for, Airron had no clue.

"Unless, of course, you would like to even the score?" he suggested.

Violet eyes blazed his way.

With a laugh, he shed his clothes and bodyshifted before she could throw something at him.

The Gangi took off down the road at a sprint. He was small, but his legs were lithe and powerful. It didn't take long for him to pick up the trail of the human. And, just as soon, the unfamiliar scent that always accompanied the one he sought bemused him. The caustic smell assailed his nose, and he shook his muzzle in disgust.

Continuing along the road, the cave with the distinctive swirl came into sight. There is where he would find the one he tracked. It was also where he would most likely find a fight to the death.

The air flickered briefly and the Gangi shifted into a mouse and scrambled up the boulders to the cave entrance. Taking care to remain out of sight of any humans, he peered cautiously inside, but even from his low vantage point, he could clearly confirm the devastating truth.

It was empty.

Airron sprouted up from the mouse form and examined the area. Beck had been here, of that he had no doubt, but he was gone now. Disappointment surged through him as he slowly walked around the cave, the bright sunshine from outside lending him plenty of light from which to see.

A stone table and several seating areas were carved directly from the cavern walls. Avalon must have created this hideaway well before Rogan's wedding. But, again, he had to wonder, why Beck? He could understand if she kidnapped *him* to gain revenge for their altercation years ago or Kiernan for ransom, but why was it Beck that she chose? The strongest man on the island? He had something that she wanted obviously. But, what?

He walked to the back of the cave and noticed that there was another exit. The trail did not end here as he had assumed, but continued on by way of another road.

He resumed his perusal, but there wasn't much else to see. He turned to leave, but a flicker of white caught his eye. There, underneath the stone table fluttered a piece of parchment.

He picked it up and opened it.

It was a map. A map of the southern portion of Deepstone with a location marked southwest of the Koda River. *Is this Avalon's or a discard of some other person?* It could take him well out of his way if he simply followed it blindly, but unfortunately, his choices were few and far between.

His best friend was in the hands of a monster.

# CHAPTER 13

## Changes

Avalon rode behind her Cyman guard with the sudden, crucial need for a female human form pressing in on her.

By this time tomorrow, they would reach the Koda River and there, in the river settlements, she would be able to find one. She knew from previous visits that the mining community where they were now headed was made up of several families from Iserlohn, including women and children.

It was very well-known that the southern portion of Deepstone offered a veritable payload of precious gems, marble and granite—the primary sources of exported income for the Dwarves. Prior to the war, no Dwarf in existence would ever have considered parting with their closely guarded mining expertise, but in a show of fostering island collaboration, King Erik allowed a limited number of men and Elves into the country each year to learn extraction techniques from the Dwarves so they could improve the engineering of ore in their own lands. Several of these expeditions were taking place now and the miners were camped at the Koda.

Reaching into the small leather purse around her waist, Avalon retrieved a small mirror she kept there. She almost cried aloud in horrified disbelief. The visible signs of desiccation to her face were far more pronounced than they had been when she left her home in Farout Falls a few weeks ago.

Other changes were taking place as well.

Her speech had become more slurred and guttural sounding, and she found it difficult to talk at times, especially when she was tired. The other disturbing transformation was the appearance of two bony protrusions on her back just under her shoulder blades. They were extremely painful to the touch and throbbed incessantly.

When all of her attempts to create the LifeFire Tonic through traditional incantations and formulas failed, she turned to the dark sorcery she learned from her brother, Adrian, and the effects were devastating.

The unthinkable was happening.

She was changing into something less than human.

Oh, yes, she needed a female body very soon. Of course, she would have Beck Atlan's form very soon, but she required the body of a female for tasks only a woman could carry out. She could have taken Gemini's likeness after she killed her, but it never would have worked. The High Priestess was too well known and thus of no use to her. Discretion was, and always had been, her greatest ally.

She wondered if the sorceress she had recruited from the Bardot Academy had achieved the goals Avalon set for her. The girl was in Bardot to study fireshifting, but the lure of power and wealth turned her to Avalon's cause. Truth be told, it was never very difficult to find accomplices for her plans. She could always depend on the inherent greed of people, their covetous hands forever reaching for further possessions and status.

Unfortunately, the little twit did happen to retain at least a modicum of decency and refused to kill Gemini, which meant that she had to travel to Bardot and commit the act herself. It had been a risky undertaking, but she was now satisfied that she had been forced to do so. It was only right that she be the one to end that witch's life when Gemini's brother, Galen, had been the one to take her brother from her.

*That one was for you, Adrian.*

Afterward, she had traveled to Kondor right on the heels of the royal *Savitars*. Fortunately for her, the watershifters' prerequisite for traveling their waterways was shifting ability, not good intentions.

Thinking of the *Savitars*, she reached up to touch the scars on her face, a habit of hers over the years. Whenever she touched them, she remembered the foe that put them there. In her entire existence, he was the only one of her intended victims that had ever escaped her alive.

*Wait a minute.* Her breath hitched in her throat when a disturbing thought came to her. That despicable Elf that gave her these scars was at the wedding of the Dwarf! When the Cymans reported no sign of pursuit, she had not bothered to hide their trail. Even though the stone road they traveled left no mark of their passage, surely their scents would be traceable, and the Elf was an expert bodyshifter! Her face bore the truth to that fact.

The growing certainty built in the pit of her stomach. He would be tracking his earthshifter friend, and his animal forms would allow him to do so very easily. There could be no doubt. In fact, he could be upon them at any time.

"Cyrus!" she shouted to the Cyman in the lead of their party. She looked back at Beck stumbling behind her horse with his hands tied at the wrists by a rope attached to her saddle.

Cyrus jogged to her side. "Yes, Mistress?"

Vanity caused her to pull her hood close around her face. "We're being tracked, so we will need to pick up the pace. We won't be safe again until we are back home at Farout."

He looked confused but didn't question the validity of her statement.

Beck suddenly tumbled to the ground behind her, but she didn't stop, and his body dragged along the stone road.

"We must continue pushing ahead until dark. Scout ahead and find us cave well off the road to spend the night. Once there, I will cast a spell of invisibility over our party while we sleep for a few hours and then we will need to move out again. We must shake our pursuer, Cyrus, at least until we reach Farout Falls. If he manages to find us at that point, I will be only too glad to settle the score with that one."

Cyrus nodded as he walked beside her horse, and then glanced back uneasily at Beck.

She saw the look and grunted in frustration. Adrian had been right, the Cymans were much too soft. She sighed. The earthshifter probably did need water, as she couldn't recall the last time she had given him any.

Not that he deserved one single drop, she abruptly realized! This was all Beck Atlan's fault.

She stopped her horse and dismounted.

The earthshifter was lying on the ground, bloodied from scrapes and abrasions. He was no longer under the glamour spell, but in no condition to fight her either. She walked over to his prone body and kicked him in the ribs. "Why didn't you tell me?"

He lifted his head groggily. "Water," he said faintly. "I need…water."

She reached down and grabbed a fistful of hair lifting his head. "You will get water when you answer my question. Why didn't you tell me that the bodyshifter was trailing us?"

He shook his head dazedly. "Bodyshifter?"

"Your friend, you idiot! You must have known that he would come after you. Why didn't you warn me?"

One side of his mouth lifted in a small smile. "Maybe because I…want him to catch up…and kill you."

She smiled, too, as she balled up her fist and hit him in the mouth.

He worked his jaw woozily. "I've had worse. Do you remember…Citrine? Now, that woman…could punch. Well…before you murdered her anyway."

Avalon tensed her body and began to pummel the earthshifter with blow after blow, stopping only when he fell unconscious.

Smoothing her dress and pulling the hood of her cloak back into place, she turned to Cyrus. "Wake him up and give him some water. I don't want him to die before I have the chance to kill him."

****

The sight of Etin's Eagles looting the city of Nysa caused Maximus to seethe in anger. The cowardly bastards stalked the streets like arrogant thugs, taking by force the hard-earned coin of any innocent who stumbled in their path. The legionnaires must have been promised the spoils of victory, but at such a cost? How could the renegade nobles not realize the damage they were causing both to the city and in the hearts of the people? Even through his closed window on the third floor of the palace, he could hear the sound of breaking windows and the screams of citizens followed by the laughter of the vandals.

He imagined it was much like this in Iserport. These soldiers, with their mob mentality, had been without discipline or structure for a long time now it seemed. The corruption so extensive that the young men of Etin's army had lost sight of their humanity and their morals and were taking extreme delight in defacing the beauty of the royal seat of Nysa, the highest symbol of authority and power in Iserlohn.

Guilt raked at him for choosing to remain behind a locked door, but he knew that in order to have a hope of saving the city, he had to bide his time until his allies could intervene. He just hoped that his careful planning would lead to triumph. Not for him, but for his people. He would give up his life right this instant if it meant that the citizens of Nysa would be spared, but if he made such an offer to Davad Etin, he would be trading his life for naught. The devious Lord was clearly insane. The mayhem allowed to run amok outside as well as his actions over the past few months proved that much. If the noble wasn't exorcised from Nysa very soon, the havoc would have a lasting, demoralizing effect on the families Maximus had sworn to protect.

Unfortunately, he had been unable to protect Darin Morel and now a second Saber Captain had made the ultimate sacrifice for him. The death of Colbie Nash tore him to pieces during the Demon War and now he had to deal with the pain of losing Darin.

And, Gemini.

He still found it impossible to believe that someone had managed to penetrate the High Priestess' imposing defenses. It was even more impossible to imagine a life without her.

He had thought often over the years of asking Gemini to marry him. Him! Marrying a sorceress! Had she said yes, she actually would have been the second woman he married with the gift of magic. His Gracie, Kiernan's mother, had been a shifter although he had always pretended not to know.

He regretted now that he never acted on his desire to marry Gemini. He had grown to love her very much over the years and so did Kiernan, Beck and Kenley. Now, it was too late. It broke his heart to know that he would never see those twinkling blue eyes of hers again or hear that infectious laughter.

"Your Grace, can I get you anything?"

He turned from the window. Eden, the young sorceress who had been unfortunate enough to end up on the wrong side of the door with him, stood there. She had come to Nysa to inform him of Gemini's death at the same time the combatant soldiers descended on his chambers.

"No thank you, Eden."

"Miss Belle and Larkin have taken an inventory of the supplies you asked them to stock and there is no need to worry. We have enough food and water for many days yet."

He nodded.

His suite of rooms included a sitting room, bedroom and small library and, although they did not know the reason at the time, he had ordered Larkin and Belle to stockpile foodstuffs in his chambers for days before the attack.

"Captain Franck and Saber Ryan have also just finished constructing a privy and wash room out of your library," she reported with an embarrassed look.

"Very good. Maybe it will get more use now than that stuffy old library ever did," he teased. "I'm sorry that you have been caught up in this mess, Eden. I promise to do all in my power to keep you safe."

The young brunette smiled. "And, I promise to do all in my power to keep you safe, Your Grace."

He grinned. "Yes, it seems we may have to depend on each other for a little while yet. Tell me. What are you studying at the Academy, Eden?"

"Fireshifting, but I must confess that I haven't had much luck as of yet." She snapped her fingers and a small yellow flame danced above her hand. "That is it, I'm afraid. Although, I can still cast quite the spell when I need to."

"About that, Eden," Maximus started. "I thank you for using your sorcery to remove a threat from my presence, but it is prohibited to do more than that. You do understand that, don't you, Eden?"

There was no trace of a smile on her face this time. "Now that is a promise I cannot make, Your Grace."

****

"Make it happen," demanded Ava Conry angrily.

"Be reasonable, Ava," Davad Etin implored. "We can be married immediately after I'm crowned King. I promise you." They were lying in his bed in one of the spare rooms in the royal palace. Although acceptable for now, soon he would be living in more lavish accommodations. Today, he was the Lord from the south fighting for justice. Soon, he would be the King of Iserlohn.

He leaned over and kissed Ava's forehead, while brushing the nipple of her right breast with his thumb.

She pushed his hand away and stepped out of the bed, padding naked to the night cloak thrown over the back of one of the chairs in his room.

He traced her movements critically. She was a little plump for his taste, but he could certainly suffer that much, and more, to achieve his goals.

She turned back to him once the cloak was in place. "When, Davad? You have been stringing me along far too long for my liking. If you think you can pull this off without the support of House Conry and the Badgers, just say the word. Maybe the loss of two thousand men will not make a difference to you?" she challenged. "My Captain has implored me to have a change of heart and abandon this attempt to topple Maximus, and I should probably listen to him."

Panicking, he jumped out of the bed and clung to her. "Ava, don't say that! It's you that I care about. Your men at arms mean nothing to me if you're not in my life!" She snorted as he nestled his face in the crook of her neck. "I can't do this without you," he whispered. "Don't leave me now." He felt her soften, felt the effect his words were having on her.

"Three days," was all she said.

"Three days? But, Ava—"

"All right, make it four, Davad! We will be married in four days or I will take my forces and join with Gregaros. Do I make myself clear?"

He wanted to punch her in her fat face. "If that is what you wish, my darling, then I will make it so."

She nodded. "Fine. I will go now and inform the Captain of my army that we will not be leaving Nysa after all."

He kept the smile in place as she dressed and left his chambers. As soon as the door closed, he slammed his fist into the wall and then grabbed the sides of his head.

*The voices!*

They urged him to dispose of Ava, but deep down, in the place where reason still existed, he knew he couldn't do that yet. He still needed her and her soldiers. If she left him now for Gregaros, he would lose everything.

Stumbling over to the wash basin, he almost sent it toppling when he grasped the rim and dunked his head into the warm water. Coming up for breath almost a full minute later, the voices were still there, but he felt somewhat better. He picked up the towel hanging on the side of the basin, dried his face and sat on the bed.

He began to hum. Humming helped to rid the incessant buzzing of those bloody voices in his head.

Sounds of the soldiers ransacking the city echoed through the open window. He knew he should stop what they were doing. This was going to be his city soon, and he did not wish to see it destroyed.

*Where is Abram?* He might be able to help.

*And, where is Ava?*

He shook his head. *Yes, yes, Ava just left, didn't she?*

In a brief moment of clarity, he also wondered what had become of the spy they sent to Bardot. He had not yet returned, and Davad was anxious for news of Lord Gregaros. Fortunately, wherever the former Saber was, it seemed as though he had no intention of entering the fight.

*Fight? What fight?*

It didn't matter. He needed to rest. Tomorrow was a very big day.

He had a wedding to plan.

# CHAPTER 14

## Old Enemies

Airron's eyes popped open precisely at sunrise. The internal clock that signaled the time for the Morning Song to Elán was abiding and unfailing in each and every child of the forest. He yawned and stretched. Last night, he attempted to construct a bed out of his horse's saddle and some blankets, but it was no use. It was simply impossible to get a good night's rest on a bed of stone.

Ever since they left Kondor, Melania chose to perform the Morning Song alone, but she was awake now, sitting across from him with an expectant look on her face.

He sat up and brushed back his silver hair. "What?"

"As husband and wife, I have decided that we should perform our prayers to Elán together. She would wish it so."

"Oh, she would, huh? Well, I would never want to disappoint Elán," he told her with a smile. He stood and held out his hand to her.

She hesitated briefly before placing her hand in his and the contact sent a blaze of electricity through his body. He sucked in a steadying breath and pulled her to her feet.

A bit awkwardly, they pressed both of their hands together and held them high, fingertips pointed toward the sky. Since it was just the two of them, the required pose caused them to stand very close together. The faint odor of rose soap on her skin touched his nose. She must have used the delicate petals when she took her brief dip in the pool yesterday and it still clung to her like an exotic fragrance.

Melania started to sing, and he immediately joined in, drawn to the beauty of her voice and the stir of the words. This very personal, very moving experience was made even more so by the heat of Melania so very close.

He opened one eye.

*Ethereal.* It was the best word he could come up with to describe his wife's face at this moment, upturned in prayer with the silver frame of her hair casting her features in an enchanting glow. Although he had yet to discover that something special that Loren promised he would find if he gave Melania a chance, he did feel a very real, very visceral attraction to her. The image of her by the pool crowded his mind until he could think of little else. But, attraction alone was not enough. Not for him.

The song almost at an end, he pushed his thoughts aside and lost himself in the final refrain. At the close of the prayer, he opened his eyes to discover Melania staring at him, her features gentled. Purple eyes captivated him and her full lips begged to be tasted. Before he could stop himself, he leaned in and kissed her.

She returned the kiss dispassionately as if it were a chore she had to carry out but derived no real pleasure from. Desperate for a reaction, he reached out and pulled her close, but she stiffened and pushed him away. "If we are to find your friend, we must be going."

He groaned silently. *Just splendid! I'm married to the only woman on the island who can resist my charms!* Angry now, he turned from her without a word and packed his belongings. Mounting the Haventi, he directed the horse back to the road without waiting for her. She could catch up on her own.

He remained out in front of her as the day wore on, hot and dusty, and it gave him plenty of time to reflect over his feelings. He wasn't sure exactly what prevented him from accepting Melania completely and unequivocally. He knew he had only to say the right words and she would be his wife in truth. Perhaps it boiled down to his continued detachment to the Elven people as a whole. He had lived in Haventhal for six years now but still felt like an outsider among the Elves. No matter how hard he tried, it just didn't feel like home to him. *I can't even master their blasted magic!*

Airron shook his mind clear. Beck depended on him to be vigilant right now, not lost in useless introspection. Tomorrow they would reach the Koda River where they could replenish their supplies. Maybe Avalon, arrogant in her abilities, would stop at the riverside town to spend the night, and he would be able to catch up to her there.

Deciding he needed another scent, he walked his horse off the road and undressed, not bothering to tell Melania his plans. Obviously, she wanted nothing to do with him and that was fine. Two could play that game.

He transformed into the Gangi, whose phenomenal nose could pick up the trail of a wraith, and not long into the search he caught the scent of blood—the blood of the human he tracked. The trail of blood appeared to him in the form of smears instead of droplets, and the Gangi recognized it as a kill drag.

He continued to follow the scent, anticipating carrion at the end of his track. The smell took him into a sharp left turn off the road and then abruptly disappeared. Confused, he circled the last spot of the smear and lifted his head to try to gain a scent on the air.

It was no use, the trail was gone.

He wasn't sure if it was a sudden movement, a smell or an imperceptible sound, but his animal instincts warned him of danger, and he leapt into the air to run. The action saved his life. The arrow aimed for his heart, hit his hind leg instead.

The Gangi yelped in pain and then morphed into a black wolf, head whipping around and fangs bared in a vicious growl.

The smell came to him then. The bitter scent that had been there all along, mixed with the scent of the human he tracked. The dog didn't recognize the scent, but the wolf did.

He had fought these creatures before.

The large hulking figure emerged from a gap in the rock formations at a run, thinking to find a dog, but came up short when he saw the wolf instead.

His one eye widened in surprise and he skidded on the stone road as he tried to turn back the way he had come.

The wolf was upon him in seconds, leaping into the air and onto the back of his assailant. He ignored the pain of the arrow still lodged in his leg and thought of nothing but the kill.

The attacker, still holding the bow in his hands, turned his body and smashed the weapon into his head. It dazed him for a moment, but he shook it off and sank his teeth into the vulnerable, blood-filled flesh of the neck. His natural senses told him that if he didn't eliminate this threat, it would kill him and the Elven girl. He shook the neck with such ferocity, it snapped in his jaws. The creature's now paralyzed legs folded beneath him and they both crashed to the ground. Distracted by thoughts of the one he protected, the wolf left himself vulnerable and the attacker managed to reach around and, with a last dying act, plunged an arrow into his flank.

The wolf howled out in pain.

"Airron!"

He heard the shout just as he bodyshifted into his Elven form, but couldn't move for a moment winded from the fight and from the pain that laced up his side.

"Oh, Airron!" cried Melania, dropping by his side. She quickly ran her fingers over his body and must have seen the two arrows because she gasped.

She jumped to her feet, and he heard her grunt with effort as she pulled at the enormous Cyman who lay partially flung over his body.

Apparently giving it up as impossible, she knelt beside him once again. "Airron, can you hear me? Are you all right? Oh, dear Elán, please let him live!" She reached out and stroked his hair back from his face. "Airron, can you hear me? Please don't die on me. Look, I…I know I haven't been a very good wife to you, but I promise I will change." She paused. "If…if you want to know the truth, I've loved you ever since you first came to Haventhal. Of course, you didn't know I existed, so I begged King Jerund to let me be the one for you. To be the one chosen as your wife. I was so happy when my wish came true, but then you seemed so displeased with the wedding and me that I acted the fool. My feelings were hurt, Airron, and I tried to act like you didn't mean anything to me, but you do. Oh, Airron." She leaned over his chest.

Airron picked his head up and she drew back with a startled squeal.

"As much as I am enjoying this," he said, "do you think you could extract the two arrows stuck in my flesh before continuing?"

****

The pain in Kiernan's lower back intensified with every step she took as she strode along the empty corridor in her home in Bardot. She tried to ignore it, allowing her thoughts to drift to the news she received earlier of the impending marriage of Davad Etin and Ava Conry. *A wedding? In the midst of an overthrow attempt?* If she wondered before, she knew without a doubt now—Lord David Etin was completely mad. If she needed more evidence, there were also the reports of his erratic behavior and a new habit of talking to—and answering—himself.

Sane or not, his decisions were helping instead of hindering the plans of House Everard. A large celebration would provide just the right distraction she needed.

According to Gage's calculations, there were close to four thousand combatant soldiers in the city. Until they could marshal all of their forces spread out across Iserlohn that meant that they were outnumbered, Gage informed her with a smile, but not outmatched. He proposed a quick and focused strike that would require only a small number of Sabers to enter the city. Hit the opponent from several points simultaneously to give the impression of a much broader attack, he told her. In the ensuing confusion, the Sabers would make an attempt to release the allied soldiers in the warehouses.

While the Sabers fought to take back the city of Nysa, Gage would lead the remainder of the combined armies south to confront Hugo Bassus and the main branch of Etin's army.

Kiernan agreed with the plan with the provision that she be part of the unit to breach Nysa. In the midst of the chaos, she could take Kirby Nash and go to her father. She knew passageways in the palace that no one else was aware of and was confident that she could gain access to the third floor corridor without being seen. The floor would be heavily guarded, but the wedding celebration and the carefully orchestrated diversions from the Sabers should thin them out enough for her and Kirby to fight their way through those that were left.

For a desperate and brief moment, she thought how much easier it would be if the shifters and their magic could be used. The rebellion could be put down very quickly and with little, if any, loss of life. But, she supported the mandate unequivocally. Magic could not be used to fight swords. Ever. It would cast an irrevocable stain on the image of magic that the shifters would not soon recover from. It could even result in the reinstatement of their exile.

She took a deep breath out of frustration. She could only deal with so many issues at once. Thoughts of Beck niggled at her incessantly, but she learned to banish them in place of other pressing matters and concerns. One of which she intended to deal with right now.

Holding her belly, she descended the stairs to the second floor where the guest chambers were located and turned right down the balconied hallway. Finding the room she wanted, she knocked softly on the door.

It opened almost immediately, and the chestnut haired beauty who answered looked at her with concern.

"I'm very sorry to bother you so late, Helenite...," she began, but the Sect Leader for Healing opened the door wide and pulled her in.

"Don't be ridiculous. Are you having pains again?" she asked, taking Kiernan by the shoulders and holding her at arm's length to inspect her up and down.

She nodded. "They are pretty constant now."

"You are probably in the early stages of labor, Kiernan. You really should be on bed rest."

"You know I can't do that, Helenite."

The healer shook her head and put her hands on her hips. "So, you really plan to go into Nysa and carry out a rescue attempt of your father from thousands of armed men? Let's see...seven, close to eight months pregnant?"

"Yes."

Helenite looked Kiernan in the eye and grabbed her hands. "Let me do it. I'll go to Nysa and free your father."

"No, this is something that I must do, my friend. It is my responsibility. Just give me more herbs to dull the pain, and I'll be like new again."

With a dramatic, almost childish sigh, the healer walked to the bureau in her room where several containers had been laid out on top.

"Besides, I have time yet, Helenite," Kiernan tried to justify. "And, I won't be in any real danger with the Sabers shadowing me."

The witch snorted. "Here," she said and handed Kiernan a folded paper with the herbs. "Just be careful."

Kiernan took the medicine with a grateful smile.

"By the way," Helenite said. "Just how do you plan to enter a city manned by rival soldiers?"

Kiernan raised one eyebrow. "Right through the front gates, of course."

# CHAPTER 15

## "I Have a Dwarf on My Head"

"Hit me one more time, and I'll break your arm," Rogan snarled.

The Halfie Tribe Leader dropped down next to him on a small hummock just east of the town of Janis to watch the Iserlohn Army sprawled out across the open plains. "Sorry, rude Dwarf," Vinni replied, sounding anything but.

Traveling with fifty Halfie warriors had proven to be the most trying experience of Rogan's life. It was like traveling with a pack of unruly children. Yet, they did move fast and required very little sleep, which suited his purposes. The first night he met up with the imps, they set out straight away in a trek across Haventhal to Havenport. There, they piled onto ferries to convey them across Traverse Lake to Iserport. And now, six days and a stomach ulcer later, he had his first glimpse of his quarry.

Rogan pulled his scowl from Vinni and went back to his scrutiny of the Iserlohn Army before him.

Legionnaires of House Etin mostly but, surprisingly, a fair amount from House Everard as well. In the distance, a stark division in the ranks of soldiers stood out to him. Compared to the clean and straight lines of the tents of the main body of the army, a large section at the back looked an unruly mess.

Now at least, Rogan understood why there were no people in Iserport. When they arrived at the Iserlohn port city, he was shocked to find it almost completely deserted. The city had been crawling with soldiers and people the last time he had been there, but stepping onto the Iserport docks two days ago was like entering a ghost town, eerily quiet and abandoned.

A handful of treacherous eyes peeked out from alleyways and decrepit buildings, but the owners must have decided against confronting their large party as they walked through the city.

The reason for those empty streets now appeared before him armed with pitchforks, shovels and axes. Seana had informed them that a mob of citizens had joined the army, but he had not been prepared for the scope of numbers of those involved. Dissatisfied with their impossible living conditions, the people probably felt as though they had no other choice but to wage war in a demand for change.

This definitely limited Rogan's options for stopping the army.

He looked over at Vinni. "You know what you have to do?"

"Of course, rude Dwarf. We will sneak into the army camp while they are settling in for sleep and set their supply carts afire. We will also cut as many picket lines as we are able and set the horses free."

"Very good."

"Are you sure we cannot stab them?" he asked, his cherub face lighting up in a hopeful smile.

"No. We just want to disable their ability to continue not hurt them."

"You promised me a fight," Vinni growled.

He was right. And, he needed the Halfies to stick with the plan. "You know what they say about poking a sleeping dog, Vinni. You may just get bit."

Vinni laughed and Rogan realized it was the first time he had ever heard the Halfie do so. Usually, his mean little face was screwed up in malice. "No Halfie will get bit, rude Dwarf, I promise you that."

That was the truth. The Halfies had a way of disappearing into the long grasses of the plains and even he had a hard time locating them when he knew exactly where they were. No, the soldiers of the army would never catch sight of their tormentors.

"Fine," he relented. "You can poke them a little. But, just the soldiers, mind you!"

Vinni stood in a crouch, anxious now to deliver the good news to his warriors.

"Wait! Do you have the cloak I asked you to find?" Once the Halfies started their bedlam, Rogan and Janin would be unable to conceal themselves as easily, so he asked Vinni to steal a cloak of House Etin from one of the legionnaires that they could use as a disguise.

"Of course, the red and blue, like you asked and right from under their noses. I gave it to the other Dwarf."

"My wife, Vinni. She is my wife."

"Whatever."

*Demon's breath, let this be over soon.* "Let's go then, but make sure you give us time to reach the camp before you start."

The Halfie nodded, gave him a barefooted kick in the ribs, and ran off.

Rogan cursed and crawled back down the hill. The sun had set an hour ago and the slate sky offered the perfect cover for their plans. He found Janin waiting for him. "Ready?"

Reluctantly, she handed him the cloak she held and adjusted the short sword at her hip. "Are you sure about this, Kal Rogan? It sounds a bit…desperate."

"It's the only way. We can't disappear as easily as the imps which means that we will be vulnerable to the roused dog without a cover of some sort."

She sighed. "Fine. Bend down."

He bent into a crouch and she climbed onto his shoulders. When he tried to stand, he let out a heavy breath from the exertion.

"What was that?" she immediately demanded.

"What was what?"

"Was that a grunt?"

"What?"

"A grunt? My weight is the same as when we first met, Kal Rogan, so don't you dare imply otherwise!" She hesitated. "Well, maybe I have put on a pound or two but that is to be expected after all these years, right?"

"Your weight is fine, Janin." Standing upright now, he readjusted her weight and another deep gasp burst forth.

"Really?" she asked loudly. "Another grunt?"

Ignoring her, he handed up the cloak. "Put this on."

She ripped the cloak from his fingers. Wiggling on his shoulders, she managed to place the cloak securely around the two of them.

With all her maneuvering, he couldn't help the sound that issued from his throat.

"Kal Rogan, why are you grunting?"

He rolled his eyes in frustration. "I am grunting because I have a Dwarf on my head! That's why!"

Janin's body started shaking uncontrollably.

"Why are you shaking? Stop that!"

"It's called a laugh, you bumblehead. Oh, Highworld, Reilly and Jala are going to have a chuckle over this one when we get back."

"We should be more concerned with surviving the night," he muttered.

"I bet they won't even want to hear the story of you barreling out of your family home during the Demon War and falling off the porch anymore."

"I did not fall! That was a carefully executed dive and roll."

"Whatever you say, my husband."

Rogan shook his head skeptically but gratefully. Although his wife was most certainly not as contrite as she wished him to believe, at least the shaking had subsided.

\*\*\*\*

Airron stretched his long legs out in front of the fire with a slight grimace. Fortunately, the pain in his side was subsiding and the wound in his leg no longer troubled him at all thanks to Melania. She quite capably extracted both of the arrows from his body and applied herbal poultices that worked wonders. To his relief, she told him that his injuries would be completely healed within a day or two. That was good news because he would need all of his strength and more when he finally caught up to Avalon Ravener. Having fought the bodyshifter sorceress before and coming out on the losing end, he did not wish to relive that experience.

His chances would be better if Melania wasn't traveling with him. His worry for her was distracting him in a way he didn't truly understand.

Careful not to let it show on his face, he smiled inside when he thought of her embarrassment the day before. She had said little to him since, and he knew that she regretted pouring her heart out to him when she thought him unconscious. *Could she actually be in love with me? Or, were those desperate words of terror at the possibility of being left alone in a strange land?*

He still struggled over his own feelings. There was an attraction there, certainly, and a desire to protect, but what did it mean? He barely knew the woman even if she was his wife.

"Are you all right?" she asked him, looking up from her work boiling bandages for his next poultice.

He smiled. "Yes, thanks to you."

She didn't return the smile.

*Is this bloody woman going to hold her confession against me forever?* He tried a different tactic and asked her to tell him more about her life in Haventhal. In hushed tones and with her features cast in the soft glow of the flames, he learned that she had two sisters, made a living as an medicinal herbalist, and loved to play the harp. She came from one of the most prominent noble families in Sarphia, but he had already known that much.

"Your turn. Tell me more about Airron Falewir."

"You are the one who claims to know me so well. Tell me what you see," he challenged.

She paused for a moment in her stirring. More to herself than to him, she said, "I see a man who is unquestionably brave. I used to sit and watch him practice with the Gladewatchers for hours when I was younger. My friends called me foolish when I left them to go to the sparring field every day just to see if he could keep his undefeated streak going." She swished the ladle in the cook pot. "I see a man who is handsome and unbelievably kind. I have seen him reach into his purse to give coin to the poor on occasions too numerous to count. I also see a man with a sense of humor, but who sometimes uses laughter to hide what he is truly feeling."

Airron sat up straighter.

"I see a man who is in pain because of a tremendous loss in his life. A man who feels lost and adrift even among his own people. A man who lives in Haventhal, but it does not feel like home to him. And, a man who roves from woman to woman because he is afraid of commitment. Afraid to love again, because he does not wish to ever experience that same level of loss again."

He turned from her, unable to look at the truth in her eyes. "It seems you know me better than I know myself. How is it that a woman can know me this well, and I do not know her at all?"

"If you were looking, you would have seen me. I have been by your side for years, Airron Falewir."

He didn't know what to say. Not even Beck, Kiernan or Rogan knew him as well as this stranger sitting across from him seemed to.

"And, just so you know, contrary to popular belief, not *all* Elves can communicate with animals. Most can, but not all. You are not deficient in any way so don't believe that to be true."

Airron felt relief at hearing this bit of news. For years, it gnawed at him that he was unable to command what he thought was an innate Elven ability.

"Where do we go from here?" he finally asked.

"I would like to be your wife, Airron, in every way. But, I will not do so until you can tell me that you also wish to be my husband. I want you to choose me as I have already chosen you."

An uncomfortable silence followed while she extracted the bandages from the boiling pot and finished her work. Still, he did not respond.

Finally, with a cheerless shrug and a sad smile, she rolled into her bedroll, turned her back on him and went to sleep.

Sleep did not come as easy for him, and he lay awake most of the night. Words unsaid haunted him. *Why are the most important sentiments, the hardest to put into words?*

In the morning, they said their prayers separately and struck camp without saying a word to each other. The morning's trek continued as all the days before with their two unyielding companions—the heat and the hypnotically repetitive landscape. Leagues passed by with no discernible change in their environment, and it was a terribly lonely existence. In his mind-numbed state, Airron could almost believe that there were no other people left in the world. It was just him and Melania and the stone.

When the Koda River and a small village finally came into view, he shuddered with relief at just having something new to look at. He risked a glance behind him at Melania and noticed her sun chafed lips and skin. Hopefully, they would be able to take shelter from the heat and eat a decent meal before crossing the river.

To add to his list of frustrations, Beck's scent had gone cold.

Airron's first order of business at the village would be to seek confirmation that he was at least on the right trail. Surely, either Beck or Avalon would stand out in such a small place, and he hoped to obtain confirmation that they had indeed passed through. If not, Airron would find a suitable place to board the horses and arrange for ferries to transport them over the tributaries of the Koda to the destination on the map.

Melania asked for water, and he handed her one of the bags. "Why don't you finish it? I will have it filled in town."

She took the bag with a grateful smile. "*Sinsai.*"

The sound of horses approaching caused Airron to look up. He expected the inhabitants of the settlement to be made up of all Dwarves, but the riders bearing down on them were men.

"Hold there," one shouted when he was within hearing range.

Airron held out his hand to stop Melania, and then put the Haventi slightly ahead in front of her Pinto.

"*Asha*, good folk," greeted Airron. "We have come seeking a stable and passage across the Koda."

A dark-haired man with a short beard spoke up. "You have picked a bad time to visit, Elf. One of the young girls at our camp has gone missing. As you can imagine, strangers are not a welcome sight at the moment. You wouldn't happen to know anything about it, would you?"

Airron quickly shook his head. "No, of course not. When did she go missing?" He knew that Avalon, if he was still on her trail, was a day ahead of him.

"Yesterday. She is the daughter of one of the miners here with our expedition, and the family had been sleeping in tents on the periphery of the settlement. The father heard a scream in the middle of night and went to investigate. He found a large tear in the tent holding his daughter and she was gone."

"And, you have seen no sign of any strangers in the vicinity?" asked Airron.

The man shook his head. "No one. But, one of the ferries is missing. We just assumed it came loose, but now I'm not so sure."

Airron was torn. He had to find Beck. Nothing was more important than saving the life of the man who had been like a brother to him his entire life. Yet, now, there was this missing girl. As a shifter of the island, he had a duty to serve and protect. It was what defined him. What shaped the essence of magic that flowed through his veins.

Melania addressed the men. "My husband is an incomparable bodyshifter as well as a Gladewatcher and *Savitar*. He will find the missing girl."

Airron looked at her with raised eyebrows. Somehow, she must have reasoned out that he would have personal misgivings about the choice before him and acted to take the decision out of his hands.

*Sinsai, my wife.*

The men dismounted and approached Airron to shake his hand. "*Savitar*? Thank the Highworld you're here! Do you really think you can find her?"

Airron nodded. "I can find her." But, his instincts were already screaming at him that it would be too late. When a body disappears in the path of an evil bodyshifter, there is only one conclusion that can be made.

*Hang on, Beck. I am coming for you. On that you can depend, my friend.*

# CHAPTER 16

## Turncoat

The carriage bounced roughly over the uneven terrain of the marketplace outside of Nysa's front gates. Normally, the hub that operated outside of the city would be bustling with activity even at this late hour, but now it was vacant. There was little money to be had from a city besieged by civil war.

Kiernan gritted her teeth as every turn of the wheels rattled her bones. Across the seat from her Kirby Nash sat utterly composed. *How can he be so bloody calm all the time?*

"Tell me, Captain. What are our odds at pulling this off?"

"Twenty percent."

"Twenty…that's it? Only a twenty percent chance that we'll be able to free my father?"

He shook his head. "Only a twenty percent chance that we'll make it through the front gates."

She frowned. "Did you not think this was an opinion you should have shared with me before now?"

"I did, Your Grace, but you chose not to listen."

He was right, of course. She didn't listen to any of her advisors, including some pretty irate sorceresses, who insisted that this gambit was foolhardy and dangerous. But, they didn't understand her duty or her blood oath. Danger and percentages of success did not always factor into her decision making.

She guessed she was just hoping that Kirby had a little more confidence that their plan would succeed. Certainly, the fact that seven of the Sabers were able to enter the city under various pretexts without difficulty should account for something. There seemed to be a substantial lapse in security from Etin's allied legionnaires.

"Halt!"

The cry came from outside, and the carriage rumbled to a stop. Kiernan tried to control her nerves as she pulled the hood of her cloak closer around her head. This was the riskiest part of their plan. Once admitted into the city, they could disappear within the mass of people and soldiers, but if found out now, it would be over.

Kirby's blonde curls, dyed black, bounced around his face as he shifted to peer out of the window of the carriage. He wore a well-tailored, plain black tunic and leggings, a complement to her stylish, lightweight linen cloak. Her distinctive, long blonde hair was pulled back into a severe chignon. A ruse designed to make them appear prosperous enough to afford a carriage, yet not among the highborn which would precipitate a discussion regarding House affiliation.

"Are you an idiot?" the soldier at the gate questioned harshly. "The city is closed!"

The Saber disguised as their driver answered. "Yes, sir, I am aware, but the Mistress Downey of York is with child and is seeking permission to enter the city to visit her midwife."

Kiernan let out a wail. "Ahh!"

Angry footsteps strode to the door of the carriage and it was yanked open. "What is the matter with you, woman?"

Kiernan gasped and kept her head averted as she held her belly. "It is time! Please, sir! I must be allowed into the city!"

Kirby held her hand and played the concerned husband perfectly.

"You will have to come back. We have a wedding tomorrow and no one—"

"Ahh!"

"What is it, Fasso?" This, from one of the archers who lined the top of the outer wall.

Fasso poked his head back out of the carriage. "A woman with child who wishes to see her midwife," he shouted up to the wall. Then, a little softer, "She's pretty big, Lieutenant."

There was a pause as the soldiers discussed what to do.

"All right, send her through."

The heavy iron gates of Nysa groaned as they slowly began to open.

The soldier called Fasso leaned in once more. "You may enter." He put his hand on the carriage door to close it and then hesitated. "Wait."

Kiernan cursed under her breath. Looking over at Kirby, she saw him reach down and remove a dagger from his leather boot, slipping it into his palm.

"Let me see your face," Fasso ordered.

Kiernan held the cloak tight around her face and glanced at the soldier with her eyes lowered, hoping he had never seen her close up.

"Let me see your eyes."

Kiernan let out a breath and brought her gaze up to the soldier.

Fasso's eyes widened in recognition at the same time that Kirby's left fist drove into his temple like a hammer. Kiernan immediately reached out and grabbed the man before he fell, and Kirby dragged him into the carriage, the open door blocking the view of the legionnaires on the wall. "Quickly!" he hissed. "Help me take off his cloak! That's all we have time for, so it will have to do."

Kiernan unlaced the cord at the man's neck and Kirby swung the cloak around his shoulders and rammed the helm with the Wolf sigil blazoned on the front down on his head. Agile as a cat, he jumped from the carriage and closed the door, pounding the side with his open hand. "Get moving!" he shouted up to the Saber driving.

The carriage lurched and the unconscious soldier rolled onto the floor. He was too heavy for her to lift by herself, but she was able to squeeze her feet from underneath him and curl them under her body on the cushioned seat. While Kiernan held her breath, the carriage rumbled through the gates and onto Dannery Row.

*Well, done, Kirby.* She leaned her head back with a sigh of relief, but knew that she couldn't let her guard down for one moment. Not all of the legionnaires would be as easy to fool as the sentries at the gates. Darkness was their ally now, but tomorrow it would be more difficult to hide her identity.

Prestigious noble estates lined the boulevard on both sides of the road and then gave way to the commercial district where the more prosperous merchants plied their wares. She hoped Kirby had been able to slip away from the guards. She comforted herself with the fact that an alarm had not been raised and would have by now if Kirby had been discovered.

The carriage took several turns and finally turned down Penny Place, a neighborhood of modest homes and businesses, and pulled up in front of an inn called the Draca Den. Anxious to leave the confines of the carriage, Kiernan waited impatiently for the Saber to open the door, indicating that all was clear.

It swung open a moment later and she quickly alighted, instructing her Saber driver to dispose of the soldier in the carriage in whatever way he deemed reasonable—short of killing him—that ensured he didn't cause trouble for them before tomorrow night.

The streets and walkways were crowded with boisterous legionnaires, and terrified citizens hurried along their way with heads hung low as they tried to avoid notice.

"Hear ye! Hear ye!"

Kiernan turned to the town crier dressed in a bright red coat, white breeches and tricorne hat, his hand bell ringing in time to his words to garner the attention of an audience.

"Hear ye! Let it be known by one and all! The King has fled Nysa! The monarch of this great land has abandoned the people in their bleakest hour! Hear ye! Hear ye! King Maximus is gone!"

Another crier further down the block touted the fact that Lord Davad Etin had assumed administrative control of the city and would not forsake the people, as had their King.

Livid at the brash dissemination of outright lies, Kiernan pushed through the throng to the front door of the Draca Den and entered. Unlike most taverns and inns, this particular establishment wasn't packed wall to wall with legionnaires. Instead, families sat quietly eating their meals in the illumination of a blazing fireplace that provided a warm and inviting atmosphere lacking elsewhere in the beset city.

She knew this innkeeper personally, and he would never tolerate loud and drunken behavior in front of his clientele. The legionnaires must have quickly realized this and looked elsewhere for their fun leaving the Draca Den a safe haven in the turmoil for the citizenry.

She caught the eye of the innkeeper busy wiping down his bar with a white towel. He gave her a brief nod. She walked the perimeter of the room and took the stairs on the south side of the building up to the second level.

He was behind her a few moments later, unlocking one of the room doors and ushering her inside.

He quickly lowered his bulk to one knee. "Your Grace."

"It's so good to see you, Jase." Kiernan met the innkeeper years ago when he had managed the Lantern Inn in the town of Janis. Since then, he had married and relocated to Nysa to open the Draca Den with his new wife. He was also one of the largest men she had ever seen in her life. In spite of her anger, she couldn't help but smile fondly at the man who had become a friend to her. "Please rise."

He stood and shook his head. "Terrible times, Your Grace, just terrible."

She removed her cloak and hung it on the single peg on the back of the door. "I just heard the town criers' drivel."

He waved his hand in the air. "Bah! Nobody believes that nonsense. We're not as ignorant as the nobles like to think. Present company excluded, of course."

"But, the soldiers, Jase. Where are their commanders?"

He shook his head in regret. "I don't know. These are Iserlohn men and I am ashamed to admit it!"

"Poor discipline and an insane leader, I guess. But, I promise you, I will do whatever is necessary to rid the city of this infestation. You have my word on that."

"Of that I have no doubt, but do you think I can talk you out of it, Your Grace?" he asked with a nod at her burgeoning stomach. "You can leave the riffraff to me. I have a mind to go out there and strap a few over my knee anyway."

She laughed. "And, *I* have no doubt that you would do just that. But, please, don't bring trouble on your head. Leave this to the Sabers."

His large face turned pink. "No offense, Your Grace, but that feels like the cowardly way to me. This is my city now. I played the coward in Janis and will not do so again."

"A mindshifter had been involved in the events with Cara," she reminded him. "You were no coward, Jase. In fact, you were the only one to stand up to her husband."

"Not soon enough," he mumbled. "But, enough of this. You need your rest, so I will leave you to it."

She reached out to grab one of his big, beefy hands in hers. "Thank you, Jase, for everything. You are very brave to put yourself at risk to help me."

He smiled down at her from his enormous height. "Flattery, my Princess, will get you the affections of an innkeeper for life."

"I hope so."

With a promise to send Kirby to the room as soon as he arrived, the big man said a final goodbye and shut the door behind him.

Kiernan went to the small window to look down on the streets while she cradled the swell of her unborn son. *Was Helenite right when she said I may be in the early stages of labor?* She hoped to the Highworld not. She couldn't have this baby now.

Not when a battle loomed.

Not without Beck.

****

*I can't just sit here, Baya.* Kenley paced back and forth restlessly in her bedroom, and the Draca Cat's green eyes tracked her movements.

*What do you propose?*

She stopped and peered into the outer room. Good. Her guard was still asleep in the armchair. *My Maman needs me! I have to go to her, Baya, but how am I to saddle a horse? Anyone I ask for help will just send me back here to my room if they find out what I'm planning.* She paused in thought. *Kirby would help me if he were here.*

*Kirby? This is not about Captain Nash again, is it?*

Kenley stopped pacing. *What do you mean?*

*You still think you are going to marry him one day.*

Her hands flew to her hips. *I am going to marry him! You just wait and see.*

*I thought humans usually choose mates closer to their own age?*

*Not me! I'm going to marry Captain Kirby Nash some day. Mark my words, Baya. But, right now I have to figure out how to save him and Maman.*

*I will take you.*

She looked at her friend in puzzlement. *You?*

*Yes, you can ride on my back.*

Kenley shook her head. *That is a crazy idea, Baya.*

*No, it is not. If you stand on a stool, you can easily reach my back to put a saddle on me, and I will take you to Nysa.*

*But, you are my friend! I could never ride you!*

*Does your Maman need our help?*

*Yes! Of course, but how can I ask that of you?*

*You have not asked, I have offered.*

She took her lower lip between her teeth and looked once more in the outer room at her sleeping caretaker. *It might work, Baya.*

*I will keep you safe, little one. I promise.*

She made up her mind and nodded. *Let's do it.*

*Keep in mind, Princess, that my gait is much different from a horse. You will need to hang on very tightly.*

*I will.* She approached the Draca and hugged her around her snowy neck. *Thank you, my friend. I love you.*

*And, I you.* Baya tilted her head in thought. *You know, Princess, they say that long ago, my ancestors, the Draca Cats, were used in battle. Are we going to battle now?*

*I think so. From what I overheard, Nysa is in trouble.*

Baya's green eyes took on a dangerous glint. *Then, we ride for Nysa!*

**\*\*\*\***

Maximus gazed into the low-burning fire lost in thought. The rest of his companions, Belle, Larkin, Eden, Bo, and Saber Ryan were asleep, but he was finding it hard to do so this night.

Tomorrow would be the seventh day of his self-imposed sequester and probably one of his last. The food supplies that Miss Belle and Larkin had so meticulously transferred to his chambers had inexplicably gone bad, so they no longer had any food to eat. Today, the water supply they kept in a lined wooden barrel tipped over leaving them without a drop.

He knew that Gage Gregaros would be planning a rescue attempt, but when? He granted a Lordship to the former Royal Guard Captain for the man's valor in the Demon War. The stories were legendary now. Without the slightest concern for his own life, the former Saber had thrown himself at the enemy with loyal abandon. Most certainly, Maximus would not be alive today if not for Gage. But, he wouldn't be alive much longer without food or water. If his liege Lord did not arrive soon and win back the city, Maximus would be forced to come out of his chambers.

He snorted softly. *Starvation or hanging? Are those really my only choices?*

He wondered if Kiernan had returned to Bardot. If so, he hoped that she stayed right there. In the midst of this ridiculous succession war, it would be her best chance of survival for herself and her children. He wasn't sure where Beck could be, he only knew what Davad told him—that Beck would not be returning any time soon.

It was all just so frustrating to be sitting inside this room instead of confronting his nemesis! Subjects had expectations that their King will keep them safe and sheltered from harm and, right now, he could do neither. Furthermore, the situation would only get worse before it had a chance to get better. When Gage did arrive, there would be loss of life—on both sides—as that was the unfortunate, but inevitable, fact of war. *Damn Etin and his greedy ambitions!*

A shadow passed over the fire, and he turned. "Ah, Eden, please sit down and join me."

The brown-haired sorceress walked around and sat in the armchair next to him. She wore a salmon-colored gown and her hair was pulled back in the plait favored by the sorceresses.

"You are up late, Your Grace," she observed.

"Yes, my mind refuses to let me rest I am afraid."

"It will be over soon," she commented flatly.

"Yes, it appears so."

They remained quiet for a few moments, and then he turned his head to study her profile. "Tell me, Eden, what did he promise you?"

She turned to him. "He?"

"Yes, Lord Etin. I know what you have been up to." The sorceress turned back to the fire and didn't respond. "It was you who dumped our water supply."

"I was only attempting to move the barrel from underneath the window," she tried to insist.

"With your foot?"

Her face hardened.

"Your sandal imprint is on the wood, Eden."

She sighed, but remained quiet for several long moments as if deciding what to say. Maximus had just convinced himself she wasn't going to reply when she said, "Not he. She."

"Who?"

"Avalon Ravener."

He cursed loudly into the silent room. "Dear Highworld, Eden, why?"

"Oh, well, she made all of the usual promises, Your Grace. Money, power, status. All of the things I could never hope to achieve on my own." She looked at him, but then rolled her eyes and turned her head. "What would you know, King Maximus? You can't possibly know what it's like to grow up a poor farmer's daughter and watch your family struggle to survive. To have hunger gnaw at your belly when you go to bed at night. To see your father work himself to the bone until he dies behind his plow horse." She shook her head. "You can't know what it's like to be whisked off to live with strangers at the age of sixteen because of a magical ability you neither understand nor want. You simply have no frame of reference for the life I lived, so you can't know."

No, he didn't know and the admission hurt more than her betrayal. The poverty and misery of the people of his country lay at his feet and his alone. He couldn't even blame Lord Etin. The suffering of Eden's family occurred on his watch.

"So, why haven't you killed me yet, Eden? What are you waiting for?"

She laughed. "I didn't know that we would be locked away with so many witnesses, Your Grace. I do want to be able to live in this city and enjoy my wealth once you are gone."

"I see. So, you figured you would destroy our ability to remain in this room and force me to walk into the hangman's noose on my own two feet. That way, your hands remain clean."

"Precisely."

# CHAPTER 17

## Changed

The bitter cold woke Kenley from her exhausted sleep. Misty clouds of vapor formed in front of her mouth with every breath she took. She snuggled closer against the warm body of Baya, thanking the spirits for her beautiful and brave friend. *I would have been really scared of all the noises in the woods if not for her.*

*Good morning,* she breathed into her living fur blanket.

*Good morning, Princess.*

She sat up. *Baya! That was so much fun last night! Riding you is much more fun than riding a horse.*

*Hrmmf,* the Draca snorted. *Do not get used to it, little one. I made that offer due to an urgent situation. You will not be putting that saddle on me to ride for pleasure.*

Kenley giggled. *I won't. It was fun, though.* She got to her feet and brushed the dirt from her tunic. *Come on. First thing I am going to do when we get to the palace is sneak into the kitchens and get some honeycakes!*

*For me, too?*

*Of course.*

Kenley crept along the forest edge but kept a close eye on the granite wall that surrounded the city fifty feet away. There were no soldiers in sight, and she thought this odd. Captain Bo Franck would be very upset if he knew that the guards were shirking their duty.

Moving silently ahead, it didn't take them long to reach the cliff that rimed the Arounda Ocean and served as the western border of the city. Waves crashed loudly against the rocks on the other side and the smell of salt hung heavy in the air.

Kenley shook her hands to bring life to her frozen fingers. She would be glad when she finally reached the palace and not just for the heat. She missed her Maman. She tried not to think about her too much or she would cry, but if her Maman was in trouble, Kenley wanted to help her. She didn't worry about her Daddy that much. He was so strong and powerful that nobody could harm him. And, Uncle Airron was helping him. There was no one to help her Maman.

She wiped a tear that fell from her eye. It would be up to her and Baya, and she would be brave like her Maman and not let her down.

Taking a deep breath, she sniffled one last time and then looked over her shoulder at her best friend. *Ready?*

Baya nodded once and together they sprinted the distance between the forest and the curtain wall. A few months ago, she discovered a small gap where the wall butted up against the cliff.

*I don't think you will fit anymore, Baya!*

Baya nudged her aside to inspect the opening. *It will be tight, but I think I can.*

*Follow me closely. We must not be discovered before it is time.*

*When do we go to battle, little one?*

*When we hear the fireworks.*

\*\*\*\*

The orange light of burning supply wagons lit up the early morning and thick smoke created a gray haze that hung low in the air. Rogan—with Janin still on his shoulders and under the legionnaire-issue cloak of House Etin—carefully picked his way through the pandemonium that was the Iserlohn Army.

Disorder reigned throughout the encampment. Animals ran loose, men groaned, and officers screamed at their disoriented troops to line up into formation. The Halfies had performed their jobs well, and the legionnaires still had no idea who or what had caused the repeated attacks during the night. And, now, the stain of another army on the horizon bore down on the beleaguered camp.

So far, the disguise Rogan and Janin wore worked, but they had been traveling mostly among the civilians. Now, they were making their way to the front lines in an effort to identify the Houses of the advancing army.

"Stop, there!" The angry shout directed their way caused Rogan to turn. Through a gap in the cloak, he saw an officer of House Etin rushing toward them.

He hoped Janin had her cowl pulled closely around her head as it would not be unusual to be cloaked in the stinging cold of the morning.

"What are you doing?" the man yelled. "Just out for a causal morning stroll, legionnaire?"

Janin must have shaken her head.

"Can't you see what's happening? Find your unit and get into formation or so help me I will kill you!" The officer leaned in inches from Janin's face. "Do you hear me?"

Rogan's fingers twitched toward the short sword on his hip, not sure if his volatile wife could hold it together. If she couldn't, and the officer tried to harm her, he would find himself with one less hand.

But, she simply nodded, and pressed her left heel into his ribs to guide his movements to the left. Needing no further prodding, he took off at a run, slowing only when he was sure that the officer had been left far behind. Melting back into the throng of soldiers once again, he realized with tremendous satisfaction that he had done all of this without a single grunt.

Close to the front line now, he searched out the banners flying at the head of the approaching Legion. His eyes slid over the sigils of House Everard and House Gregaros. It would be hard for him to imagine Gage Gregaros ever turning on the Everard family, but he couldn't rest on that belief. Especially, since he was already surrounded by legionnaires in the scarlet and black of House Everard.

During his traipse through the rear of the army over the course of the night, he learned that many of the Everard soldiers and even some from House Etin were uneasy about this conflict and on the verge of abandoning their duty and running. Blindly following the orders of superiors during war with an enemy was one thing, they said, but to march against the King they had sworn to protect? It wasn't sitting well with many of them. In fact, Rogan had heard talk that some of the legionnaires had already defected back to Iserport in the middle of the night.

The lines were becoming more ordered as Rogan progressed toward the vanguard. He was among the Calvary now, their enormous warhorses stamping and snorting malcontent at their stationary stance. A dangerous place to be, but he had to know the intentions of Gregaros.

A few Cavalrymen glanced down at them curiously, but most had their eyes directed upward at the threat looming closer.

Janin gave him an urging kick, so he strode faster to the very front of the line. Warily, he stepped out of the column to provide both him and Janin a view down the long row of horses. Commander Hugo Bassus sat tall astride a barrel-chested Haventi, a hauberk covering his red and black tunic. His shoulder length hair, mostly gray, lined a focused profile that appeared made of stone as he studied the army before him.

Across the plains, Gage Gregaros, the wiry, gray-haired Lord who was once a Scarlet Saber, rode at the head of his procession, standing upright in the stirrups with a range finder held to his eye. All was quiet as the army advanced.

Gage finally halted his men several hundred feet from Bassus' line. Running his horse along the column, Gregaros chose a small parley group of six men who then peeled away from the others and joined the Lord in his approach toward the waiting army.

To Rogan's surprise, and probably Gage's surprise as well, Hugo Bassus made no move to receive the parley. That was enough of a cue to Rogan to get the bloody hell out of the way. Bassus' actions made it clear that he had no intention of accepting any form of truce that may be offered and meant to fight through Gregaros.

At least, Rogan thought with relief, it did confirm that he and Gage were still fighting on the same side. He turned and threaded his way back through the horses, responding to the touches of Janin's heels and his own sight through the cloak to navigate the sea of muscular, restless animals.

Rogan glanced back through a narrow opening and saw Gage pull his party up short.

"In the name of King Maximus, you are charged with treason to the Crown, Hugo Bassus! Stand down or you will be cut down!"

"To the Netherworld with King Maximus!" laughed Bassus. "The reign of Everard is over! Iserlohn needs a new leader! Preferably one who can't have us burnt to a crisp at a whim."

It was Gage's turn to laugh derisively. "And, you think Etin is the man? Come now, Hugo. I have known you for too many years to believe that."

"He is the man for now," Bassus admitted. "Who knows what opportunities may open up in a year or two."

"I don't want to kill you, Hugo. Stand down."

"Join with us then, Gage! You will be entitled to keep your lands and title, I can assure you of that. Bend your knee to House Etin!"

"Etin does not have a legitimate claim to the throne!"

"Etin means to be King, Gage, and if he must inherit a broken crown in doing so, so be it."

"That is precisely why I cannot support him! He has no idea what it takes to be King! The people will never love him."

"You fool! It is obedience he commands, not love!"

The naked fury on Maximus' liege Lord was unmistakable. "For the sake of our friendship, I ask one more time for your sword!"

"You may ask, but you will not receive!"

"Then, I will take your head instead!" Gage and his legionnaires wheeled their mounts around and headed back toward their line to regroup.

Bassus, abandoning all of the rules of parley, thrust his sword into the air and kicked his Haventi forward before Gregaros was halfway back to his men. "Charge!"

****

Beck yanked harshly at the chains holding his arms and legs pinned to the cavern wall with a snarl. The manacles didn't budge, and all he managed to do was cause the metal to cut deeper into his skin. Avalon already told him that his bonds were infused with magic, but he kept trying anyway, hoping brute strength would somehow prevail.

Early on, he realized that his earthshifting would be of little use to him with the lack of loose stone or earth within range. He could probably try to bring the mountain down on top of all of their heads—he had brought down a mountain once before—but that would only serve to kill him in the process. There may come a time when it became necessary to do it, but it hadn't yet arrived.

His face was still bruised and swollen from the beating Avalon had given him on the way to Farout Falls, but he was healing. One thought held him together. Airron was coming, and he was pinning all of his hopes on his friend.

This remote location that Avalon called Farout Falls was devoid of all people. They traveled unseen for leagues to this hideaway of hers, hewn from the southern cliffs of Deepstone. He was so physically spent by the time they arrived that two Cymans had to carry him up rough stairs that rose seventy feet or more to the cave entrance above.

Once inside, he was surprised to find Avalon had managed to fashion a comfortable home out of the massive cavern by using the natural pillared formations to create separate rooms. Colorful tapestries and carpets adorned the walls and floors. Heavy, ornate furniture of mahogany covered in richly decorated brocades and silks lent a distinctly feminine touch to the starkness of the stone. Dancing yellow flames in copper braziers created soft light and provided a source of heat to take the chill from the air.

A low, whistling sound roused him from his thoughts and he looked up as the tip of a black leather whip narrowly missed his face and bit into his shoulder with a loud snap. Beck cried out in shock and excruciating pain.

"The Mistress 'as ordered five lashes of the whip for your deception," the Cyman guard said sorrowfully. "Just 'old still and it will be over soon."

If possible, the second strike to his chest hurt worse than the first because he now knew what to expect. Tears formed in his eyes, but he refused to let them fall.

Crack.

Lash three hit his stomach followed by a fourth to his upper thigh. He bellowed out in agony.

Crack.

The last crossed the second strike to form a red laced x on his chest.

Blood seeped from the wounds and trickled down his body, and he felt faint from both the burning throb and the sudden brutality of the act. Head hanging down, he smelled her musky scent drift to him before she spoke.

"I predict that this will not be the last time you will force me to have you whipped, Prince Beck." Her voice sounded unusually raspy and the speech garbled.

He didn't respond but looked down at her with a murderous glare only to find her face hidden within the folds of her cowl.

"I know this because I can still see it," she observed. "It is still there."

He had no wish to communicate with her, but needed answers. Needed to know why she had kidnapped him and what she was after. "What? What can you see, witch?"

"Hope. You still have hope that you are going to make it out of here alive. Am I correct?"

Despair washed through his body. The conviction in her voice that the opposite was true seemed to confirm an inescapable conclusion. He was going to die here.

"You hope that your Elven friend will find you. You hope he will charge in here at the last moment and free you from your bonds. And, you hope to see your family again." She waved her hand in the air toward him. "It is written all over your face, earthshifter."

"I do hope those things," he admitted quietly. "More than anything."

"Anything? Well, we shall see if that holds true. Let me start first with one of the reasons I have asked you to be my guest here at Farout Falls. The Protetor, my dear progeny of Galen Starr. Where can I find this most valuable of all treasures?"

"That is what this is about? The Protetor?" The book suddenly felt heavy in its location in his trouser pocket, but he knew he had to stall. He had to buy time for Airron to track him. "You are welcome to it. I never wanted to accept the book in the first place, but Mage Starr insisted. You will have to travel to Bardot to retrieve it. It is located in my office at the Academy."

She began to pace back and forth below him, a dark hooded shadow gliding across the floor. "Where in your office?"

"On my shelf where I keep all my books. It's small and black and free of markings."

She spun toward him. "You keep such a valuable item on a bookshelf? Where all have access to it?"

"I didn't consider the book valuable," he lied. "I told you. I never wanted to accept it in the first place."

She nodded. "Very well. I will travel to Bardot to retrieve the book. You better not be lying to me or you will be very sorry."

"I'm not."

"Good. However, now that that's settled, I think I can spare a day before I leave to dispose of the Elf."

Beck swallowed his fear. "He has probably gone back to Haventhal by now."

"Another deception, Prince Beck!"

"Please, don't—"

"The book can wait," she interrupted. "I need the LifeFire Tonic to stay alive, yes, but I'll never be the same. My body is too far gone."

Even though she stood directly in front of him, her face and body were shrouded by her cloak. *What did she mean by that?*

She inched closer. "Whenever you feel hope creep back into your heart, earthshifter, remember this." She lifted her hands to remove the cloak and let it fall to the ground.

Beck shrank back in horror at the hideous creature that stood before him. Bent and skeletal with curved hands and toes that ended in claws. Skin so translucent and mottled that it reminded him of an animated corpse. Dark circles caused her eyes to look like sunken marbles, and deep cracks sectioned her face like a broken mirror.

He was unable to tear his eyes away as the thing that had once been Avalon Ravener unfurled a pair wings behind her back, membranes pulsating with what looked like black blood.

He couldn't help himself.

He screamed.

# Chapter 18

## Clash of Swords

After Hugo Bassus gave the order to charge, Rogan barely managed to dive free of the last column of horses before the stampede. The cloak fell off Janin's shoulders when she rolled across the ground, but it was just as well. The disguise would only be a hindrance at this point.

His wife fell into a crouch and unsheathed her sword. With the ease of an old dance, she pressed herself against his back at once, and they began to fight their way through the mass of foot soldiers running ahead to close with House Gregaros. With battle lust raging in their eyes, few of the soldiers seemed to notice the Dwarves in their midst and fewer yet that they were fighting against them.

The wound on his thigh where one of the Halfies stabbed him back in Haventhal began to throb in earnest, but he pushed through it, inching closer and closer to the allied forces. Janin, in her element again, screamed her fury at any who ventured too close.

The brutal collision of the two armies and the ensuing clash of men, animals and weapons was deafening. Soldiers younger than he slipped in grass now sodden with blood in their haste to rush to the fight. The full weight of one wounded and staggering soldier hit him from behind and drove him to the ground in a tangle of limbs. Rogan twisted and looked up at the man. He wore a crazed bloody smile on his lips, but his eyes were already glazing over toward death.

Rogan pushed the dying man off him and jumped back to his feet just as another legionnaire rose up and swung a large broadsword at him. He knocked it aside and Janin made a running leap to bury her blade in the man's neck.

Rogan hated this.

Men—boys really—sacrificing their lives in combat with their fellow countrymen. For what reason? Rogan witnessed firsthand how distressed King Maximus had been when he learned that the living conditions in Iserport had not improved. Given the opportunity, the Iserlohn monarch would have addressed the issue, of that Rogan was certain. But, the nobles had their own agenda for starting this war and it most likely had nothing to do with Iserport or involved any altruistic motive for what was in the best interest of the citizens.

Janin cried out when a soldier rammed his elbow into her face and she fell to the ground. The legionnaire jumped on top of her and lifted his fist to strike her again.

Rogan shook as he fought back the desire to kill, to drag his sword across the soldier's neck and watch while the blood spilled from the man's throat. It would take very little effort. Instead, his foot connected with the legionnaire's cheekbone, and he heard the distinctive crunch of bone.

The soldier fell away from Janin.

Rogan stood over the man now cradling his face in his hands and pointed south. "Get out of here! Now!"

The young soldier didn't have to be told twice and scrambled backward to get away from the enraged look in Rogan's eyes.

He went to Janin. "Are you all right?"

"Nothing broken, but I don't think I can say the same for the other guy," she noted with a feral smile.

In the next instant, a large of amount of blood sprayed across their faces from two combatants fighting next to them. Rogan growled with the desire to summon fire. *To the Netherworld and back with the law!* Janin's life was in danger, and he would not stand by and let her be killed when he had the power to stop it.

Instead, he grabbed her by the elbow. "Come on, let's get—"

A loud angry bellow rent the air and a hole opened up in the melee when the legionnaires stumbled back from the shout. The fighting came to an end as all turned to watch Gage Gregaros and Hugo Bassus, off their horses now, circle each other—the former allies now enemies.

"Come on, you bastard!" screamed Bassus, making a clumsy lunge for Gage, and Rogan saw why. The Commander was bleeding from a deep cut on his thigh. The gushing blood told him that the former Saber had sliced Bassus' femoral artery. Unless the Commander received care within the next few minutes, he would bleed to death.

But, the man didn't have even a few seconds.

Gage walked over and with both hands on the hilt of his sword, took the head of the traitorous Hugo Bassus as promised.

Seeing their leader cut down broke the resistance of many of the legionnaires, and they threw down their swords and knelt to the ground. Two Cavalrymen wearing the plumes of officers on their helms dismounted and bent before Gage. "Yield! We yield to you, Lord Gregaros!"

As word of the surrender passed back through the ranks, the warfare ground to a halt.

Rogan and Janin stood out among the kneeling soldiers and Gage's blood spattered face froze in shock when he saw them. He immediately strode over and held his hand out to Rogan. "I can honestly say that you're one of the last people I expected to see here."

Rogan took the outstretched hand, but before he could reply, the high-pitched squeaks of the Halfies echoed loudly behind him.

Gage pointed to the sprites actively routing the army from the plains with their spear points and sending many soldiers sprinting at a dead run south back toward Iserport. "Your idea?" he asked with a chuckle.

Rogan shrugged. "I needed an army."

Gage informed him then of Lord Etin's plot and his seizure of Nysa. "I will send a runner back with news of Bassus' defeat to Princess Kiernan immediately. She will want to know that the threat has been eliminated."

"Has there been any word of Beck?" Rogan asked hopefully.

But, Gage shook his head. "Nothing."

Rogan felt a tug on his sleeve and turned to find a gleeful Vinni Vee. "Thank you for the fight, rude Dwarf."

Guarding all of his vulnerable parts, Rogan faced the imp. "It is I who must thank you. We will meet again when this is over, Vinni, and I promise you that I'll find you a home. You would like that, wouldn't you?"

To Rogan's surprise, the Halfie turned his back on him, and he wondered if he offended the Tribe Leader with his offer.

When Vinni finally turned around, Rogan thought he detected a small tear building at the corner of the Tribe Leader's eye. "That's all we have ever wanted, but most people do not understand that."

"I do, because it's all I ever wanted, too. Until we meet again, Halfie."

"Until we meet again, rude..." He shook his head fiercely as he fought his natural instincts to be mean. "Until we meet again, *Savitar*."

****

The burning sun hung directly overhead as Airron stepped off the ferry and held his hand out to Melania to help her onto the dock. After their fifth ferry in as many hours, and he was grateful to be on dry land again.

He rubbed his neck in exhaustion. It had been impossible to sleep the evening before after obtaining the confirmation he dreaded. Avalon Ravener had indeed passed through the small mining community, and the proof insulted every moral fiber of his being as a bodyshifter and caused his blood oath to rage. The shrunken corpse of the young woman had been unceremoniously wedged in an outcropping of rock not far from where the miner family slept in their tents. It left Airron to explain to the father that a fellow bodyshifter had committed this heinous crime.

After that, the man looked at him with disgust in his eyes and Airron couldn't blame him. The father could not possibly be expected to distinguish Avalon Ravener with any other bodyshifter on the island. Magic had killed his daughter. That was all he knew or cared about.

Melania tried her best to explain who Avalon Ravener was and how they were on her trail to stop this from ever happening again. But, in this father's eyes, they were too late. He cared nothing for justice at that moment. He just wanted his daughter back.

Despite Melania's passionate words, the townsfolk asked the two of them to spend the evening away from the settlement to give the family an opportunity to grieve without the presence of a bodyshifter nearby.

He understood. And, for the first time since this journey across Deepstone began, he felt grateful to have Melania with him. The rebuke had him feeling unexpectedly despondent, and her presence at his side soothed him.

The miners told him they would encounter no other people west of the tributaries of the Koda. On foot now and alone, they walked through the searing heat of the day. The inhospitable barren landscape of exposed sandstone punctuated by the occasional rolling badlands spread out for leagues ahead of them. With the exception of lichen and moss, the plant life that was so sparse east of the Koda, was nonexistent here.

He found himself glancing over at Melania often. For a highborn, spoiled Elven, she endured the conditions better than he expected. Earlier, she trimmed a scrap from her emerald dress, dampened it with water, and wore it tied across her forehead to keep cool. She carried a pack of supplies and three water bags across her shoulders without complaint.

The sight of her tall and proud twisted his insides. *I'm falling in love with her, but I can't say the words.* As soon as the thought popped into his mind, he chased it away to focus on Beck. Now would be a good time to try and pick up his scent again. Although doubtful Avalon would be careless now, he had to try something.

After informing Melania, he shifted into the Gangi. It took him by surprise when he found the trail instantly. Where it had completely disappeared a few days ago, it was now stronger than ever, almost as though Avalon were enhancing rather than hiding her passage.

The implication glared at him.

When they made camp that night, he told Melania about the conspicuous trail during a cold meal of dried beef and cheese purchased at the miner's camp. A hot meal was out of the question since the wood he brought was long gone, but it wouldn't have mattered anyway since the only living creatures he was able to spot from the air were a few snakes and lizards, and Melania absolutely refused to eat either.

For the light alone, he wished he was able to build a fire, but a blanket of stars winked down from the night sky to lend their help. The pinpricks of radiance reminded Airron of the glow worms in Aquataine.

"You know it's a trap, do you not?"

He nodded. "I suspect as much."

"Yet, still you go?"

He looked at her profile in the starlight. *Highworld, but she's beautiful.* "I must. He's my friend."

"And, his life means more to you than your own?" she asked incredulously.

"It's the nature of a shifter, Melania. For a woman who knows so much about me, you must see that."

She lowered her eyes. "I do. I guess I was just making one last attempt to see if you would choose me. To see if you would decide that a life with me was more important than your death."

*What is wrong with me? Why can't I tell her what she needs to hear? Am I really that much of a monster, unable to love?* The thoughts disturbed him, just not enough to act on them. "Now, how can I die with the best medicinal herbalist on the island with me?" he asked, hoping a little levity would lighten her mood.

It didn't.

"I have decided to go home," she announced abruptly.

"I see."

"I'll take a ferry up the Koda to Deeport and then another boat directly to Havenport. From there I will travel on foot to Sarphia."

"I'm not sure I like the idea of you traveling alone."

"Don't pretend to care for my welfare now. I am well traveled and have done so by myself many times before."

"But, I do care about your well being. Very much."

"I realize now that I was wrong."

"Wrong about what?" he asked, genuinely curious. Despite his apparent flaw, he wanted to know more about this lovely creature sitting next to him.

She shrugged her slim shoulders. "I thought that I loved you enough for the both of us, but I have since realized that one side is not enough. You cannot force someone to love you simply because you wish it were so. I was wrong to marry someone who did not love me back. I want more than that for my life."

"Melania…," he began, unsure what to say.

She stood and gathered her bedroll under one arm. "It is as it is meant to be. I'll go with you to free your friend and then you will be free as well. Good night, Airron Falewir."

# CHAPTER 19

# The Hunt

For what must have been the tenth time, Kiernan checked the scabbard at her back and lifted the sword a few inches to convince herself that it was seated correctly and free from obstructions. That she would need to put it to use within the next hour was almost assured. She meant for this eighth day of the siege of Nysa to be the last.

The wait inside her room at the Draca Den for Kirby Nash seemed interminable. The herbs were doing their job in numbing her pain, and she wanted to be doing something—anything. She just wanted out of this room that she had been holed up in since the evening before.

The door opened at last and Kirby slipped inside. "It's time," was all he said.

She nodded and swept her cloak around her shoulders and raised the hood. She would soon be walking among the people—her people—and she had to take extreme care not to be recognized.

Kirby led the way down the stairs to the common room of the inn. She noticed Jase behind the bar wiping down glasses, but he didn't so much as glance in her direction.

Exiting the inn behind Kirby, she pushed her way into the unusually large crowd of people. Siege or no, the promise of a wedding, it seemed, had brought out every citizen in Nysa.

There were other Sabers in the throng, but she didn't look for them or try to make eye contact with any of the people on the street. Too many knew her. Too many knew the distinct color of her eyes.

A shout rang out and a swell of murmurs rippled through the air. Kiernan craned her head to look in the direction of the others. A white, open carriage came into view, making its way around a bend in the road. Davad Etin and Ava Conry sat together on the red leather bench seat of the carriage and waved to the cheering onlookers.

Kiernan noticed with intense satisfaction that the applause came only from the occupying legionnaires. The citizenry of Nysa remained coolly aloof.

The carriage rattled by and looking into Davad Etin's smug face, Kiernan wished more than anything that she could mindshift a thought into that big head of his. The audacity of this man to seize the royal city and then conduct a wedding ceremony right in the middle of the coup before the outcome was even decided.

The carriage turned the corner and headed toward Dannery Row and the central square where the ceremony was to take place. Kiernan turned away in disgust and pressed against the tide of spectators to walk in the opposite direction toward the royal palace. Realizing time was short, she moved faster. The Sabers would be in position now to create their diversions— minor explosions, fireworks, and a staged fight near the Calvary that would spook the horses—all designed to create confusion and disorder. If the plan worked, it would take some time to sort through the chaos and give Kiernan the time she needed to free her father and the Sabers time to free the allied soldiers.

The crowd thinned near the palace. As she suspected, it would be impossible to enter through the front doors. There were at least a dozen guards standing on the wide palace steps, pointing and laughing.

*Laughing?* She traced her eyes to the subject of their taunts. In the palace courtyard, four men and a woman were bent over with their heads and arms locked in wooden stockades. Yellow yolk dripped down their faces and the remains of eggshells littered the ground in front of them.

"Keep moving, Your Grace," whispered a voice behind her and only then did she realize that she had stopped to stare, her anger bubbling to the surface once again.

"But—"

"Move, Your Grace."

With difficulty, she turned from the scene and walked west, following the cobblestone road for several minutes before ducking into an alleyway. The narrow corridor was dark, but she did notice several figures standing on a second story balcony above. A few men yelled out to her, but she ignored them and hurried along until she reached the end of the alleyway and a wooden fence eight feet high. Kirby laced his fingers together to give her a boost up, and she managed to get her bulk over to the other side.

Despite the nerves and the exertion, she was still pain free. *Thank you, Helenite.*

They were at the periphery of the royal gardens now, and she scaled the waist-high wall that encircled the grounds. Quickly scanning the area, she ran at a crouch to the southern side entrance that led to the lower level servant rooms of the castle. Normally, several Sabers would be guarding this entrance, but now it was deserted.

She went through the door cautiously, and Kirby materialized at her side and slipped in behind her. They ran along the hallway lined with closed doors on both sides. One opened and a servant put her head out, but let out a squeal of fright when she saw them and slammed the door closed again.

Kiernan turned into a shadowed recess that led to the back staircase to the upper levels of the palace, and she started up. Despite the herbs, she had to stop once between the second and third floor to catch her breath before continuing. The baby pressed on her diaphragm making the physical exertion difficult.

A few breathless seconds later, she nodded at Kirby's questioning look and they made their way to the top. At the door to the hallway, the Captain held up a hand to indicate that he wanted her to wait, but they didn't have to wait long. The timing of the Sabers proved impeccable when a loud explosion ruptured into the night.

Kiernan heard raised voices on the other side of the door and then the sound of running boots sprinting off in the opposite direction down the corridor.

At Kirby's nod, they pushed through the door together. Four soldiers whipped around in surprise.

Kiernan threw off her cloak and drew the sword of Iserlohn over her shoulder. One soldier closed with her and two engaged Kirby mistakenly thinking him the bigger threat. The fourth hung back and waited to see where he would be needed.

She grunted with effort as she parried his first strike and swept it wide. The soldier's eyes slid down to her belly and grew wide in shock, causing him to hesitate. She didn't waste the opening. She slammed the flat end of her sword against the side of his head and he dropped like a stone.

The soldier waiting in the wings, not so concerned about fighting a woman with child, rushed her. Sparks flew when their swords met. In an obvious attempt at a feint, the man stepped close with a quick flick of his blade. Kiernan leaned toward it instead of away as the man intended, and he lost his footing. She swung her leg around and kicked him behind the knees sending him to the floor. She used the hilt of her sword this time and delivered a vicious blow to the man's neck and he also crumpled to the ground.

She spun around to Kirby. One of the aggressors was down, but he was still occupied with the second. Wanting to end this quickly, she shouted and the man turned with a swing of his blade meant to take her head off. She ducked and then came up under the momentum of his arm and pierced him in the stomach. While he looked on in stunned disbelief, she leapt into the air to land a kick in the chest that sent him flying on his back. He didn't move again.

Kirby looked at her sheepishly. "I thought I was supposed to be protecting you, Your Grace?"

She looked around at the four men on the ground and shrugged. "You are. You got one, didn't you?"

He shook his head, but she didn't notice, turning to the door of her father's suite. High-pitched whistles from the fireworks sounded outside of the palace, and the shouts in the streets were becoming louder and more frantic.

She banged on the door. "Father! Open up! It's me, Kiernan!" She put her ear to the door and thought she heard a scuffle.

"Kiernan! Move from the door! Now!" Her father barely managed to get the words out before she heard him grunt as if he had been hit. Sensing immediate danger, she backed away from the front of the door and dragged Kirby with her.

"*Ejektelo!*"

The spell exploded both doors of her father's suite off their hinges and across the hallway where they crashed into a twisted wreck. A curtain of dust hung in the hair, and Kiernan scattered the particles from her face with her hand.

A young woman stepped out of the ruined opening with her hands raised, and Kiernan recognized her as one of the students from the Academy. "Eden! It's me, Kiernan. The soldiers are down!"

The girl turned to her and looked at her stomach. "Good. You're still pregnant. This should be easy then."

Kiernan's blood ran cold. She lifted her sword in front of her, knowing it would be no match for a sorceress.

"Stand back, Kiernan," said a voice behind her. "Leave this one to me."

Kiernan turned in surprise. It was Sapphire, and the dark-haired sorceress had her hand held out toward Eden.

"*Bindeno!*"

Had the spell worked, it would have glued Eden's arms and legs tightly to her body, but the sorceress was able to issue a counterspell that deflected the curse.

Kiernan peeked into the room while the two witches circled each other. "Stay inside!" she ordered.

Sapphire looked at Eden with disappointment in her eyes. "You are my sister, Eden. You took a vow to protect and defend the coven. What would make you cast aside your oath?"

Eden didn't answer. Instead, she tried to cast another spell, but she was dealing with the Sect Leader of Spell Casting. She never had a chance. Sapphire countered the spell and rushed her, placing both hands on top of Eden's head.

"*Morbendi.*"

She said it softly, her voice laced with regret.

It was a killing curse.

Gemini once told Kiernan that for a sorceress to take a human life, the spell required her to physically place her hands on the intended victim when uttering the incantation. Accidental killing wasn't possible—it had to be a very up close, very personal decision.

Eden slumped to the ground.

Sapphire turned to Kiernan with a pained expression. "I hope I never have to use that curse ever again."

"But, how did you know Eden turned?"

"I didn't. Diamond had a feeling that a sorceress was involved in this mess so she sent me after you, but that is all that I had the authority to do. Now, that the threat of magic is over, the rest will be up to you."

Kiernan nodded and without another word, Sapphire turned and went back through the door to the stairs to the servant quarters.

The King walked out of his now doorless chambers, hurried over to her, and took her in his arms. He had a bloodied gash on the side of his head. "I was so worried for you."

"Is everyone all right?" she asked.

He nodded and stepped back, and she saw Captain Bo Franck, Saber Ryan, Miss Belle, and Larkin step out of the room.

She hurried over to Miss Belle and Larkin. "The danger has not yet passed," she told them tiredly. "Go to your rooms and hide there until the fighting is over. Hurry now."

Miss Belle looked at her as if she were mad. "Like demon's hell, child! I have lived in this city for more than sixty years, and I refuse to *hide* in my room while murderous thugs roam the streets. I still have a thing or two I can teach those ruffians! Come on, Larkin!" The stout woman hiked up the sides of her dress and ran down the corridor.

Larkin shrugged her shoulders with an excited grin and took off after her.

Kiernan watched them go in frustration. She turned back to Kirby. "We need to secure the castle. Preferably before those two women have a chance to get themselves killed."

Captain Bo Franck spoke up. The scar he received in the Demon War created a jagged line from his temple to chin. "I will see to it, Your Grace. Come on, Ryan." He paused to wink at her. "I'll keep an eye on old Belle, don't you worry, girl."

The two soldiers hurried off.

The clash of swords and shouts of fighting men echoed throughout the palace. Kiernan just hoped that the sounds meant that the Sabers had been successful in freeing the imprisoned legionnaires. If the Sabers were fighting alone, they wouldn't stand a chance.

"We need to find Etin and put an end to this charade once and for all," she told her father and Kirby.

"Your Graces!" A Saber skidded around a bend in the corridor and raced toward them. "Word has just reached the city. Commander Hugo Bassus is dead! Lord Gregaros defeated Etin's army on the plains near Janis!"

Kiernan let out a breath of relief. "Finally, some good news! Any word of Lord Etin?"

"In the midst of the diversions, he left Lady Conry by jumping out of the carriage and running this way toward the palace. I was tracking him, but he managed to slip away. He's in here somewhere, I'm sure of it."

Her father grabbed her arm. "I must go out into the city, Kiernan. It's imperative for morale that the troops and citizens see that I am freed."

He was right. She nodded, and he turned to go. "Wait! You can't go alone! Where is Captain Morel?"

The obsidian eyes glazed over. "Dead." With that, he turned and resumed his flight.

Kiernan looked at the Saber that delivered the news of Bassus. "You're now the King's primary guard. Protect him with your life."

He banged his fist to his chest. "On my oath as a Scarlet Saber, Your Grace," he confirmed and was gone as well.

She had her own mission.

She was going hunting.

Hunting for a Lord.

****

The intense sting of Beck's wounds from the whip and the bloody welts where the shackles cut into his wrists and ankles woke him with a start. He didn't know how long he had been hanging against the cavern wall, but it felt like a lifetime. Every so often, he would drift into an exhausted slumber only to be awakened by the pain.

Almost worse than the pain was the image in Beck's mind of the monster that Avalon Ravener had become. He discovered that morning that she was still able to bodyshift and wanted nothing short of her death when she transformed into the figure of a young, dark-haired girl. It sickened him to think of what the girl went through at the hands of this creature that cared nothing for human life.

Grisly images of the same thing happening to Kiernan and Kenley paraded through his mind and he knew that he could stall no longer. He would hand over The Protetor to Avalon as soon as she reappeared. If he gave her the book she so desperately wanted, she would have no reason to go anywhere near Bardot. If it cost him his life, so be it.

Not for this first time, he wished that he had fulfilled the request of his grandfather and become a Mage. If he had, he wouldn't be hanging here as helpless as an infant. Powerful as Avalon was, her witchcraft would have been no match for the sorcery of a Mage.

Thinking of what might have been, he slipped into sleep once again. When he awoke sometime later only to find himself still trapped in the same nightmare, his heart started racing and he found it difficult to breathe. He blinked in surprise when the ceiling and walls of the cavern shifted and began to move. *They're closing in on me!* Gasping, trying in vain to pull air into his burning lungs, the walls continued to move steadily closer, preparing to crush his body in a vice of stone. Suffocating in his own terror, tears sprang to his eyes and he moaned in sheer helplessness.

"What is it?"

He physically recoiled at the voice and the act allowed him to finally suck in that desperate breath. Panting, he glanced down at the Cyman standing before him. The same guard who brought the whip against him. Was it yesterday? Or longer? He looked back up. The walls had stopped moving, his fears chased away by the guard's presence.

"It was just a dream," the Cyman assured him.

Beck nodded self-consciously. *It had seemed so real.*

The kindness of the guard reminded him of Titus. The young Cyman he befriended in the Demon War spoke openly of the Cymans' desperate quest for freedom and the torture they had to endure in Nordik. They viewed the Demon War as a chance at liberation from their evil oppressors and, for the survivors, that desire was realized.

"I don't suppose I could talk you into letting me go?" Beck asked with a shaky voice.

Another guard standing at the cavern entrance glanced his way, but the Cyman he addressed said nothing.

Feeling stronger, his curiosity got the better of him. "Tell me, Cyman, why you remain here on the island with Avalon Ravener instead of back with your own people in Nordik?"

The guard straightened. "What did you say?"

"Your people were freed at the end of the war, and they returned to your home. Why are you still here?"

"You are lyin', earthshifter!"

Beck shook his head. "It's true. I give you my word that if I live, I will personally escort you to a stronghold called Northfort in northern Iserlohn where you will be able to secure passage back to Nordik." Beck waited while the Cyman processed the information. "In return, I don't even propose that you free me. All I ask is that when my friend arrives that you do not intervene. Allow him to fight the black witch without interference."

Beck didn't know what the Cyman's answer would have been because Avalon sauntered into the main chamber in the form of the dark-haired girl. She stood directly in front of him and looked into his eyes. "Oh, dear. There it is again, earthshifter. That look of hope." She shook her head as if he were a willful child that had deliberately disobeyed. She looked over her shoulder. "Cyrus, you will whip this man twice a day, once in the morning and once in the evening. Without fail! Do you understand?"

The Cyman nodded. "Yes, Mistress."

She turned back to him. "I have decided to leave for Bardot immediately after all. Before I go, I will cast an invisibility spell around the cave to make it impossible for your bodyshifter friend to find you until I return. If you must hope for anything, Prince Beck, hope that you were not lying to me when you said that The Protetor was in your office at the Academy." Her cruel glare cut through him. "If it's not there, your wife will not survive my visit."

Beck swallowed and said softly, "There's no need to travel to Bardot. I have The Protetor with me."

Dead eyes narrowed into razor sharp pinpoints. "Where?"

"In the back pocket of my trousers."

She gestured to the Cyman called Cyrus, and the guard strode to him and turned his body on the chains to gain access to his pocket. Shooting pain flooded into his limbs and he gritted his teeth against the agony.

"I 'ave it, Mistress," the guard said and pulled out the small book.

"Bring it here," she ordered.

She ripped the book from Cyrus' outstretched hand and flipped through the pages. "Is this some kind of joke?"

"No."

"There's nothing here! The pages are blank."

"The book is bespelled and only I have the ability to read the pages."

She glowered at him with an expression of such loathing that even the Cymans shrank back from her. She let out a primal scream. "You think you are so clever!" she spit at him, dribble flying from her mouth. "But, you are a pathetic, disgusting excuse for a man. Look at you, hanging there like a side of meat. Helpless! And, weak! How are you going to feel when I string up your wife the same way you are right now? I promise you this, earthshifter, I will not stop to eat or sleep or even blink an eye until she is dead! Are you feeling clever now, Prince Beck?"

Beck struggled wildly against his bonds and snarled in fury. *I have to do something!*

She grabbed the whip from her guard and flicked the lethal tip toward him. It came fast and furious, striking him in the cheek and setting his face on fire.

*The time has come, but I will die my way, not hers!*

He lifted his fingers in a summons to the mountain of rock Avalon called Farout Falls. The tortured stone groaned audibly and began to tremble.

Avalon shrieked as she tried to maintain her balance under the shifting floor beneath her.

All of a sudden, the Cyman on guard at the cave entrance flew back onto the ground with a loud grunt.

"Hope I'm not late."

Beck whipped his head toward the entrance. Brighter than all of the angels from the Demon War combined, stood his smiling, silver-haired savior.

# CHAPTER 20

## A Colorful Revelation

Davad Etin raced along the passageway of the servant quarters frantic to find a place to hide, but every door was locked. *There!* Up ahead, he spotted one room with the door ajar. He sprinted toward it and darted inside, but found the room filled with servants huddled together waiting out the battle for the city. The terrified faces peered at him in shock as he cursed and backed out again.

The sounds of combat drifted through the palace corridors, intensifying his panic. He tried three more doors until finally, the last door in the corridor came open at his touch and he flew inside.

It was empty.

He slammed the door closed behind him and threw the bolt. Leaning back against the door, he clenched his fists. "Shut up!"

The voices would not stop! There were too many now and all talking at once! Pushing away from the door, he flung himself down on the narrow bed in the room and began to hum.

When had everything gone so wrong? One moment he was preparing to be crowned King of Iserlohn and the next, he was…planning a wedding?

*Yes, the wedding was Ava's idea and this is all her fault,* one voice whispered insidiously.

Davad pounded his fist into his palm. That was his way out! He could blame this whole disaster on that cow, Ava Conry!

*Now, you are thinking.*

He stood and began to pace, still humming.

*Yes, lay everything at Ava's feet, Davad, and the King will forgive you,* another voice encouraged.

*He may even bestow a medal on you for thwarting her plans.*

*Do not forget Abram Winslow,* one reminded.

*True. Maximus no longer trusts his old friend.*

These troublesome voices were finally talking sense. Maximus was a fair and compassionate King. Despite Davad's crimes, if he played his cards right, he would be shown mercy, he was sure of it.

A soft knock on the door startled him and he let out a small scream. He looked around quickly for a window or door to escape through, but there was nothing.

"Master Black," called a sharp, urgent voice from the other side. "Open the door. It's me."

Master Black?

*Yes, that is you. Open the door to your ally,* one of the voices ordered sternly.

The voice was right. Davad recognized now who it must be and sighed in relief. He hurried to the door and threw the bolt back. The tall man standing outside slipped in furtively and shut the door quietly behind him.

"Thank goodness you're here, Master Red."

"What in the bloody hell happened, Black?" the man demanded.

Davad shook his head. "I don't…I don't know. Somehow, Gregaros must have taken the gates."

Master Red shook his head. "No, Gregaros was never anywhere near the city, you fool. He was too busy engaging your army out on the battlefield. Master Blue was killed."

Davad's panic returned, and he reached around Master Red to open the door. "I don't want to die! I am just going to have to throw myself on the mercy of the Court."

Master Red grabbed his wrist in a steel grip. "You will do no such thing."

"Ouch! You're hurting me. Stop!" The man kept his arm lifted high, walked him back to the bed, and forced him to sit down.

Davad rubbed at his wrist, and a bit of his fiery spirit resurfaced. "Lay a hand on me again, and I'll kill you." One look at the man's face, however, made him back down quickly. "If you're so smart, what do you suggest?"

Red ran his hand through his hair in an agitated manner. "You really have screwed everything up, Black."

"It is not too late! We have thousands of soldiers in the city!"

"No, I am afraid that part of our plan is over. But, there is still a personal score that I must settle with the royal family."

"What are you talking about? We still have a chance! Your presence here has convinced me of that!"

"Look at me," Master Red commanded forcefully.

Davad lifted his eyes to the man's gaze.

"You are a liability, Master Black."

*No!*

Davad nodded his head and stood. "Yes, I am a liability."

*This man is dangerous! Turn away!*

"You must die."

*No! He will kill us all! Turn away!*

"Yes, I must die."

Face slack, Davad Etin unsheathed the dagger with the eagle tip that he always wore at his hip. He took the hilt in both hands and held the dagger outstretched in front of him. At a small nod by Master Red and without the slightest hesitation, he thrust the weapon backward and buried it into his chest, silencing the voices forever.

****

Kiernan and Kirby crept along the servant quarters in their hunt for Davad Etin. As of yet, there had been no sign of the spineless Lord.

Every door they checked in the silent corridor was locked.

"Your Grace!" whispered Kirby, and pointed with his head to the last door on the right. Kiernan rushed to his side just as he stormed into the room, naked sword in hand.

She stepped in after him and pulled up short, shocked. "Roman Traynor! What are you doing here? Is Beck with you?" she asked and held her breath, hope flaring to life within her like a pulsating beacon.

Beck's personal guard dropped to his knee and shook his head regretfully. "No, Your Grace. I stayed in Kondor for several days, but there was no word about Beck or Airron Falewir in that time. I thought I could be of more help here than sitting around a Dwarven castle."

Kiernan wanted to lash out at the Saber. Not because his actions were incorrect, but because the sight of Roman without Beck seemed to presage a permanent separation. With Roman actively involved in the search, there was still a chance. But, when Beck's friend and protector had given up, what was left for Kiernan to hang on to?

"Please rise."

"The good news is, Davad Etin is dead." Roman stepped aside and revealed the Lord's corpse on the floor, an eagle-tipped dagger protruding from his chest.

Kiernan bent down next to the body. She found it hard to believe that the handsome Lord she had known all her life and had shown so much promise at one time was dead. Although, Roman may have yielded the weapon, the man's own greed and apparent mental illness had been his true killer. It was just unfortunate that so many innocent people had been sacrificed along the way.

She stood and turned back to the two men.

"When did you get here?" Kirby asked Roman. "I saw you briefly in Bardot before we left for Nysa, but didn't get a chance to bring you in on our plans."

Before Roman could answer, the clamor of a violent skirmish sounded outside of the room. The two men raced out, and Kiernan unsheathed her sword and followed.

At the end of the passageway, three legionnaires stepped into their path, a dead Scarlet Saber at their feet. All three were Badgers of House Conry.

Two of the soldiers rushed Roman and Kirby, and the third swung his blade in a one-handed downward stroke at Kiernan's head. She lifted her sword, barely managing to block the forceful strike and turn it aside. The impact of the blades vibrated painfully through her hand.

She stepped back to give herself room to fight. The man was much stronger than she, but his overconfidence made his intended moves easy to read. Pivoting on the ball of her right foot, she ducked underneath his second blow and swung her blade in a full circle before delivering a slashing cut to the man's stomach. It was a lethal wound, and he staggered backwards and crashed to the floor. She left him to die.

From the opposite direction and coming through the outer door to the royal gardens, another Badger appeared, and Kiernan ran at him with a scream. As his blade flashed toward her, she jumped to the floor in a slide and passed between the man's legs with her sword in the air, gutting him from sternum to groin.

The soldier went down, but her reckless act caused a shooting stab of pain to arc wildly throughout her abdomen. She dropped her sword, curled into a ball and groaned in pain, but had enough sense to realize that if another legionnaire appeared now, she would be dead. In a haze of agony, she listened to the clash of swords for several minutes before all finally fell silent.

"Pick her up," she heard a voice order.

She felt two people lift her from the ground and begin carrying her down the corridor and up the back stairs. At this point, she didn't care who it was. Her pain-clouded mind left little room for rational thought.

At the top of the stairs, her carriers pushed through the door to the main level of the palace. She heard Roman Traynor curse and lifted her eyes. The corridors were swarming now with soldiers, both allied and enemy.

Roman and, who could only be Kirby, ran with her between the fighting men. Behind, she heard a woman's voice shout out. "What are you doing? Where are you taking her?"

*Miss Belle.*

Ignoring the woman, Roman yelled out, "There!" and pointed with his chin to the open doors to Grace Hall. The Saber directed their movements into the vast room and as soon as they were inside, he dumped her unceremoniously onto the floor. If not for Kirby still holding onto her other arm, she would have gone down hard.

Roman ran back to the door and tried to slam it shut on Miss Belle, but the woman used her bulk to barrel inside.

She looked in shock at Kiernan on the ground writhing in pain. "Do you realize this woman is about to give birth?"

Roman grunted and shut the door. He turned toward Kirby. "There's no lock for this room. We need to barricade it as best we can. Use chairs, tables, whatever is available on hand."

Kirby nodded and started to drag the chairs stacked neatly along one wall across the marble floor to the doors.

"Are you all right, child?" Miss Belle asked her, dropping next to her with a grace that belied her size.

Kiernan's contraction subsided, and she could finally breathe enough to talk. "It is time, Miss Belle. Dear Highworld, I did not want this to happen now."

Miss Belle stood again and rushed to grab a linen from one the dinner tables spread throughout the hall. Returning, she lifted Kiernan underneath her arms and helped her onto the white tablecloth. "Nothing to be helped for it now, child, but I will not leave your side until this baby is delivered safe and sound. I promise you that!" She threw an angry glower over her shoulder at Roman. "I thought he was in Kondor."

"He was, but..." Suddenly, a blatant impossibility surfaced in Kiernan's mind. If Roman stayed in Kondor for several days before leaving, how could he have been in Bardot two days ago? Even if he left straight away, he couldn't have traveled that distance on horseback in the time she had last seen him in Deepstone. Even in her current state, she was able to arrive at an undeniable certainty. Roman Traynor traveled through Aquataine to get to Bardot. And, the only way that was possible was if Roman Traynor was a shifter.

She sat up and turned to face the Saber. He had heard Miss Belle's question and the sneer on his dark face confirmed her suspicions. She managed to clamp her mind shut, just as she felt the first mental probe of his mindshifting.

"Kirby! Watch out."

The Saber Captain crouched, but it was too late. His face went slack, and he stood back upright with a jerk and remained there, motionless.

"You are good, Your Grace," said Roman. "Although, if Captain Nash had not seen me in Bardot, you never would have figured it out until it was too late." He shrugged. "Actually, it already is too late."

"Don't look at him, Miss Belle, he is a mindshifter. Roman Traynor has turned on us."

"Turned?" the Saber questioned sarcastically. "I was never yours to begin with!"

Kiernan screamed as another contraction griped her in its throes.

Miss Belle threw her body over her. "You come near this woman and I will kill you Captain Traynor. So help me, I will kill you!"

"Move!" he screamed.

Kirby, oblivious to what was happening in his mindshifted state, began dragging furniture once again across the floor toward the door to finish his barrier.

Kiernan knew that Roman would never allow her to give birth. Doing so would only restore her mindshifting ability, the most powerful in the land, and he would be no match for her then.

Roman grabbed Miss Belle by the hair and dragged her off Kiernan's body. Highworld bless her, the woman kicked and scratched the entire time, but Roman had enough and landed a crushing blow to her face that rendered her dear protector unconscious.

It was only her and Roman now.

He picked up an edge of the linen tablecloth she was lying on and started to drag her up the aisle of Grace Hall.

Numbly, she gazed up at the mural of the city of Nysa high above her head and thought of her mother, the Queen Grace Kenley Everard, and wondered what she would do in Kiernan's place. She also thought of Beck, Kenley, and finally her unborn son. Tears trickled down her anguished features.

Roman looked back at her. "Don't cry, Your Grace, your suffering will be over soon. I promise."

When the next pain racked her body, she was thinking that it might not be such a bad thing.

# CHAPTER 21

## A Rise From the Ashes

At the sight of Airron standing at the cave entrance, Avalon bent over and in a brief shimmer of air, shed the young girl image for her own, newly misshapen form. When she straightened, her white, translucent body, plagued with black splotches, looked even more grotesque than Beck remembered. Black wings unfurled wide and, and Avalon bellowed a high-pitched screech at the top of her lungs.

If Beck could have covered his ears, he would have.

"Whoa, Avalon," remarked Airron. "Wish I could tell you time has been good to you, but quite obviously that would be a lie."

With a guttural growl, she took a running leap and flew the rest of the way at Airron and his body disappeared under a flurry of beating wings and slashing talons.

Cyman soldiers rushed into the main chamber from rooms beyond, but skidded to a stop at the spectacle of the fighting bodyshifters. The guard, Cyrus, thrust his big arm out to halt the soldiers when it looked as though they may join in. He then swung his one-eyed gaze up to Beck as if to question in his mind the validity of Beck's statements.

Beck nodded once in confirmation and then forgot about the Cymans, his concern all on the struggle below.

Airron's clothes fell to the floor in a mound as he shifted into an eagle. The ferocity of the combat between the two winged creatures as they tore at each other was frightening to watch. Beck couldn't imagine how either one could survive the horrific injuries being inflicted.

Beck drummed his heels against the cave wall in despair, wishing he could go to Airron's aid. "Get me down from here!" he screamed, but knew it was useless. Cyrus would not cross that line and Beck even told him he didn't expect it. He just felt incredibly impotent watching his friend battle for both of their lives.

The air took on a shimmering sheen, and Airron shifted again—into the black Grayan wolf this time. Avalon responded with her own wolf, this one light gray in color but just as imposing in size.

The gray lunged, but the black hunched down causing her to tumble across the floor and almost out of the cave entrance into the night air. Somehow, the gray scrambled upright mere inches from the lip of the shelf, bared her teeth in an angry snarl, and attacked, jaws snapping in the air. Again, the black evaded the gray's strike by seeming to disappear into thin air.

Airron's mouse grinned up at the gray wolf from the floor and darted into a crack in the cave wall. Avalon responded with her own rodent and followed right behind Airron, wiggling into the tight opening and vanishing from sight.

Beck could hear the scuffling of tiny feet and the distressed squeals of the fighting mice through the walls, and then one mouse reappeared. Airron sprouted up into the air and stuffed his shirt into the crack.

He turned to Beck. "That won't hold her long. How do I get you down from—"

The cave wall exploded outward in a hail of rock already loosened by Beck's earlier summons. The mountain groaned as chips of stone and dust coated the air. An enormous gorilla stepped out of the haze of debris and beat its chest with a ferocious bellow.

"Airron! Watch out!"

The primate grabbed Airron around the neck with large, human-like hands and slammed Airron to the ground. His friend, unable to break his fall, landed hard with his head striking the stone floor with a terrible thud.

Avalon shifted into her winged body and stood over the unconscious Airron. Beck screamed at her, but it did no use. She didn't even look up at him. She had her prize in her sights—the bodyshifter who scarred her for life—and she was going to exact retribution.

Her sinister laugh rang through the cave, and then she finally did look up at him and pointed with a curved, yellow talon. "You are next!"

She leaned over Airron and her mouth opened abnormally wide in jerky movements, gruesome rows of tiny, pointed teeth reaching for his throat.

"No!" Beck thrashed helplessly, his heels now making indentations in the stone behind him. With his mind so close to the breaking point, at first he thought he was imaging things when a female Elf reared up behind Avalon.

She held a long knife in her hand.

The Elf landed a powerful, swift kick to Avalon's temple that toppled the winged creature to the cave floor. Avalon hissed and turned on her back to get a look at her attacker, but before she could cast a spell, the Elf dropped down beside her and plunged the knife into her chest. A last tormented scream erupted from the witch's deformed mouth, and then she was still.

The deed complete, the female Elf simply stood and dusted off her emerald dress as if killing the most dangerous sorceress on the island had been of no great import.

Airron began to stir, and the female went to him. "Are you all right?" she questioned tenderly, probing the back of his head with her fingers.

"Ouch!" said Airron groggily and waved her ministrations away from him. He looked at her with one open eye. "I thought I asked you to stay at camp?"

She rolled her violet eyes. "Really? Now, what good would that have done you, my husband?"

"Husband?" asked Beck. "Master-I-will-never-tie-myself-down-Falewir?"

The female grimaced. "That explains everything."

Airron looked up at him as if seeing him for the first time. "Oh, hey, Beck. How are you doing up there?"

Beck shrugged. "Besides the agonizing pain, the unquenchable thirst, and the ravenous hunger? Not bad, actually."

Airron sat up gingerly.

"You have a hard head," his wife proclaimed. "You will be just fine."

He threw her a sarcastic smile. "Lovely, isn't she?"

Airron leaned over to feel the pulse at Avalon's neck. "The witch is dead," he confirmed. When he stood, he noticed the Cymans standing at the back of the cavern. "Good guys or bad guys?" he questioned Beck and bladed his posture for a potential fight.

"Good, I think."

The Cyman leader spoke. "I am Cyrus, and we do not wish to battle with you, Elf. We 'ave done as the earthshifter asked and we did not intervene. 'E must now 'old up 'is end and allow us a peaceful return to our 'ome in Nordik."

"My friend's word is good," Airron told him. "You can trust in that."

The Elven woman went to the far corner of the cave ledge and picked up two packs, throwing one to Airron. He caught it and walked over to his clothes trapped underneath the rubble of the cave wall. His naked body was covered in angry-looking scratches and bite marks, but he quickly dressed back into his now dusty tunic and leggings.

"Airron! Let me treat your wounds first."

"No time, but you can help Beck. Looks like he was in a fight with an alley cat. An enormous and enraged alley cat." Airron looked at the Cymans. "Who has the keys?"

Two Cyman warriors rushed over and unlocked Beck's shackles and lowered him to the ground. He could do nothing more than sit there for a moment as his weakened and cramped muscles refused to support his weight.

Airron's wife approached with a small bag and began to dress his wounds. "I am Melania by the way."

"I can honestly say that I have never been more relieved to meet anyone in my entire life, Melania. If you had not shown up when you did, we would be dead right now. Thank you."

She bowed her head.

"She is a remarkable herbalist, Beck," interjected Airron. "Your wounds will heal in no time."

Beck nodded gratefully and then looked pointedly at Airron. "A wife? Is this what you wanted to talk about after Rogan's wedding?"

"Yeah, it was weighing on my mind."

"I can see how a secret marriage might do that."

Airron waved his hand. "We will have to postpone the talk once again. We have another disaster to forestall. The city of Nysa has been besieged by a rogue noble army and—"

"What?" Beck interrupted. "Where's Kiernan?"

"If I know your wife, right in the middle of the fight."

Beck groaned and politely gestured to Melania that he had had enough. He struggled to stand, but did manage to keep himself upright when he got there.

Melania walked over to Airron. "I guess this is it then. You travel north, and I go east."

He nodded. "I guess so. Are you sure you will be all right?"

Her violet eyes welled with tears. "Yes." She turned and stuffed her medicine bag into her pack and then looked at Airron, immense pride stiffening her back. "You know, Airron, you still have time to choose. You have only to say the word, and I will stay."

Airron's features remained stoic as he gave her a terse shake of his head.

Her face contorted in pain, but she nodded in resigned acceptance and walked out of the cavern and apparently, Airron's life.

****

Cyrus peered out over the valley of Farout Falls and for the first time in his memory, a smile lit up his face. In all likelihood, he had smiled as a child, but couldn't remember actually doing so. Couldn't remember ever having anything *to* smile about.

He did now.

After six long years on the Island of Massa, it looked as if he finally may be able to go home and return to the wife and children that he prayed still waited for him, but who in all probability believed him long dead.

He tried to visualize how Nordik might look and wondered if sunlight and new growth had returned now that the Mage was gone. Life had a way of doing that. Resurrecting out of the ashes. Blossoming in the least expected ways. There was no force more powerful than the will to exist.

He turned to look back at the body lying on the floor behind him. It still made him shudder to look at her—at what she had become.

The earthshifter, who had left a few moments before with his Elven friend, promised to be back and Cyrus believed him. He just hoped it didn't take too long.

"Are we really goin' 'ome, Cyrus?"

He turned to his friend, Arlen, with his newfound smile. They had fought side by side in the war and managed to survive with their lives if not their freedom. Mercifully, that was all about to change.

He nodded in response to Arlen's question. "It looks like it. I can't wait to see the look on Crissa's face when she sees me agin."

Arlen snickered. "The great mighty Cyman warrior, Cyrus, back from the dead! I feel like dancin' I am so 'appy."

Cyrus patted Arlen's back. "Settle down, my friend. It may be a week or more before the earthshifter returns."

"Well, I'll be waitin'! Come on, Cyrus, let's get somethin' to eat. We don't even 'ave to worry about our rations anymore. We can eat whatever and whenever we want!"

Cyrus shook his head in wonder at his friend's casual statement. So simple, yet so meaningful. Never in his entire life had he ever been able to eat what he wanted. To hunt or grow his own food and prepare it however he wished. He ate the little that was handed out to him—no more, no less. There had never been any other choice. Choices were for his betters. Now, thanks to the earthshifter, a world of choice had opened up for them.

"Just think, Cyrus! We can sleep when and where we want! Wear what we want! Sing! Dance! Oh, spirits, this is goin' to take some gettin' used to."

With another smile, Cyrus turned to follow the ecstatic Arlen back through the cavern. When he neared the corpse on the ground, he realized that they would have to do something with it soon.

Stepping gingerly around the pale, translucent body, a scream tore from his mouth when a taloned hand seized his ankle in a vise-like grip.

"You are going nowhere, Cyman."

****

Through the torture of her contractions, Kiernan scanned the great hall searching for a weapon—anything—she could use against Roman. Miss Belle lay unconscious and Kirby Nash sat against his furniture barricade with a blank stare.

It was up to her alone to somehow survive this madman. She still wondered at his motives. Did this also have something to do with Beck's disappearance? *Of course, it does! How could I have been so blind?* The only way Beck Atlan could have been kidnapped under Roman Traynor's watch, was if Roman himself had allowed it to happen.

Beck's protector was working with Avalon Ravener. *That bastard!*

"Roman!" she screamed at him. "Tell me why, traitor! Why would you align yourself with Avalon Ravener against Beck? Your friend!"

Roman stopped and turned back to her. "Avalon Ravener? I know nothing of that witch. Your husband was kidnapped because of an influential group of dissenters who wanted to see change on this island. Beck and Maximus were targeted so that Davad Etin could be crowned King of Iserlohn. It's that simple."

*So, he is in league with Davad Etin and not Avalon Ravener? Not simple. It doesn't make any bloody sense!*

A sharp contraction coursed through her again and she thought she was going to die right there before Roman Traynor had an opportunity to lay a single finger on her. She panted through the pain while the Saber looked down at her with a smirk.

"Looks like it hurts," he observed mockingly.

"And, me, Roman?" she asked through clenched teeth. "Am I to be killed for the same reason? For political gain?"

His laugh was scathing. "Oh, the faction wanted you dead, but their reasons are not mine. I want you dead, Your Grace, because six years ago, you helped my mother kill my father."

Confused, Kiernan was about to question him further when he dropped down to his knees by her side and grabbed her hair. "Harden Sullivan, Your Grace! Do you recognize that name? It was my father's name! His friends called him Sully! Are things becoming clearer now, Your Grace?"

Kiernan responded softly, her tone filled with regret. "I was trying to help your mother, Roman. Your father had—"

With his free hand, he slapped her across the face. "Shut up! No more lies!"

Letting go of her hair, he stood and walked back toward the double doors. "Nash! Look at me!"

He needed to mindshift Kirby again. His magic wasn't as strong as hers, so he had to keep reinforcing Kirby's shifted state.

She struggled to stand, but couldn't do it as pain once again raked her body. This time, though, it felt different. She suddenly realized with horror that the baby was coming! Now! There was no more time.

"Ahh!" Her body felt like it was ripping in half when she felt the baby's head pushing out of her body. *No!* Her magic, dormant for months, flared to life within her and she knew then that the preservation instinct of her power was progressing the delivery in an act of survival.

She sat up and tried to stop the birth, but it was no use. Bearing down on her lower belly, she gave a tentative push and a low primal moan ripped from her throat as a dark-haired head popped free. One more frantic push with all of her waning strength, and the baby slid the rest of the way clear of her body onto the linen tablecloth.

She looked down with a sob.

Beck was right.

It was a boy.

A beautiful, defenseless babe, and she had brought him into this world under the most devastating of conditions. Tears poured down her cheeks as she looked at his tiny body covered in blood. With trembling hands, she unsheathed the dagger at her thigh, cut the cord and tied it. Grabbing one edge of the tablecloth, she swaddled him as best she could and lifted him to cradle against her breast. How many minutes did she have? How many seconds to love this precious little baby in her arms?

She heard another scuffle behind her and realized that Miss Belle had gained consciousness and was attacking Roman again.

Suddenly, another contraction shot through her abdomen.

*What is happening?* The pain should have subsided now that the baby was born!

To her complete astonishment, she felt another being try to thrust its way out of her body. With a fearful groan, she laid her wrapped son next to her side and looked down at the crown of light hair on the second baby. She pushed with all of her might, but this one wasn't as easy. It took several silent but painful grunts of effort before the head emerged. She gripped the little shoulders when they appeared and with a gentle pull, guided the child free.

Another son.

She could hardly see him through her blurred vision, but she knew he was as beautiful as his brother. She used the other end of the linen now drenched in red to wrap this baby and then picked up the first one once again. Lying back down on her side, she brought her knees up and sobbed, holding her two cherished bundles close to her heart.

She didn't know how long she lay there. Seconds probably, but it felt longer. She flinched when she heard Roman's angry footsteps striding back down the marble aisle.

Thump, thump.

He was coming for her.

Thump, thump.

Coming for her babies.

Mercifully, exhaustion filled her mind and body with an almost peaceful acceptance of what was to come. She was simply not capable of anything more. She had lost quite a bit of blood and couldn't even remember the last time she had anything to eat. But, how silly to be thinking of that now, she chided herself, when she should be treasuring these last seconds with her sons.

Thump, thump.

She smiled as she looked down at their little faces one last time. *Oh, Beck, you should see them! You would love them as much as I already do!*

Kiernan's shoulders jerked violently and she gasped in fright when a splintering explosion resounded through Grace Hall. Instinctively, she covered the babies with her body as wooden fragments from the furniture barricade rained down on top of them. She heard Kirby Nash cry out and looked up as his body went sailing through the air, smashed into one of the marble pillars that lined the aisle and then slid to the floor in a broken heap.

Fighting through her frailty and the lethal maelstrom, Kiernan rolled to the side, grabbed a handful of the linen and dragged her sons underneath one of the heavy dinner tables.

She tucked her body underneath and waited for the sounds of the onslaught to fade. When they showed no signs of abating, she mustered her strength and heaved her body to her knees to peek up over the table.

Kenley!

Her daughter stood in the entrance to Grace Hall with her arm lifted. She directed a turbulent tornado of air out in front of her while she searched the room for danger. Baya, at her side, bellowed a howl of aggression that made Kiernan's spine tingle.

The sight of her daughter sent a torrent of adrenaline flowing through her. "Kenley, look out for Roman!"

Her daughter's black ringlets swirled around her head as she sought out the Saber. It was disconcerting for Kiernan to see her daughter wielding so much power and so resolute upon destruction.

She was just five years old.

Suddenly, Roman let out a roar and charged through the rubble toward Kenley. He was bleeding from multiple cuts on his face and blood droplets flew from him as he ran.

Kiernan left her sons under the table and began crawling up the aisle. She had to get to her daughter! "Kenley!"

She watched Kenley make a rotating circle with her hand and then thrust it out toward the advancing Saber. A powerful airstream hit Roman in the chest and threw him back onto the floor. He tried to get up but it was Kenley now advancing on him. She stalked toward him with her arm still out, holding him in place. His body slid backward on the marble, and he tried to scrabble away from the force of the airstream she commanded, but he was powerless against her magic. Kenley flicked her wrist and drove the Saber to the edge of the floor and up the wall where she pinned him flat against the stone.

"Maman?"

"Yes, Kenley, I am here."

"What should I do with him?"

Kiernan shook her head in remorse. A five-year-old should never have to face the prospect of such violence. She also realized that her daughter had not yet been marked. There had been no time. If she had, she would not have asked that question.

"Don't kill him, Kenley," she said softly, regretfully.

"I'm not sure if I can stop it, Maman!"

"You must," she mumbled weakly.

Kiernan could see the strain of effort on her daughter's face and then Kenley dropped her arm and Roman fell to the floor with a grunt.

A growl echoed throughout the hall, but it did not come from the Draca Cat. "There's no blood oath holding me back!" Miss Belle cried out as she ran toward the Saber with the leg of a broken table raised before her like a club.

Roman took one look at the charging woman and stood, taking off at a run to dive through one of the stained glass windows of Grace Hall.

Miss Belle caught up at the broken window and looked down at the one story drop. "He's running away! Coward! Come back here again and I'll show you what happens to traitorous filth like you!"

Kiernan had been making her way up the aisle toward Kenley, but with Roman now gone, she began crawling anxiously back to her sons. She just now realized that she had never heard either one of them cry.

"Miss Belle! My babies!"

"Babies? You had the baby?" Miss Belle asked, obviously confused as both she and Kenley rushed past Kiernan to the table with the linen tablecloth peeking out from underneath.

Kiernan got up onto her hands and knees so she could move faster. Leaving her own trail of blood on the marble floor, she began crying again.

Miss Belle had already moved the table from over the boys and Kiernan almost refused to look, terrified that they were dead.

But, she did look, and her body trembled with an emotional ecstasy that only a mother could understand.

Twin sets of pudgy little fingers wiggled in the air as her two sons cooed contentedly.

Men were running into the hall now. She heard Captain Bo Franck's voice above the victorious shouts.

"It is yours, Your Grace! The city is yours!"

# CHAPTER 22

## Loose Ends

Five days after the defeat of the uprising from the Houses of Etin, Conry and Winslow, Beck and Airron rode through the gates of Nysa. While all agreed it was a triumphant military campaign on the part of House Everard, the city did not walk away unscathed from the revolt. Fifty Scarlet Sabers were dead and at least that same number of citizens.

Instead of the somber tone Beck expected from a city just back from the brink of war, the opposite was true. Jubilant Nysians had taken to the streets in celebratory glee. Dannery Row teemed with drinking and dancing citizens grateful to be rid of the marauding soldiers who had caused such turmoil in their peaceful lives.

Few recognized Beck as he passed by, unaccustomed to seeing the Prince of Iserlohn without an entourage by his side.

He glanced at Airron. His garrulous friend was unusually quiet. They did not talk very much on the long journey from Elloree, choosing instead the privacy of their bunks to recover from their mutual ordeals. Beck suspected Airron's sullenness had something to do with the departure of his wife, but he let it be. His friend would talk when he was ready.

When they finally managed to pick their way through the congested throng to the royal palace, Rogan was waiting for them.

Beck dismounted and the two friends embraced tightly.

"The watershifters sent word that you were on your way," Rogan said, patting Beck on the back. "I can't tell you how good it is to have you back safe."

Beck pulled back and looked down at his friend warmly. "I hear you have your own tale to tell?"

"I do, but first things first." The Dwarf held his hand out to Airron still sitting atop his horse. "Pay up, Elf."

Airron feigned indignation, but then smirked and reached into the purse at his waist.

"What's this?" Beck asked.

"Oh, our overconfident friend here made a wager with me that he would be the first to return to Nysa."

"I'll give this one to you, fireball," Airron conceded. "But," he said boastfully, "I did manage to kill Avalon Ravener. Can you top that, my friend?"

Beck cleared his throat. "Technically, since this is an official bet and all, your wife killed Avalon, not you."

"Aha! I knew it! You're trying to cheat!" Rogan growled. "Not only did I make it back here first, but *I* defeated Etin's army and saved the people of Nysa!"

Airron shook his head. "Technically, Lord Gage Gregaros and the Halfies routed the army. We heard all about it."

"Well, I was there, and I still won our bet."

Airron tossed a silver tenet down toward the Dwarf. "Yes you did, and you know what they say. An Elf always pays his debts."

"I thought the saying was—"

"Never mind, you two," growled Beck. "I want to see my family."

Rogan hissed loudly.

"What is it?" Beck questioned. "Is everything all right?"

"Yes, everything is fine, but you may want to wait before visiting your wife. She is busy at the moment entertaining a few men in her room."

"What? Speak sense, man!" He shook his head. "No, never mind, I'll find out for myself." Beck threw Chasin's reins to Rogan and ran up the palace steps. The movement caused the lash marks on his body to throb painfully, but he ignored it.

*Two men? What could Rogan possibly be talking about?*

A Saber passing by looked at him in surprise when he entered the palace and, seeing that he was alone, quickly fell into step behind him.

Anxious now to see his wife and daughter, Beck sprinted across the foyer and took the stairs two at a time until he reached the third floor.

*Entertaining two men?*

He raced down the corridor until he came to his chamber suite. Two Sabers, neither one Roman or Kirby, stood in front of the door. Both knelt when they saw him.

"None of that nonsense now!" he snapped. "Open the door!"

The Sabers jumped to their feet. "Congratulations, Your Grace."

His head spun with the mixed messages he was receiving, and he burst through the doors like a madman and stormed into the bedroom he shared with his wife.

The sight of Kiernan, lying on the canopied bed, with Kenley on one side and a bundled baby in her arms collapsed him to the ground.

His son had arrived.

There were so many hours over the past days with Avalon Ravener that he never thought to see his family again. And, now, here they were right in front of him and with the newest member of their household.

"Come here, my love," Kiernan said, and he looked up to see her hand reaching for his.

He staggered to his feet and went to the bed. He took Kenley into his arms and held her tight to him, breathing in the clean scent of her dark curls.

"Hi Daddy. I missed you so much!"

"Me too, Ken, me too," he croaked out.

Kiernan smiled at him. "You were wrong, Beck, you do not have a son."

His grin widened as he looked at the little baby swaddled in white. "Another daughter, then. One who will help her sister spoil me in my old age, I hope." Kenley giggled when he tickled her under the chin. He set her back down on the bed and reached for the baby. "Can I hold her?"

Kiernan shook her head. "You don't understand. You do not have *a* son. You have *two*." She looked down and drew his eyes to another bundle lying on the other side of the bed.

"Twins?" he asked incredulously.

She nodded. "I would like to introduce you to Kellan Jaimes and Kane Maximus. I hope you do not mind that I named them already."

They had never discussed names before, and he was touched that she would name one of his sons after his father. He leaned down and kissed her forehead. "The names are perfect. Just like you."

Sitting on the edge of the bed, he picked up one of the twins, and the stories unfolded regarding Roman's betrayal, and Kenley saving her mother and siblings with her airshifting power. Next, Kiernan described how she had delivered their sons in the middle of the nightmare, single-handedly.

He smiled and said all the right things in all the right places, and told his girls how proud he was of them, but the remarkable bravery of his family only underscored what he had been feeling for days.

He had failed in his duty to his family and in his royal obligations to the people of Iserlohn.

He had let them all down when they needed him the most.

\*\*\*\*

Smokey filaments undulated through the tavern as though alive, obscuring all they touched in gray shadows. The gloom suited his needs just fine. Relieved to have made it out of Nysa alive, he traveled directly south to his home town of Janis, but had no desire to engage in idle conversation. The silky screen provided a convenient barrier in keeping the other patrons at bay.

Before becoming a Saber, Roman had spent many a long, enjoyable night in this bar called The Wild Boar with his father. He still would be enjoying them if not for Kiernan Atlan.

How could all of their carefully laid plans have collapsed into such ruin? Admittedly, he never met a plan that fell into place exactly as intended, but this was a disaster.

Master Black was dead.

Master Blue was dead.

And, Kiernan Atlan was still alive.

According to a watershifter he talked to that morning, so was Beck Atlan. What did it take to kill these people?

A young serving girl approached his table. "Hi," she said shyly. "What happened to your face?"

His hand involuntarily rose to the cuts on this face from his dive out of Grace Hall. He shook his head. "Nothing."

"There is a woman at the bar who wishes to know if you would like company."

Instantly alert, he asked, "Who?"

"The dark-haired lady at the bar."

Roman looked around the serving girl. He immediately spotted the woman as she was the only female there, but didn't recognize her. "What did she say?"

"Only that you were the best looking man in The Boar tonight and that she could really use some company. And, coin, if you get my meaning."

He did. If he decided to accept the woman's invitation, she wouldn't be the first whore he had taken to his bed. He shrugged his shoulders. What else was he going to do tonight? A little relaxation to take his mind off the impossible events of the past few days would be a welcome distraction.

"You can have me for free," the serving girl offered. Her prospects in the small community of Janis limited, she probably hoped that the act would lead to marriage so she could leave the drudgery of The Boar and start a family.

He thought about the proposal while he again looked at the dark-haired woman at the bar. If you could call her a woman. She appeared extremely young. Still, a spasm of desire rushed through him when he studied her profile. There seemed to be a mystery about her just begging him to unravel. "No, thanks," he said to the serving girl. She threw him a disappointed look and turned to leave. He grabbed her arm and pressed a coin into her hand. "Tell the woman I am staying at The Lantern, second floor, first door on the right."

She nodded reluctantly and walked toward the bar to deliver his message.

Roman picked up his mug, drained the rest of the ale and walked out into the night. He didn't have far to go, The Lantern Inn was directly across the street.

With the exception of The Wild Boar, the conservative town was closed up for the night, most people long abed at this hour. The public turned a blind eye at their men folk enjoying a drink or two in the local tavern, but that is where they drew the line, and those same men would be the first through the doors to church on Sunday morning. It was a little incestuous for his taste, and that's why he left. The serving girl would do well to follow his example and get out while she still could.

When he stepped off the wooden platform that surrounded the business district, he remembered that it was on this very street that the shifters first came to Janis and humiliated his father in front of the whole town. Later that evening, the man had been pursued out of the gates like a wild animal and murdered in cold blood.

He lost both parents that night as he had been unable to forgive his mother for her part in the killing with the aid of Kiernan Atlan. Although the Princess had not been the one to deliver the final blow, she had been the catalyst that started events in motion, whispering dark insinuations into his mother's ear. He knew his mother, and she never would have committed this act on her own. Before Kiernan Atlan came to town, his mother was a gentle, caring soul who knew her place in the world. To his way of thinking, whatever his father may have done to his mother in the past, he did not deserve to pay for those actions with his life.

With a snarl of satisfaction, he took comfort in the fact that he was still alive, and that meant that there would be plenty of time to see justice carried out. Now, though, another form of comfort filled his mind.

He entered The Lantern Inn and wasn't surprised to find the common room empty. A man named Jase once owned the inn, but now the proprietor was a mousy, nosy woman who asked too many questions. He already had to tell her to mind her own business earlier that evening.

A door behind the bar opened up, and she came out and eyed him as he walked to the steps to the second floor. Undoubtedly, she would also notice when the woman from The Boar come to his room as well. He laughed. That would give her something to gossip about.

Outside of his room, he opened the door cautiously with his hand on the hilt of his sword, Saber instincts on high alert. He didn't think anyone knew he was in town, but he couldn't take any chances.

The room was as he left it, his belongings arranged in the same positions. Entering, he lit the lantern for more light, unbuckled the scabbard from his waist, and hooked it on the back of the only chair in the room. He was just splashing his face with warm water from the basin when a soft knock sounded outside.

*That was quick.*

He walked to the door. "Yeah?"

"You know very well who it is," said an arrogant female voice.

He opened the door and admitted the woman from the bar. Again, he noted how young she was, but now also observed how her manner and confidence were that of a much older woman. She wore a light linen cloak that she removed and threw on the chair next to his sword.

He gave a mental shrug. Arrogance could be easily tempered.

Crossing the room, he grabbed her shoulders and swung her up against the door. His hand shot out and ripped away the lace bodice of her dress until he exposed her breasts. With one arm holding her in place across the throat, he groped her cruelly, twisting one of her nipples.

Undaunted by his rough handling, she brought her hands up to his chest. "My, my, an anxious one."

Her smug face infuriated him and he slapped her across the face. "Don't talk. You know what you're here for." He briefly considered mindshifting her, but found himself aroused by the game.

Her tongue darted out and she licked at the small cut his strike left on her lip. "How about a drink first?" she suggested.

"How about you get naked and spread your legs on that bed?"

She shook her head and squeezed out of his hold. "I promise it will be worth the wait."

He gazed at her with irritation. "There's a bottle on the table. Make it quick."

While she poured her drink, he undressed and lay on the bed. Originally, he thought to have his way with the woman and quickly send her on her way, but changed his mind. He still had a great deal of frustration to unload and she would provide the perfect outlet. His eyes scanned the room for a gag to use that would silence her screams.

The girl walked over and held the glass out to him. "There is only one glass. Your turn."

He grabbed the glass from her hand and downed the contents. "You have had your drink, now give me what I want." He pulled her on top of him.

"I don't think so."

"I know so," he sneered. "And, if I have to beat you into submission, all the better."

"Hmm…like father, like son."

The comment startled him and he sat up on the bed. Immediately, his head began to spin, and he thought he might vomit. "What do you know of my father?"

She shrugged. "Uncovering facts about those I work with has always been a priority for me."

*Work with? What is she talking about and why is it becoming so hard to think?* His Saber training screamed at him that all wasn't right with this woman. He tried to push her away, but his arms felt weak. She leaned forward to kiss him and as soon as their lips met, the air shimmered in front of his eyes.

"Ahh!" he screamed. The woman was gone and in her place—pressing hard, thin lips to his—was a balding man with strange eyes.

Master Orange!

Roman fell out of the bed and dove for his sword, but his movements were clumsy, and Master Orange easily beat him to it. From his back on the floor, he looked up at the blurred image of a man he once thought an ally.

"Don't even think about mindshifting me," Orange said. "The herbs I put in your drink have quite efficiently robbed you of that ability."

"You're a bodyshifter?"

Master Orange nodded. "Among other things."

*Bloody hell. Can it be?* "Avalon Ravener," he voiced aloud in a slur.

"In the flesh," Orange confirmed.

"I thought you were dead."

"Unfortunately for you, no. An Elf plunged a knife in my chest, but missed my heart. It was easy to cast a spell over my body to make me appear dead, but after the assailants left, my Cyman guards took care of my wound, and here I am." Master Orange shook his head. "I hate Elves."

"What do you want with me?"

Master Orange smiled. "Oh, just eliminating loose ends. I never did like to leave behind people that have personal knowledge of me. I even killed my own lover once rather than leave him behind."

Roman opened his mouth to scream, but Master Orange cast a spell that paralyzed his vocal chords and then kicked him under the chin. "That's for the bloody lip!"

Roman struggled weakly in a pitiful attempt to fight back, but it was hopeless. A baby could have overpowered him at this point.

"Farewell, Master Red."

For the second time, Roman saw a faint flicker in the air and then a winged creature hovered over him. The beast opened its mouth in a hiss, and multiple rows of tiny sharpened teeth gleamed with saliva in the light of the lantern.

As the repugnant abomination began to tear at his body with gnashing teeth and claws, he finally had the answer to a question that puzzled him for a long time. A fatal mistake, it turns out, that he didn't look for the answer sooner.

For he now knew Master Orange's motive.

He was pure evil.

# CHAPTER 23

## The Trial

Kiernan smiled down at her two sons sleeping peacefully in their cradles. Only a week old and already the differences were noticeable. Kellan, her firstborn son, was dark-haired and larger than his brother by almost two pounds. *My little earthshifter.* He was also much more vociferous about his needs and demanded more of her attention. Her second son, fair-haired and more reserved, appeared not to mind acquiescing the limelight to his twin. His eyes were a shade of brown so light they looked yellow. She couldn't venture a guess as of yet as to what shifting ability he would have.

Now that they were asleep, she decided it would be a good time to seek out her husband. Beck had been very withdrawn since he came back to her from his ordeal with Avalon Ravener, and she was determined to discover why. She had not asked for any details of his captivity and he in turn had not offered any. It was obvious that he had been whipped—the scars on his body were horrific—but, something else was bothering him. Something more personal.

She left her bedroom and walked into the sitting room where Kirby Nash and Kenley were playing a board game called Dragon's Fire. The object was to roll a dice and move the game piece the corresponding number along a checkered board without touching the square holding the dragon figurine. It belonged to Kiernan when she was Kenley's age, and she adored playing this very same game with Captain Bo Franck.

Filled with guilt, her daughter had not left Kirby's side for a moment since he had been injured at her hand. Baya had since healed the Captain with the Healing Breath, but his eyes still looked haunted for some reason.

Miss Belle, the right side of her face sporting a large purple bruise, sat in an armchair knitting, and Baya as usual was curled up by the fire.

Miss Belle immediately rose when she saw Kiernan and put aside her work. "Should you be up, child?"

Kiernan waved her back down. "Yes. I've been stuck in these rooms for days and I need some fresh air before I go stir crazy." In truth, she did feel a little wobbly, but refused to let it show. "I'll be back soon," she said and walked out of the door before Miss Belle had a chance to question her further.

Anton LaFrae stood outside of her chambers. She nodded to him and walked toward the stairs, the Saber following silently behind her.

She wondered where to begin the search for her husband. If this were Bardot, he would seek solace in his private office at The Academy, but they were still in Nysa to allow her time to recover from the twins' birth.

She hurried down three flights of stairs and outside into the sun-filled afternoon. She noticed Airron sitting on the edge of the fountain in the royal gardens but, completely absorbed in his thoughts, he did not look up. He seemed just as preoccupied now as he did when he came to visit her and the boys earlier. It seemed her husband's disposition had affected Airron as well.

It suddenly came to her that Beck was probably hiding out in the stables. After a brief return to Bardot, Beck rode Chasin back to Nysa yesterday and a visit with his old horse always had a way of lightening his mood.

She walked the brick pathway through the gardens and two more Scarlet Sabers joined Anton. It didn't bother Kiernan the way it did Beck. Except for her time in Pyraan, royal protection had always been an inescapable facet of her life as a Princess.

The sound of pounding hammers and the rasp of saws filled the air. The royal groundskeepers were constructing a wooden dais for the trial this afternoon of Abram Winslow and Ava Conry, accused of treason to the Crown. It had been a very long time since a public trial had taken place in the city of Nysa, but the seriousness of the crimes and the vast number of innocents who suffered injuries demanded that the people be allowed to stand witness.

Besides the workmen, the streets were unusually quiet due to the late nights of revelry. Those few that were out knelt and offered shouted congratulations to her on the birth of the two new Princes. Kiernan acknowledged all with a gracious nod or wave. The sun and the smiles made her realize just how much she had to be thankful for. Her family and friends were safe, her father was free, and Avalon Ravener was dead. For the first time in years, she could live her life without feeling like she had to constantly look over her shoulder for the sorceress.

As she suspected, Beck was in the stables grooming Chasin. At the open double doors, she stood and stared at him a moment. The cut on his cheek was healing, but it made her heart ache to think of the pain he went through. She vowed to make it up to him somehow.

As if he could read her thoughts, he turned to the door. When he saw her, he gave her a small smile and she walked over to him. "If I didn't know you better, I would think that you were hiding from me," she said, reaching out to pet Chasin's nose.

"Of course not," he replied and continued his strokes with the brush.

She reached out, grabbed his arm, and forced him to look at her. "What is it, Beck? You know you can tell me anything. I would never judge or hold against you whatever you have to say. I give you my word."

He turned away and put his head down.

She decided it was best to just come out and say what was on her mind. "All those days you were in captivity, did you and Avalon…?"

His head snapped up. "No!" It was his turn now to take her arm. "I promise you as your husband that no such thing ever happened. What would make you ask that?"

Relief flooded through her. "You have been so withdrawn lately that I just figured it had something to do with whatever happened to you."

"It has everything to do with that! Don't you see, Kiernan? I failed. I failed you, Kenley, our sons, Maximus, Gemini Starr, Darin Morel, and the list goes on."

She was confused. "Why are you shouldering the blame for something that you had no control over? Those deaths belong at the hands of Avalon Ravener and Davad Etin, Beck. Not you."

"There will always be evil people in this world, Kiernan. So, what will happen the next time a Davad Etin rears his head? Will I be just as powerless? And, how many people will die then? Will it be you or one of the children?" His tortured features begged for her understanding.

She did understand. "This is about you becoming a Mage, isn't it? You feel that if you had the powers of a Mage, those lives could have been saved."

His blue eyes were full of conviction. "I do."

"I don't agree. Like you said, there will always be evil. Even as a Mage, you can't possibly save everyone from harm. It is unrealistic."

"No, not everyone, but I can save you, Kenley, Kellan, and Kane," he said softly.

She turned from him then and rubbed her arms to rid her body of the awful premonition that gripped her whenever they had this discussion. She turned back, tears in her eyes this time. "I never told you this before, but Diamond had a vision about you and it concerned a journey you would take one day." She looked him in the eye. "It ended with your death."

"Kiernan…"

"I believe in my heart, that if you leave me to become a Mage, you will never come back."

He took her hands. "You know that Diamond's visions are never that cut and dried. And, it doesn't mean that it was *this* journey that she saw. It could have been me journeying into the Grayan Forest for a blacktail hunt at the age of ninety-nine. I will be back, Kiernan, I give you my word."

"No." She turned her back on him. "You are asking me to choose between the safety of a family that is not in danger and you. I can't do it, Beck. I will not gamble with your life. Living without you is not something I can survive. Please don't ask me again."

When he did not respond, she walked out of the stables.

****

Beck knew he was late and raced through the palace corridors tugging at the sleeves of his black coat. He spent more time in the stables than he intended and when he arrived back at the suite, Kiernan had already left.

Straining his neck to catch a glimpse out of the row of windows as he ran, it looked to him like every citizen in Nysa had turned out for the trial.

The courtyard and streets beyond were crammed full of spectators. Opinions regarding the fitting punishment for the felonious nobles ranged from a public stoning to a life sentence in the palace dungeons. Beck was just as curious as the people to see how Maximus would rule.

The Sabers at the front doors held them open for him, and he dashed out into the courtyard. Hastily stepping up onto the newly constructed dais, he nodded to the drastically reduced Court members before taking his seat next to Kiernan. She didn't glance his way. She stared straight ahead as she sat regally and breathtaking beautiful in a scarlet, silk dress and arm veils.

"Still angry with me?" he whispered.

"I could ask the same of you."

"Why would I be angry?"

"Because of how weak I am when it comes to you."

He reached out and turned her chin his way. "You are the bravest and strongest woman I know. And, the discussion is over. I will not ask it of you again."

She reached over and squeezed his hand. "Thank you."

The royal trumpeter heralded the appearance of the King. A procession of Scarlet Sabers in their crisp scarlet tunics and black sashes marched out of the palace and down the stairs, shiny Sabers glinting in what was left of the late afternoon sun.

All those seated rose to their feet.

"Where is Kenley?" Kiernan asked him in a hushed voice.

"In the suite with Kirby and Miss Belle. She's not very happy to be confined to the rooms."

"I wonder where she gets that stubborn streak of hers?"

Beck turned to her and lifted his eyebrows. "Yes, I wonder, indeed."

Kiernan slapped him in the arm just as Maximus made his appearance and descended the palace steps. Usually, Kiernan's father shunned wearing the royal crown with its surfeit of rubies and black onyx, but it sat atop his head today

The King strode to the dais and took his place on the throne in the center. "Please be seated," he ordered, and all on the platform sat back down with the exception of Lord Gage Gregaros.

Gage walked down one stair of the dais to address the crowd. "We are gathered here today to stand witness in the trial of Abram Winslow and

Ava Conry. Will the guards bring the accused forward." Stepping back, Gage returned to his seat.

A murmur rippled through the crowd as four Iserlohn guardsmen brought forth the two former members of the King's Court.

Beck was shocked by the appearance of both. Abram, nearing his ninetieth year, looked even older, his face gaunt and hollow and his clothes hanging on his thin frame as he shuffled along between two guards. Ava Conry, usually dressed in the finest of clothes, wore a plain, disheveled dress and her face was streaked with dirt. Unlike Abram, though, she walked tall, her chin jutting forward.

"Hang them, I say!" someone shouted from the assemblage and cheers of support followed. Beck noticed Ava's shoulders flinch when a tomato thrown from the crowd hit her in the back and the juice splattered over her dress.

The guards led the nobles directly before the dais, and all quieted as the King rose to his feet.

"Ava Conry, step forward," he demanded.

The guards let go of the woman's arms, and she stumbled slightly before righting herself to approach.

She knelt before Maximus.

"Ava Conry, you have been accused of high treason against the Crown in an attempt to undermine the lawful lines of succession, plotting murder against your Sovereign, waging war against your Sovereign, and conspiring to spill the blood of your compatriots."

Ava's composure began to crack under the charges and she let out a tiny sob.

"How do you plead?" the King asked.

She reached for Maximus' hand. "I...I plead guilty, Your Grace, but I beg you to show mercy. Lord Etin tricked me with his lies and duplicity. I am as much an innocent victim in this as the rest of Nysa."

"Bah!" a man shouted from the crowd. "Soldiers follow the orders of their liege! One of Conry's legionnaires killed my son when he did not move out of the man's way fast enough! Lady Conry was there and did nothing to stop it! No clemency was shown to my boy and none should be given to Lady Conry!"

Cries of support for the man echoed through the gathering and more tomatoes were lobbed at the kneeling woman.

King Maximus held up his hand and the people settled down quickly, anxious to hear the King's decree.

"Ava Conry, I could show you mercy for conspiring against the Crown." Ava looked up hopefully. "But, I cannot show mercy for the death of innocent people due to your actions. For your crime of high treason, I sentence you to death by hanging."

Ava screamed and then fainted.

King Maximus gestured, and two guardsmen rushed forward, picked her up and carried her into the palace, presumably to the cells to await her execution.

"Abram Winslow, step forward."

The ancient man shuffled forward and knelt before the King.

"Abram Winslow, you have been accused of high treason against the Crown in an attempt to undermine the lawful lines of succession, plotting murder against your Sovereign, waging war against your Sovereign, and conspiring to spill the blood of your compatriots. How do you plead?"

"Guilty, Your Grace."

"Abram Winslow, I could show you mercy for conspiring against the Crown, but I cannot show mercy for the death of innocent people due to your actions. For your crime of high treason, I sentence you to…" The King paused. "I sentence you to banishment."

The crowd gasped in collective surprise.

Abram lifted his watery eyes to look at his old friend. "Your Grace?"

"As of this day, you are stripped of all lands and title and banished from Iserlohn. You will be allowed time to pack a modest amount of provisions and then you will be escorted to the city gates. Go to Deepstone or Haventhal or to the northern shores of Nordik. I care not which. If your family wishes to join you, they may do so with impunity."

A single tear dripped down Abram's face. "Why, Max?"

The King moved down the dais. "Because your grandson was being held against his will and you were under extreme duress when you made the decisions that you did. I have since learned how you reined in your legionnaires and ordered them to protect the people of Nysa when Etin's and Conry's were out of control. Many of your soldiers saved innocent people who otherwise may have died."

Abram nodded. "But…but I still was unable to save my grandson. I don't know where he is or if he is alive or dead."

"Oh, he is very alive, Abram."

The old man struggled to his feet when the guards brought a teenage boy out of the palace.

"Grandfather!" The boy ran down the steps and into the arms of the man who had given up everything in an attempt to save his life.

Abram looked at Maximus. "But, how did you...?"

"The moment I heard that Davad was holding the boy, I sent the Sabers in search of him. It didn't take long to uncover his whereabouts in the basement of Davad's estate." The King shook his head remorsefully. "I just wish you would have come to me first, Abram."

"I am a stupid old man, Max."

"Old, yes, but not stupid. Desperate would be a better word." Maximus turned and walked back up the stairs. "You have one hour, Abram Winslow, to pack your belongings and depart Iserlohn never to return."

The former Lord turned to go, but Beck saw Abram straighten his shoulders when Maximus said loud enough for him to hear. "May the Highworld favor you, old friend."

# CHAPTER 24

## A Cryptic Passage

Once the King and members of the Court departed, the gathered Nysians began to disperse as well. Standing on the platform still, Kiernan looked out over the heads of the people and scanned the crowd for Airron, Rogan and Janin. She knew the two Dwarves were anxious to return to Kondor to reunite with their children and she wanted to say goodbye to them before they left.

She noticed Airron right away, his silver hair and tall frame easily identifiable in the throng. She waved to him, and he began making his way toward her.

Her eyes still on the crowd, she noticed a head of black ringlets dashing through the mass of people and growled.

"What is it?" asked Beck.

"It seems your daughter has managed to escape her confinement." A flash of white also caught her eye, and she grinned. Although often as impetuous as her daughter, the Draca Cat would never let harm come to Kenley.

The courtyard had thinned considerably now, allowing Airron, followed by Rogan and Janin, she was pleased to see, to approach and climb the dais.

Airron was gnawing on a piece of grass, but removed it and used the green blade to point at her. "Don't even think about it."

"Think about what?" she asked in confusion.

"Grilling me about Melania. You know how I feel about marriage. I refuse to tie myself down, and I don't care how beautiful she is. Or smart. Or talented. Did you know she could play the harp?" He shook his head sharply. "It doesn't matter! It just wouldn't work and that, my friend, is all I'm going to say on the subject!" His rant over, he shoved the grass back into his mouth.

Kiernan shrugged. "So, end the marriage."

The grass fell from his opened-mouth gape. "End the marriage? What kind of advice is that?"

"Airron, I am on your side. If you feel that strongly against marriage to Melania, just end it. As lovely as she is, she will find another husband in no time."

"Another husband?"

She reached out to pat his arm. "I will support any decision you make. I do have to admit, though, that I love Beck so much that the thought of him with another woman would tear me apart. If you can imagine another man touching Melania's soft, silky skin and kissing her while they writhe together in passion, well, then you are not in love, my friend."

"I will kill him!" the Elf growled, violet eyes blinking rapidly. "I have to get home to Sarphia!"

Kiernan turned to Janin with a wink. "Like shooting fish in a barrel."

Rogan and Beck both laughed and put their arms around their friend. "He's done for," observed Beck.

"Looks that way," admitted Rogan.

The easy laughter came to an abrupt halt when a shout of alarm pierced the darkening sky. "What in demon's hell is that?" a man on the street asked, pointing to the rooftop of a cutlery shop lining Dannery Row.

Kiernan looked up at a black, winged creature perched on the tile roof.

"It can't be," breathed Beck.

"What is it? A bird?" asked Kiernan.

"No. It's Avalon Ravener," Beck hissed and jumped off the dais.

Kiernan's heart sank. The nightmare wasn't over after all.

The creature that was Avalon let out a high-pitched screech and took flight, diving toward a small group of people on the street.

"Run!" Beck shouted to the bystanders, waving his arms to get their attention.

Those that noticed the danger screamed and ran in an attempt to dodge out of the way of the flying beast. Beating powerful, leathery wings, the creature flew low over the heads of the frightened runners and slashed at one man with her front claws, sending him into a vicious tumble across the ground.

Turning in a sweeping arc for another pass, the creature suddenly pulled up and let out an excited cry. With a renewed burst of force, the beast flapped its wings furiously and shot forward. It came in over another group of fleeing people and reached out with taloned feet to grip the shoulders of a little girl running on the cobblestone road back toward the palace.

A little girl with black ringlets.

A pitiful roar erupted into the night. Baya raced below Kenley's dangling feet, leaping up into the air in an attempt to pull her free with her teeth. In order to evade the cat, Avalon wheeled around sharply and climbed higher into the air.

"No! Kenley!" Kiernan screamed and sprinted down the platform stairs.

Rogan followed her off and called a fiery spear to life in his hands. Kiernan heard the distinctive summons of fire behind her and stopped, gripping his arm. "No! If you hit Avalon, she will drop Kenley!"

Shouts and screams filled the evening, and Kiernan realized that the loudest was hers as she watched the winged abomination soar higher and higher until finally disappearing behind the rooftops with her baby.

Twenty or more Royal Scarlet Sabers swarmed out of the palace, but Kiernan knew there was nothing they could do to help.

Airron took off running in a sprint, and shifted into his eagle form, shooting into the night after the departing monster. The Sabers gave chase from the ground.

Kiernan's legs gave out and she started to sink to the ground, but Beck found her then and caught her under the arms. "Airron will find her, Kiernan," he said and pressed her face into his shoulder. "He'll find her."

*Yes, yes. He's right! Airron saved Beck, and now he would save Kenley.* She refused to think differently because any other outcome was unthinkable.

"Come on." Beck led her, Rogan, and Janin back to the dais and they sat on the steps, huddled together. A despondent and whimpering Baya put her head in Kiernan's lap. Kiernan stroked the white fur and bittersweet memories of the Draca's father, Bajan, rose to the surface.

Within moments, the King strode over to them with a trailing group of Sabers demanding to know what was happening.

She let Beck explain. She couldn't find any words within reach.

Kiernan did not know how much later, but Airron reappeared from one of the side streets off Dannery Row wearing one of the Saber's scarlet tunics. She jumped to her feet in an expectant rush.

He was alone.

Beck stood several paces away with his back to her. She saw him glance up at Airron and then he slowly turned her way with a look of fierce determination coloring his features. He simply stood there and watched her, like a racer waiting for the signal to go.

His thoughts were written all over his face. A bodyshifter couldn't rescue Kenley, but a Mage could. He was asking her to make a choice. To choose between him and their daughter.

Eyes filled with liquid, she started toward him numbly.

Airron intercepted her. "Sorry, Kiernan. She went down and then must have used an invisibility spell..."

She barely heard him.

She kept walking.

When she reached Beck, she swallowed back the lump in her throat so she could speak. "You said you would not ask me again."

"The stakes are higher."

"Where do you have to go?"

"I'm not sure exactly."

"How long will it take?"

"The book didn't say."

Green eyes met blue in a connection so deep, so pure that it defied words. But, there was another bond pulling at them that was equally as strong.

"She is so small and defenseless, Beck."

"I know."

There was a long pause.

"Go. Just go," she whispered in agony.

There was no goodbye. Beck must have known she couldn't handle it. He took off at a sprint for the royal stables and a few moments later raced by her on Chasin toward the gates of Nysa.

Despite his promise, he forced her to make a choice, and she did.

She chose Kenley.

\*\*\*\*

Beck made it to Bardot in well under two hours. The foam at Chasin's mouth and his labored breathing concerned him, but it couldn't be helped and he silently thanked his old horse for not letting him down.

Two guards stationed in front of the grate to Aquataine banged fists to chest in unison when they saw him approach.

Beck offered the same salute and asked one of the guards to take care of Chasin. "He's been running hard, so rub him down good and provide him with plenty of oats when he has had time to rest." The last words were shouted over his shoulder as he took off at a sprint for the palace. There was only one item that he would take the time to collect and that was the compass that could lead him through the tangle of magic to Callyn-Rhe. Without it, he could wander the Puu Rainforest for an eternity and never find the city.

He ignored all of the shouts and greetings on his way to the palace and back. When he returned to the grate, he yanked the grille open with a bang and dove head first onto the slide.

The usual thrill of the ride was lost on him, all of his thoughts on Kenley. He had been a captive of Avalon Ravener, and he knew she wouldn't hesitate to kill an innocent child if it brought her closer to her goals.

He splashed into the warm lagoon just outside of Barbary and kicked to the surface. He swam to shore, raced to the second cavern, and dove in, not bothering to use one of the tethered rafts or wait for a watershifter escort.

Since it was morning here, the waterways were busy. People recognized him and waved. One young boy riding a porpoise had to leap out of Beck's way as he cut through the water, his strong arms pumping vigorously. He arrived at Digby's small, limestone stilt house praying that the watershifter was home. There was no one who could get him to Sarphia faster than Digby.

He pulled himself from the water and flopped down on the wooden deck in front of the house to catch his breath. A door opened and the wide smile of Digby gleamed down at him.

"Thank the Highworld you're here."

The watershifter knelt and observed, not for the first time, "Always in a hurry, Prince Beck."

"This time is different, Digby. I need your help."

The watershifter was instantly alert. "Whatever you need, Your Grace. You know that."

Beck told him as much as he dared take the time to say. As soon as Digby heard the story of Kenley's kidnapping, he stood quickly. "Get in the boat."

Beck did as instructed, and Digby went inside his house to tell his wife, Liliana, what had happened. A few moments later, the watershifter rushed out of the door, threw a pack onto the deck of the boat, and dove into the water. "Sit back and try to relax, Your Grace," he said when his head resurfaced. "There is food in the pack. Sarphia is a two-day ride, but I can shorten the trip by picking up two more watershifters at the next port village."

Beck nodded and sat down on a crate on the deck, his mind whirling with doubt and fear. He wasn't lying to Kiernan when he told her he knew very little of the journey ahead of him. The very last passage in The Protetor said only, *"Strength lies in mastering others, but true power lies in mastering yourself. Your true power awaits you with the Malakai, the ancient enemy of Callyn-Rhe, in the tribal village of Torg."*

Tribal village of Torg? He had never heard of this place. How long would it take to get there? What would be required of him once he arrived? Who were the Malakai? He had questioned Baya once through Kenley, but the Draca Cat had never heard of the Malakai and insisted that the Moshie were her mortal enemy.

Beck remembered only too well how much the Moshies and Draca Cats despised each other. He was on hand to witness a vicious attack by the apes on Kiernan's bondmate, Bajan, when traveling with him through the Puu. The encounter left Bajan badly wounded and Airron with a broken leg.

Beck decided he would begin his search in Callyn-Rhe to speak to the Sovereign, Moombai. If anyone could lead him to the Draca Cats' ancient enemy, it would be their leader.

**\*\*\*\***

"It's called Farout Falls?" Kiernan asked Airron, studying the map on the wall in front of her. It was the middle of the night, but none of them could sleep. Until pure exhaustion overtook her body, sleep would not come easy again until her daughter was safely home.

Beck was never coming home.

Airron slapped his hand on the southern tip of Deepstone. "Yes, this is where Avalon took Beck when she kidnapped him, and she will do the same with Kenley."

They were using the royal War Room to take advantage of the palace's many charts and maps. Kiernan shook her head. "It doesn't make sense that she would take her there when she knows that you can find her."

"She wants us to follow! Think about it. Why else would she take Kenley? She wants us to follow so she can destroy the *Savitars* once and for all. Whether she is seeking revenge for the death of her brother or is simply being guided by the dark magic now flowing through her body, I don't know. I only know that she wants us dead. All of us."

Kiernan rubbed her hand over her face finding it difficult to think straight with her daughter's life hanging in the balance. Any decision she made could mean life or death for Kenley. Finally, she threw her hands up. "All right. I have to be doing something. Beck is following his path and I must follow mine, which appears to lead to Farout Falls."

"Who should we take?"

"You won't be doing this without us," declared Rogan from the door. He and Janin postponed their trip home and she was grateful for their support, but to enter this fight with Avalon Ravener? This wasn't like six years ago. The two Dwarves now had their own children to consider.

"No, Rogan. I can't allow it."

Rogan looked up at the ceiling. "Do you hear something, Janin? I thought I heard nonsense, but I must be mistaken." Then, he leveled a narrowed gaze at Kiernan. "We are packed and ready to go. Who else?"

She knew that she would never be able to talk him out of it, because she would have done the same if this had happened to Reilly or Jala. Instead, she looked at each one of her friends with gratitude and love. "Thank you," she choked out. "There are no other words for what your friendship means to me."

Rogan and Janin walked over to embrace her. She waited for Airron to crack a joke or poke fun at her for being overly sentimental, but he did neither. He simply walked over and peeled her from the Dwarves to lift her off her feet in a hug.

"I will get Kenley back or die trying. I promise you that," he whispered fiercely in her ear.

She wept then and couldn't stop.

When it went on longer than it should, her friends worried over her mental state, she could hear that much through their anxious whispers. Still, she couldn't stem the tide of emotion that poured out of her body as she sank to the floor. This time there was no one to catch her.

Janin placed a blanket over her shoulders and they left her alone to crawl back from the abyss of despair on her own. She hugged her knees tight to her body and lowered her head on her arms. A heavy despondency settled in her aching heart and in her bones. She couldn't move. Her limbs felt heavy, her mind sluggish. All she could do was sit there while dark thoughts dominated her mind.

Sometime later, she wasn't sure how long, three pinpoints of light penetrated the gloom.

Her daughter and sons.

The maternal drive to love and shelter and protect her babies shattered her grief and the thread of its powerful existence dangled in front of her. She clawed for it. And, inch by inch, second by second, one breath at a time, she climbed out of her dark hole.

At last, she rose from the floor and discarded the blanket around her shoulders. Without a word, she walked over to join her friends at the table and listened in on their discussion.

"The Sabers will have to stay behind because they can't travel with us through Aquataine," Rogan commented, eyeing her worriedly. "Kirby Nash won't be very pleased with that as he keeps insisting that he's going after Kenley."

"What about some of the shifters in Bardot? Or, the sorceresses?" Janin asked. "If there was ever a situation where the justification of their involvement could be sanctioned, this is it."

"I have a feeling that iron chains could not stop Sapphire from going," Airron responded. "I think we should also ask that spirited dark-haired witch, the Sect Leader for Combat. Citrine, right? That will make us a party of six which is still small enough to allow us to travel quickly."

"When do we leave?" asked Janin.

Kiernan glanced toward one of the windows and was surprised to see the faint rays of dawn. Feeling stronger, she said, "Now. I just need to have a word with Captain Nash, and I'll meet you at the stables."

She left the War Room and Saber LaFrae knelt when he saw her, but she barely noticed him. She ran up the stairs to the third level of the palace. At one end of the corridor, workmen were already busy reconstructing the doorway of her father's chambers. Turning in the opposite direction, she headed for her own suite of rooms.

As she suspected, Kirby Nash was still there, sitting in the armchair by the fire. He had not left the room since Kenley disappeared, his remorse over her disappearance spilling over into an irrational need to protect her sons.

And, at the moment, it was exactly what she needed.

"Where is Miss Belle?" she asked him when she entered the room.

He started to stand, but she waved him back down. "She's in the bedroom with the babies, Your Grace."

Kiernan knelt in front of him and took his hand in hers. The intimate contact took the Saber by surprise. "Kirby, look at me. You are not at fault for what happened to Kenley."

"Of course I am."

She shook her head. "You were injured and exhausted, and at the mercy of a very bright and strong-willed girl."

"I'm going with you to find her, Your Grace," he said adamantly.

"No, Kirby, I'm sorry but you can't go."

Her response deflated the Saber even more. "I am your protector, Your Grace! After all these years, have you lost all faith in me?"

"Of course not. I need you to do something far more important than protecting me. I need you to look out for my sons. I could not leave if I didn't believe that they were in the safest hands possible." She squeezed his hand tighter. "They are babies now, Captain, but remember that you guard the Princes of Iserlohn!"

Kirby straightened in the chair.

"You must remember!"

"Of course, Your Grace!"

"Not a hair on their heads is to be harmed, Saber, unless your own death precedes it! I will accept nothing less for that is your sworn oath."

Captain Nash banged his left fist to his chest. "My life before theirs, Your Grace, I promise you that!"

She nodded and stood. "Good. Now, that that is settled, I must go and bring back my daughter."

Beck was never coming home.

# CHAPTER 25

# The Malakai

Beck had no illusions that his arrival in Haventhal had gone unnoticed. He walked calmly through the Puu Rainforest and waited for the Elven Gardiens to appear. They did so almost immediately.

Wearing brown and green tunics that blended into the forest as if cultivated from the trees and plants that disguised them, one minute the path was empty and the next it was filled with Elves.

Beck searched their faces but didn't recognize anyone in the group. Fortunately, most knew who he was, and he was granted permission to go on his way. Before he left, he asked the Gardiens if any had ever heard of the village of Torg or the Malakai. None had, and they insisted that they knew every inch of Haventhal.

The news was discouraging, but if there was one thing Beck had learned, it was that not everything was as it appeared. Prior to the war, the Elves were also unaware of the existence of Callyn-Rhe, yet it had been present in Haventhal as surely as the royal seat of Sarphia.

Beck nodded his thanks and shouldered the pack Digby had given him. The watershifter insisted on waiting for him even though Beck could not guarantee when he would return.

The Gardiens now gone, he pulled out the magical compass created from the silver pendants Galen Starr had bestowed on the *Savitars*. Keeping his hand flat, he turned his body until the needle pointed east and then set off at a jog through the humid forest. There were many dangers to be wary of in the Puu including deadly spiders, snakes, jaguars, and even plant life that could stop a man's heart just by rubbing up against their leaves. He kept a watchful eye out for these things, but didn't dwell. There was no time.

The tunnel and waterfall he would have to navigate sprang to his mind. It was an experience he was not particularly anxious to revisit, but would do what he had to do for Kenley. A second in Avalon Ravener's clutches was a second too long. The thought spurred him on, and the minutes turned into hours. The rainfall, a drenching torrent whenever a break in the overhead canopy of trees opened up and an insidious mist at other times, seemed singularly determined to break his spirit. The muddy path pulled at his boots and threatened to remove them from his feet with every step he took. Rainy runnels dripped into his eyes and obscured his vision. So much so, that he didn't see the leafy wall of the tunnel in his path until it emerged out of the haze directly in his path.

He wiped the rain from his face and moved to the entrance. He had to clear the foliage that had grown around the aperture before ducking inside. Fortunately, the space did not seem nearly as dark this time without Adrian Ravener's conjured blackness to impede his way.

He pulled out a strip of beef and ate to keep up his strength as he trudged through the swirling water. Idly, he wondered what Kiernan, Rogan and Airron were doing right now. Had they gone in search of Kenley? That is what he would have done if the roles were reversed, but he had not had the time to discuss any plans with his wife and friends. If they left the morning after he departed for Bardot, they would be two days into their trip by this time.

The water rose higher, soaking his already damp trousers up to his calves. He plowed ahead, the effort of walking now considerably more difficult and soon his legs muscles were burning with exertion.

Still he pushed on.

The monotony of the journey pressed in on him and his impatience seethed as the time passed but his surroundings remained infuriatingly the same. His world had become the incessant dripping of water, the gloom of the tunnel, and the slippery limestone floor that had sent him crashing to the ground more than once.

Digby had commented often that he was an impatient man, always in a hurry. On an intuitive level, he knew it was true, but he had not always been that way. Once he married into royalty, he discovered he had little tolerance for the endless Court sessions, politicking, and rigid protocol. He was a simple man, married into a complicated life.

The water had risen to his waist now, so he mentally prepared for the stomach-turning drop into the churning rapids of the river far below. From there, he would continue east until he found Callyn-Rhe. He couldn't remember how long it took the last time he traveled this way. The hours leading up to the discovery of the land of Draca Cats all those years ago were muddled in his memory and, to this day, he had very little recollection of that final leg of the journey.

The clamor of the falls crashing in the distance came to him, faint at first, but began to build. Beck let himself be swept away now with the flow of the moving water, and the closer he drew to the opening, the more ominous the sound became. He caught a glimpse of the full moon hanging in the sky like a scoured marble and in the next instant, he was weightless, flying out over the falls in a towering plunge.

When he hit the water, it felt as though he had collided with solid ground and his body had broken into a million tiny pieces. The pain caused him to suck in his breath and he swallowed a mouthful of water. Feeling like he might drown, he panicked and fought his way to the surface. When his head broke through the roiling torrents, he gulped in the air greedily but with his lungs already holding the inhaled water, he felt no relief and only a sharp burning in his chest. Coughing violently, he swam awkwardly to the shore and hauled himself on the beach. For several long moments, on hands and knees, he could do nothing but spew the water from his lungs while taking desperate gasps of air in between. When he had nothing further to expel, he flopped down on his back, his chest still on fire.

Tentatively, he tested the movement of his limbs, but it didn't feel like he had broken any bones.

Looking up at the darkening sky, he decided to stay put for the night and camp on the shore. If he continued on now, he would be forced to spend the night in the rainforest and be subjected to, among other things, the swarming insects that would bite and sting him unmercifully while he slept.

He sat up and scanned his surroundings. He noticed that there was plenty of wood, but it was useless since he didn't have anything to start a fire with. In retrospect, it was foolish not to have at least taken a moment to pack a tinderbox. If not for Digby, he wouldn't even have any food to eat.

Instead, he curled up into a ball on the sandy beach, using the pack Digby gave him to rest his head. At first, the deafening rumble of the falls made it difficult to sleep, but soon he grew used to the sound and nodded off.

As the cold night deepened, he awoke every few minutes from the uncontrollable shivers raking his wet body. He finally gave up on the miserable evening in the middle of the night, deciding if he wasn't going to sleep, he may as well keep moving. At least then, he could warm his body and stop his teeth from chattering. He blew into his cupped hands to coax them back to life and picked up his pack.

He turned toward the rainforest and stopped.

A group of five Moshies crouched in his path.

He remained perfectly still, knowing from experience that it wouldn't take much for the apes to attack.

One bellowed out a howl and scrambled toward him on all fours in an aggressive manner, but Beck held his ground and the Moshie pulled up short in confusion and scampered back.

The Moshies moved like animals, but their faces were so *human.* That is, if you didn't consider the three-inch canines jutting forward over their lips.

Beck held his hands out. "Look, fellows, I just need to get by. No one needs to get hurt here." *Especially me.*

The Moshies stirred in agitation, but made no effort to step aside.

*Evidently, talking to animals is not going to help me.*

In frustration, he dropped his hands and looked to the Highworld. "I just need to find the Malakai! Is that too much to ask? For Kenley?"

"What did say?"

Beck started and took a step back. "Who said that?" he asked into the night.

The Moshie who had rushed him stood upright and walked to him, the cloak of an animal shedding with a human gait. "I did."

"You can talk?"

The Moshie's yellow eyes glared at him. "Foolish question."

"But…I thought you were animals," he managed to stutter out insensitively.

"Thought what wanted man to think."

"Well…since you can speak my language, maybe you can help. I am looking for the Malakai. Do you know where I might find them?"

"We are Malakai. To know that name, must be Mage apprentice."

"Yes…yes! And, I am in quite a bit of a hurry."

"I am called Odawa. Follow."

The Moshie, or Malakai rather, turned and walked back to the others. After a brief conversation that included more hand gestures than words, all four stood upright and started back on the path behind them.

Odawa turned to Beck to make sure he was following. "Torg not far. There will find what seek." He paused, then asked, "Why come by waterfall, foolish one?"

"I…that was the only way I knew to get here. I was headed for Callyn-Rhe and the—"

The Malakai charged at him with a growl. Baring his teeth, Odawa grabbed Beck under the neck. "Do not speak of enemy cats in presence of Malakai!"

*He is so strong!*

Beck nodded and held his hands up in submission.

"Foolish." The Malakai spit at his feet and turned to follow his companions once again.

Beck had no choice but to follow and after a short walk, the path opened up into the village of Torg. Even after meeting Odawa and the others, Beck could hardly believe his eyes at his first glimpse of the Malakai, a functioning society of animals that moved and spoke with human-like intelligence.

Despite the fact that it was the middle of the night, the villagers were awake and active. Small children ran, laughing and playing among two dozen triangular teepee tents and huts built with bamboo and palm tree fronds. Female Malakai cleaned fish from the river and stirred the contents of huge pots cooking over open fires. Most of the males sat back in leisure while the women worked. A cloud of smoke hovered above one small group as they puffed on long pipes.

All turned and stopped what they were doing when they saw Beck, but none of them seemed overly concerned at the man in their presence.

Odawa addressed the Malakai in a language Beck did not understand. Some commented back to Odawa and he answered, and Beck noticed him pointing several times to three small teepees sitting apart from the rest of the village under a sturdy wooden shelter.

The conversation over, the village went back to their tasks, and Odawa motioned once again for Beck to follow him. Before he could take a single step, two children ran to him and grabbed his arms. They giggled as they examined his flesh very carefully, seemingly surprised to find them without fur.

"*Nin!*" Odawa shooed them away and they ran off.

As Beck made his way warily through the village, he noticed an old woman sitting cross-legged in front of one of the tents. She was human. At first glance, she appeared to be sleeping with her head hanging on her chest, but as Beck passed, she looked up and offered him an amused toothless grin. Goose pimples broke out on his arms as he looked into the woman's eyes.

They were completely white.

Beck had the unnatural impression that she could read his mind and sense his every fear and desire. Just as he had the thought, she let out a shrill cackle. "Oh, yes, boy. Oh, yes."

"Come!" Odawa ordered sternly.

With difficulty, Beck tore his gaze from the old woman and followed the Malakai to one of the teepees. He gestured for Beck to sit on a hewed tree stump just outside of the tent opening. "This home of Odawa," he informed Beck. "Must wait until mixture ready, then go training."

"Mixture? What is that?"

"Mage potion must drink before training. Those are rules. Live with it." Odawa sat as well and picked up a long pipe, lighting the bowl with practiced ease. After blowing the inhaled smoke out through his nose, he handed the pipe to Beck. "Smoke."

Beck shook his head politely. "No, thank you."

"Not question. Smoke." He continued to hold the pipe outstretched until Beck accepted it.

Beck had seen his father smoke a pipe when he was younger, but had never done so himself. Gingerly, he put his mouth on the wooden stem and inhaled. Immediately, his lungs exploded in pain and he coughed violently, tears streaming down his eyes.

The other Malakai males in the village pointed and laughed while Beck struggled to catch his breath. Even the children laughed at him.

Odawa shook his head. "Foolish."

When Beck was finally breathing normally, he turned an angry eye at Odawa. "When will this mixture be ready?" he asked, anxious now to leave this tribe where he felt as foolish as the Malakai claimed him to be.

"On the morrow."

"Tomorrow! You don't understand. My daughter is missing! We must begin right away!"

The Malakai opened the flap to the teepee behind him and pointed to a bed of fronds inside. "Rest. Will wake when time."

Beck sighed in frustration, but the pipe smoke had made his head dizzy. Knowing he could not get Odawa to move any faster, he entered the small tent and lay down, once again using his pack as a pillow.

This delay had probably cost him his transportation from Digby. He supposed he would have no problem hailing another watershifter, but it would take time he didn't have to arrange.

The need for more information still wrenched at him. He poked his head back out of the tent. "Where will the Mage training be held?"

The Malakai pointed to the three teepees set away from the village.

Beck looked over. "In there?" he asked doubtfully. "I don't even think I will fit inside."

"Will fit."

"Who conducts the training? The Malakai?"

Odawa wrinkled his nose in disgust. "Mage do Mage training, foolish one."

*But, there are no more Mages on the island.* Did Odawa have any clue what was to happen? Starting to wonder at that, he decided to try one last question. "What will I do inside the tent?"

"Die."

# CHAPTER 26

## A Shout in the Dark

Kiernan wiped the sweat from her forehead with the back of her hand. Where moments ago she shivered from the biting cold, the air was now thick with humidity. Diamond must have seen the movement because she handed her a handkerchief.

Kiernan accepted it with a grateful smile.

The Divination sorceress refused to be left behind when she learned of their plans and that added another to their party, which was perfectly fine with Kiernan. There were no others she would rather have at her side to help save her daughter than the six people riding next to her. Surely, this assemblage of power could defeat one witch? She shook her head. No, she didn't kid herself. That one witch was centuries old with the morality of a Netherworld demon. That made her the most dangerous of all foes.

After traveling two days through Aquataine and picking up horses at the sorceresses' castle in Elloree, they started out immediately south on horseback. With a long ride still ahead of them, they alternated between a walk and a ground-covering gallop to save the horses. Sapphire offered to cast a spell over the beasts to free them from their weariness, but Kiernan declined. The spell may have served to mask the animals' fatigue, but their physical limitations were still very real. The only thing the spell would do is cause them run to their deaths instead of stumble.

Kiernan glanced up at the sun. They had been walking the horses for an hour or so now, and the grueling journey in a land that offered no break from the burning heat was wearing on her. She drummed her heels into her mare's ribs and the animal took off at a startled run. She didn't warn the others. They would follow.

Kiernan relished the speed of movement and the wind slicing over her body. With all of her concentration on the ride, it left little room for thoughts of Kenley. Yesterday, she begged Diamond to read her gem for information, but the sorceress' stone was again obscured, and Sapphire had not had any luck removing the spell this time. Of course, Diamond also reminded Kiernan, as she always did, that a foretelling did not always come true. It was a prediction of a probable event and should never be construed as fact. But, no matter what she said, Kiernan knew that Diamond's skill in the craft of Divination allowed her to distinguish between what would happen without fail and those events that were still undecided. Kiernan supposed she used it as a fail-safe answer to avoid divulging all she knew.

Racing out in front of the others over the endless sea of rock, Kiernan pulled back on the reins when she heard a shout. It took a few moments for the big horse to come to a complete stop, and even now the animal continued to dance restlessly beneath her.

"Look!" Sapphire yelled, pointing southward.

Kiernan squinted into the distance but wasn't sure what she was seeing. A gray, dense mist at least a thousand paces wide moved their way at a fairly rapid speed. "What is it?"

"Demon's breath," cursed Sapphire. "Rogan! Airron! Tie us together with rope! Quickly!"

"What is it?" Kiernan questioned in alarm.

"Death."

The word hung unpromisingly in the air.

"Everybody dismount!" Sapphire ordered. "Once that mist descends, it will try to separate us, and it will succeed unless we are tethered."

Rogan and Airron jumped off their horses and removed ropes from their saddlebags. Airron handed one end to Kiernan, and she wrapped it around her waist twice and handed the other end back to him.

"It?" Kiernan directed at Sapphire. "You refer to this mist like it is a living, thinking entity."

"It is."

"Can we ride around it?" asked Airron.

"No, it has been set on its course, and I fear that course is us. Keep hold of your horse's bridle. The mist ahead is a conjuration of dark magic. It is called the Sea of Void and it is deadly. It has the power to induce a mind-eating insanity."

"Impossible," Janin retorted.

Sapphire continued as if Janin had not spoken. "Once the Void envelops us, it will penetrate our minds to discover our deepest fears. Once it has done so, the Void will invoke graphic images of those fears in an attempt to cull the weakest from the group. Don't be scared and, for Highworld's sake, do not run! You must remain strong mentally! Everything you see will be an illusion. The Void must remain in motion to exist so it will continue to move past us. If you keep your head down and keep walking, and we are very, very lucky, we can survive this unscathed."

"Bloody hell," muttered Rogan. "Here it comes. Don't let go of my hand, Janin!"

"I will not, Kal. I love you."

"Can we breathe in it?" Kiernan asked abruptly, feeling the need to hold her breath as the mist neared.

"Yes, just keep your head down and walk," Sapphire repeated.

Kiernan took a deep breath anyway and held it as the gray sea rolled over them. The hair on her arms stood up straight as the invasive, sinister vapor slithered its way around her. The blackness of the Void blotted out all life causing Kiernan to hold tight to her mare's bridle as it was the only physical connection she had left in the world.

Suddenly, a vision appeared before their eyes. Kiernan recognized Airron's wife, Melania Shael, in bed, making love to an Elven male. A long, slim leg wrapped around the Elf as her hips arched up to meet his movements.

Airron grunted. "Thanks, Kiernan, for planting that one there."

"Sorry."

"That is your deepest fear?" questioned Rogan incredulously. "Are you serious?"

Kiernan could sense Airron's shrug. "At this moment, it's all I can think about."

The intimate vision went on in detail, in every direction within the mist, no matter where she looked. Even shutting her eyes didn't help as the image continued to play out in her mind. *How can Airron stand to watch?*

The picture disappeared abruptly, replaced by a horrifying visual of Janin standing back-to-back with Rogan in the thick of battle. A violent struggle went on for long moments before one of the faceless enemy soldiers lashed out with his blade and pierced Janin directly through the heart. She fell away from Rogan to the ground and clutched her bloodied chest.

Kiernan wanted to cry out for Janin, but Rogan was already doing so.

"I am here, Kal. I am safe," she murmured soothingly, and she heard him take a deep, calming breath.

Soon, the image faded, and tears filled Kiernan's eyes when an illusion of Gemini Starr dying in several different and brutal ways appeared. In the depicted scenes, Sapphire was always running toward Gemini to help, but always just a fraction of a second too late to save her mother as she died over and over again.

Sapphire did not utter a sound.

The Void's attempt to break Diamond came next in a nightmarish sensation of spiders crawling in a black mass over the sorceress' body. Kiernan couldn't stop herself from brushing frantically at her own arms and legs as big, hairy spiders slithered over Diamond's body and bit down on her exposed white flesh while she screamed, both in the vision and in reality.

Kiernan flinched when the mental probe of the Void penetrated her mind like the stabbing prick of a pin. Her biggest fear came to life as a simple image yet unbearable to fathom. It showed her sitting on her throne in Grace Hall surrounded by her three children, adults now, and another man standing behind her with his hand on her shoulder.

Beck was not in the picture.

Beck had never come home.

"It is an illusion, Kiernan," reminded Diamond.

"I wish I could believe that."

Suddenly, the rope around her waist tugged violently and she fell to the ground.

"Citrine! Stop!" shouted Sapphire.

Kiernan looked up. The gray mist showed a younger Citrine praying for the death of her predecessor Sect Leader so that she could be Named. The image fast-forwarded several years to the center of the Demon War. The sounds, the smells, and the colors assailed Kiernan's senses. Men screamed, weapons clashed violently, the smell of blood hung heavy in the air. In the middle of the horror, it was Citrine and not Avalon Ravener who walked to her former mentor and with a glint of glee in her eye, twisted her neck.

It was Citrine's fear that her childish, yet appalling, wish had caused the woman's death.

"Citrine! It is an illusion! Stop!"

The skin on Kiernan's knees ripped open as she was dragged on the ground. She screamed out and then the rope became slack. "What happened?"

"Citrine is gone! She cut the rope and ran into the Void alone."

"We have to help her!" Kiernan shouted, getting to her feet.

"It's too late. Keep walking," Sapphire instructed.

Kiernan shook her head. "No! We can't leave her out there! We have to do something!"

"You will die if you go after her. You will never find her and you both will die. There is no other possible outcome when dealing with the Void."

Kiernan struggled with the rope.

"You must listen to Sapphire, Kiernan!" screamed Diamond. Then, quieter, "I foresaw Citrine's death months ago. Do not throw your life away needlessly."

"You said yourself that your foretelling is not always accurate, Diamond! We may be able to change Citrine's fate if we try."

"Not this time." Kiernan couldn't see Diamond, but the pain in her voice was clear.

It took a moment for Kiernan to suppress the urge to run after Citrine, but she knew Diamond was right.

Her blood oath had not stirred in the least.

Kiernan tightened the rope around her waist once more and began walking forward. It was one of the most difficult things she ever had to do.

The party silently continued through the rolling darkness. There were no more visions. There was no need. The Void had culled the weakest and claimed its victim.

\*\*\*\*

"Kenley, darling, come over and join me for some tea."

Since disobedience brought nothing but pain and discomfort, Kenley rose from her pallet in the corner of the room and walked to the table where the Mistress sat.

She pulled out a chair and lowered herself into it gingerly.

"Still sore, my dear?" asked the Mistress.

Kenley nodded.

"Well, that lesson was absolutely necessary, young lady, but if you do not try to use your airshifting again, you will not have to learn it twice."

"Yes, Mistress." Two days ago, Kenley tried to press the Mistress up against the wall with air, and the welts where her kidnapper had taken a strap to her backside still throbbed painfully. No, she wouldn't use her airshifting again unless she was sure it would allow her a better chance at escape.

"I am much, much stronger than you, Kenley. Remember that always."

"I will."

A shadow fell over the table and Kenley turned toward the cave entrance. It was the guard that the Mistress called Cyrus.

"Well?" demanded the Mistress impatiently. "With the Dwarves out of Kondor, we cannot waste this opportunity, Cyrus!"

"They 'ave returned," he told her. "Still a few leagues away, but I can see them on the 'orizon."

"Did they succeed?"

Cyrus nodded, and Kenley recoiled when the Mistress clapped her hands in delight. "That is wonderful news, Cyrus! The earthshifter may have gotten away, but as it turns out, I did not need him." She turned toward Kenley and tickled her chin. "I got what I wanted in the end." She glanced over her shoulder and muttered, "I guess these wings are good for something after all."

Kenley remained silent. The Mistress often talked to herself and it was best not to draw attention her way while she did.

The Mistress tapped her fingernails on the stone table while she poured tea. "Kenley, the Cyman scouts tell me that your father is not with the others that are traveling this way. Do you know where he might be?"

She shook her head. "No." Then, she dared to ask. "Who is coming here, Mistress?"

The woman waved a hand in her face. "Nothing for you to concern yourself about…yet."

"When can I go home, Mistress?"

The disappointment on the Mistress' face was unmistakable.

"Kenley, how old are you?"

"I will be six years very soon."

"Then you are old enough to stop asking childish questions. I told you, that part of your life is over."

Tears welled in her eyes. "But, that is where I belong, with my Daddy and Maman and new brothers."

The teacup in the Mistress' hand fell to the stone table and shattered. "You have brothers?"

Kenley backed away from the advancing black liquid. "Yes, twin brothers. They were just born."

"Two more pureblood unmarked boys!" The Mistress stood and began to pace the chamber, her tea forgotten on the table. "With this news, I may have to change my plans."

She was talking to herself again.

"Hmm…maybe we won't return to Nordik. With that many purebloods by my side, I could stay right here and rule. Where Adrian failed, I most certainly will not now," she declared fiercely. She turned back to Kenley. "Do you realize how powerful we can be together, Kenley? Once the *Savitars* are gone, no one will be able to stop us!"

Kenley felt confused about what the Mistress was saying, but didn't ask.

"First things first. Kenley, I will need your help."

"My help?"

"Yes, and you will be a good girl and do as I say, won't you? You remember what happens when you don't?"

Kenley swallowed. "Yes, Mistress."

Another Cyman guard returned. His name was Arlen, and Kenley smiled at him. He was very nice to her and always made sure that she had something soft at night to pillow her head. He even rubbed her back at night when she cried herself to sleep.

She liked Arlen.

"The Sea of Void is gone, Mistress."

"Did it work?"

"It took one of their members. A female."

"With any luck, it was…," she turned toward Kenley. "Finish your tea, darling, I must speak to Cyrus and Arlen." The Mistress went into a corner of the chamber to talk with the guards.

*Who is coming?* The Mistress mentioned that it wasn't her Daddy, so could it be her Maman? As she glanced at the three adults deep in conversation, she briefly thought about using her airshifting to shove the Mistress out into the night air, but then quickly dismissed the idea. The woman would only turn into a bird or, worse, the winged creature that brought her here. If that happened, her punishment would be far worse than a strapping.

*Princess!*

Kenley gasped aloud at the mental shout.

The Mistress turned her way. "What is it?" she asked, angry over the interruption.

"Nothing, Mistress. I am just going to lie down for a few minutes. My stomach does not feel very well."

"Fine."

Kenley got up from the table and hurried over to her pallet and lay down with her back to the adults. She didn't want them to see her black eyes.

*Baya!*

*I am here.*

*Highworld, Baya, how did you find me?*

*I traveled behind your Maman and then passed her and the others when they stopped at the witches' castle.*

*My Maman is coming?*

*Yes.*

*Oh, no. I'm frightened, Baya, that if you or Maman come here, you will be killed. The Mistress is very mean and powerful. You must not try to rescue me!* She cried freely now.

*She does not frighten me.*

*That is because you don't know her.*

A growl sounded in her head. *Did she harm you?*

*It's not important. Where are you?*

*The land of the Dwarves. But, for some reason, I cannot scent you. Where are you?*

*I am up in a very high cave.*

*I will keep searching until I find you.*

*No! Please, Baya, I could not bear it if something were to happen to you.*

*And, I could not bear the same. That is why I must come.*

*Baya...*

*I was born to protect you.*

*Please be careful. The Mistress is a bodyshifter and can turn into an animal that could hurt you.*

*And, I am Draca Cat. It is the evil Mistress that should take care.*

# CHAPTER 27

## The Realm of Mages

They burned Citrine's remains in the dark of night. When the Void finally rolled past, they retraced their route north and discovered her body lying on the road not far from them.

Citrine's face looked tortured, even in death, and Kiernan wondered at the clumps of hair missing from the sorceress' scalp until she saw the dark strands waving from the grips of her closed fists. Sapphire told them that once The Void had Citrine in its grasp, its single purpose would have been to devour her mind. To hammer her psyche with unspeakable torment.

Fortunately, as soon as the Void claimed its victim, it began to dissipate and Kiernan felt grateful that the dark sorcery would not be able to continue roaming the island, killing indiscriminately.

Exhausted both mentally and physically over the death of their friend, the despondent party collected stones to serve as a pyre and placed Citrine reverently upon it. Rogan cast the fire that ignited her body in a mantle of flame. An emotional Diamond offered words of remembrance of her sister and Sapphire led the Highworld prayer.

Once finished, the group quickly set up camp for the night and rolled into their bedrolls without conversation. Sleep did not come easy for Kiernan. Highworld willing, she would be reunited with her daughter soon, and the prospect set her heart racing in her chest. How she longed to hold her baby girl in her arms again! The burning desire to remove Kenley from harm's way thudded through her body.

That it would prove difficult was an understatement. Avalon Ravener had the advantage. This was her game, her rules. Since she reappeared, the *Savitars* could do nothing except stumble along in her wake while she pulled all the strings. What black magic would she throw at them next? Another Sea of Void? Something new and more sinister? One way or another, the tables had to be turned. Her last thought before sleep claimed her was that they needed to change the rules of the game.

She said as much to the others as soon as they awoke the next morning.

"What do you propose?" asked Airron, his purple eyes questioning.

"You said she's in a cave, Airron, and if we go after her there, she'll just wait for us to get close and pick us off one at a time. Somehow, we have to get her to come out. Then, Sapphire can issue a binding spell, and I can mindshift her."

"So, how do we get the bat out of the belfry?" asked Diamond.

"Bait," Airron answered, his eyebrows raised toward Kiernan. "Tell me I'm right."

She smiled for the first time in a long time. "I did hear that Elves can run pretty fast."

"Like lightening when there is an evil sorceress on our arses."

"If I had any other choice, Airron, I would not ask it of you."

"And, I would be offended if you hadn't."

"It's settled then," said Rogan. "We serve up the Elf."

****

Beck came awake slowly with the oddest sensation. Feather-like touches traveled up his leg, chest and then stopped just below his neck. Disoriented, he cautiously lifted his head and opened one eye. A tiny hairy, mouth with two lethal fangs reached for his throat.

"Ahh!!!" Beck screamed and swatted the creature away. He jumped to his feet in fright and sprinted from the tent.

Loud guffaws rang out.

He turned his head with a growl.

Odawa was running away and two other male Malakai were bent over in laughter.

Beck looked down. A Puuvian goliath arachnid skittered away from the tent on spindly legs and a body at least two spans in length. The spider, native to the Puu Rainforest, was deadly. A single bite could kill a man within moments without the intervention of a very skilled healer. He glared at Odawa in disbelief. "Are you crazy? That thing could have killed me!"

The Malakai continued their ridicule with words and gestures that no language barrier could disguise. Keeping his temper in check, he bent to retrieve his pack. With luck, the mixture was ready and he could leave these prankster apes behind.

For the first time, Beck noticed that the villagers were gone, and he was alone with his three harassers. "Where are the rest of the Malakai?" he questioned.

"Middle of day. Hunt. Work. Malakai not soft like humans!"

Beck looked up at the sky and through the rainclouds, he saw the sun directly overhead. He had slept for hours! "Demon's hell, Odawa, I slept too late!" he complained in a panic. "Is the mixture ready?"

"Done long time."

"Why didn't you wake me?" he demanded angrily.

Odawa let his tongue loll out of his mouth and made a snoring noise. "Apprentice very sleepy." This elicited more laughter from his cohorts.

*Enough!*

Beck threw down his pack and stalked toward the Malakai. Their laughter stopped as he thrust out his hand and a ball of dirt erupted out of the ground.

The Malakai ran.

With a flick of his wrist, Beck sent the gritty orb screaming toward Odawa's head. Beck's tormenter shrieked in fright and ducked, but the earthen missile circled around and sped toward him again.

Furred arms swatted frantically at the air. With another gesture by Beck, the ground beneath Odawa heaved and sent him crashing to the ground amid a flurry of flailing arms. Beck pointed and hovered the ball directly over the prone Odawa and let it fall, dirt and pebbles peppering down on top of his head. "There is plenty more where that came from, Odawa. I may only be a Mage apprentice, but I am a master earthshifter. Lead me to the training now or you will be eating that dirt!"

This time it was at Odawa that the others wailed in laughter.

Odawa stood and wiped the dirt from his shoulders. Walking past Beck, he snapped his large teeth at him aggressively. "Follow."

"Now, was that so hard?" Beck asked.

"Come!" he growled.

Odawa led him to the three teepees under the wooden structure. Flora from the jungle encroached on the areas around and between the tents, indicating no one had been inside for a very long time.

"Must enter first tent, apprentice," Odawa instructed, pointing to the tent on the far right.

Beck looked at him in confusion. "Mage training is in a teepee?"

"Must enter first tent," Odawa repeated. "First tent for learn." He pointed to the middle tent. "Second tent for observe." His arm swung to the last tent. "Third tent for experience. That is all know of Mage custom."

Beck sighed. He would get no further answers from the Malakai. Best to simply do as instructed so he could get this over as quickly as possible. He strode toward the first tent, and Odawa said, "Go to your death bravely, apprentice."

Beck turned his head sharply, but Odawa had already turned and was walking away. With a snarl, he reached out to the tent opening and ducked inside. The tent was empty except for a small circle of stones on the dirt floor and a tin cup filled with a dark liquid placed in the center.

*Is someone actually going to join me? A Mage as Odawa suggested or another?* Resigned to the fact that he would have to wait, he sat on the ground and crossed his legs. There was little room to do anything else, and he again wondered how training was to be conducted in such a small space. Surely, the practice of spells and other forms of sorcery would be involved.

The minutes ticked by and the sweat poured down his face and back from sitting in the hot tent, but still no one appeared. Beck looked at the tin cup again. *Am I supposed to drink it? Is this the mysterious mixture I waited so long for?* Suddenly, an overwhelming thirst came over him and he felt compelled to reach for the cup. Compelled to drink its contents. Unable to stop himself, he picked up the cup and in one swift motion, downed the drink. Almost immediately, his eyes grew heavy and his body slumped to the side.

****

It seemed to Beck that he had been unconscious for hours when the foggy layers of sleep slowly began to dissipate, and he came awake. He was no longer in the tent. That much was obvious as a strong, cooling breeze ruffled his hair and clothing. Pushing past his lethargy, he forced himself to sit up.

He looked out at a desolate landscape similar to the terrain of western Deepstone. Gone were the lush forests, grasses and rivers of Haventhal. Barren of vegetation of any kind or people or buildings or roads, Beck saw only an infinite sea of red sandstone in every direction.

*Did the Malakai move me here while I slept? Is this another one of their pranks?*

Beck cupped his hands to his mouth. "Is anybody there?" As soon as the words left his mouth, he clamped it shut, realizing that it might be unsafe to be speaking aloud in the pall of silence hanging over the land. It was uncertain what kind of animal or other danger he could attract by making his presence known.

"Apprentice!"

Beck turned toward the voice. A towering, hooded figure in all white guided toward him, his hands lost in the folds of his wide-sleeved cloak. The newcomer finally stopped in front of Beck and looked down at him on the ground.

All Beck could do was stare.

"You do speak, do you not?" the man asked, voice deep and rumbling.

Beck nodded and then decided he should prove it. "Yes, of course."

The cloaked figure removed his hood revealing his Elven heritage. "I am Mage Arias Sarphia."

"Arias Sarphia?" Beck asked in surprise. "The original *Savitar?*"

The Mage bowed his head. "I am, and I will be your guide for Mage training. The instructors are waiting for you." He held out a long-fingered hand. "Shall we?"

"But…but, aren't you dead?" As he asked the question, he thought of the odd phrase Odawa uttered to him before he entered the tent. Had he really gone to his death? Was he at this very moment standing in the Highworld?

Arias gave a deep chuckle. "Life exists in many dimensions, my apprentice. Death in one world simply translates to life in another."

"Am I dead? I mean…in my old world?"

"No. This dimension exists for a specific purpose. You are a guest here and you will return to your world when your education is complete."

Beck thought of something. "Is Galen Starr here as well? Will he be part of my training?"

"No. Mage Starr is off in another realm at the moment, but he does send his high regards."

Disappointed, Beck nodded.

When the giant turned to go, Beck said, "Mage, I really must hurry—"

The figure waved a hand in the air. "Yes, yes, you are in a hurry. You all say that."

"All? There are more?"

"Oh, I have not seen an apprentice come through in centuries, but men are all the same. Impatient. Rash. Self-centered. This century or the next, you are all the same."

"But, you don't understand. My daughter is missing."

"Yet, you are here?"

"I...I'm hoping that becoming a Mage will allow me to save her," he admitted.

"Then, why are you still talking?"

Beck had no response for that.

"With wisdom comes patience, apprentice. Your training is over when it is over and not a moment before. Come."

Beck reluctantly followed behind and where he originally thought he was standing in the middle of a flat endless surface of rock, he could now see that they were on the lip of a deep stone valley. Beck looked down from the precipice to a city below unlike any he had ever seen. The buildings were sleek and angular, with rows and rows of windows, and the roads were covered with a black, unfamiliar substance. Lights on tall poles lit the entire city in a brilliant glow as hundreds of white-robed figures glided from one building to the next.

"The first part of your journey is to learn," Arias informed him as he started down the hill. "Here you will learn all there is to know of shifting, sorcery, and defense. A Mage must be the master of all."

Walking behind his guide, Beck had a chance to study the inhabitants of the city. All were men and most of advanced age if the heads of gray were any indication. Wrapped in their cloaks of white, he assumed that they were his instructors. When they saw him approach with Arias, a general excitement rippled through the air.

"I told you, it has been a while since we have had an apprentice. Be prepared to be inundated. Your training is about to begin."

True to Arias' word, the instructors descended on him in an ocean of white and swept him toward one of the strange windowed buildings. They led him to a massive room that seemed even larger due to the windows that covered the entire western wall. The instructors called it the preparation room, but it looked to Beck like any traditional classroom with student desks, diagramed reference charts, slate and chalk.

From that point on, Beck's world moved at a hectic pace as the lessons began by one instructor after another.

First came a review of the rudiments of the four metamagics of shifting taught to him at the Parsis Academy, but then the education branched into different forms of shifting that he never knew existed.

There was metalshifting that allowed a shifter to forge raw metal into finished products. Instead of using tools to hammer, bend and cut the material, a metalshifter used his magic to heat and mold the object into the desired shape. It made him wonder if the more renowned metallurgists in Deepstone were actually using metalshifting and unaware that their magic was involved.

He learned of sightshifting, a unique ability that allowed shifters to create lifelike illusions. One instructor created a likeness of Beck that looked incredibly real, even down to the gestures Beck used. When he reached out to touch the illusion, it disappeared in a puff of smoke.

Feralshifting allowed a summoner to commune with animals. This, Beck suspected, was the shifting ability of the Elves and must be why Airron could never learn the magic. He was already a bodyshifter, and a shifter could only master one form of shifting, the most dominant ability presenting first.

He studied how airshifting manipulated the currents in the air to move objects, create tunnels of air, and even allowed the practitioner to fly. *Kenley will be able to fly!* He wasn't quite sure how he felt about that, but was grateful that he could at least now instruct her on the safe use of her magic.

He wasn't surprised to learn that there were also more sinister forms of shifting like the spiritshifting of Adrian Ravener, dreamshifting that allowed a shifter to stalk and torment a person's nightly dreams, and soulshifting that provided the ability to steal a person's very soul.

In this realm where Beck now existed and trained relentlessly, he didn't eat or sleep nor did he feel the need to. The hours turned into days, and he was only able to mark the passage of time by the stubble growing on his chin.

From shifting, the focus moved on to a vigorous indoctrination in the arts of sorcery. He learned the principles of every incantation and curse known to the Mage. He discovered that it was a hover spell that Adrian Ravener used in the Demon War when he appeared to fly, not a form of airshifting.

He learned the art of healing and how to prepare alchemical potions including the LifeFire Tonic that Avalon Ravener was so desperate to have as it could extend life by hundreds of years.

All that he learned became entrenched in the cells of his brain, the very marrow of his bones. All filed away inside a cerebral arsenal that, he was told, would remain within reach his entire life. As his mind and body filled with more knowledge and wisdom, he felt himself becoming something more, and maybe even dared to use the word superior.

When the sorcery education concluded, Arias Sarphia reappeared. It had been days since he had last seen the Mage.

"I was beginning to think I wouldn't see you again," Beck commented sourly.

"As I told you, I am your guide and will not leave you for the duration of your education."

"Mage—"

Arias held up a hand. "It is over when it is over, apprentice." The Elf turned his back and led him out of the preparation room and back outside toward an enormous circular building. "You must now prove to us that what you have learned can be translated into skill." Arias held open a large, arched wooden door, and Beck went through cautiously.

It was an arena.

Rows of benches filled with Mage instructors surrounded an open field of bare dirt. More bright lights mounted on poles glared down on the center of the arena.

He followed Arias out to the middle.

"Your final tests in defense will not be easy. Prepare yourself for a fight to the death. You will face many opponents. Do not hesitate. Do not feel remorse. Your adversaries most certainly will not."

"Will I have a weapon to use?"

Arias shook his white head. "*You* are the weapon."

A worm of fear wiggled into Beck's thoughts. "Can I die here in this world?"

"Yes." The Mage paused. "It does not happen often, but it can happen if an apprentice is especially weak. Are you ready?"

Beck nodded, and the Mage walked away, leaving him standing in the center of the arena alone. All at once, a grating sound echoed behind him, and he spun to watch an iron grate he had not noticed previously, lift open.

Beck narrowed his eyes at the black opening. Who would he fight first? Would it be another Mage?

A figure lumbered forward.

No.

It wasn't even a man.

A beast dressed in an armored chest plate and a battle axe in each fist stepped out into the light on two hooves, and the grate clanged shut behind it. The animal resembled a bull with two curved horns, and a blunt snout with wide nostrils through which a gold ring dangled. Tufts of coarse black fur peaked up around its face and a full coat of wooly hair covered its body.

As soon as the bull saw Beck, it strode forward confidently, arms and legs bulging with muscled power as he advanced. Throwing its head back in a challenging roar, the beast hefted one of the axes in its hand and hurled it through the air at Beck. The blade tumbled end over end, unerringly on a path for his head.

Beck confidently swept out a hand and cast his first spell. "*Divergia.*"

The axe swept away out of his path and landed in the dirt. Wanting to end this quickly, Beck started running forward to close with the beast, and the animal picked up its pace in response. The other axe flew from its hand, but Beck easily sent that weapon flying wide as well.

As he ran, Beck methodically sorted through his mental cache for the best way to dispose of his opponent. That was when the bull struck first.

"*Bindeno,*" it bellowed in an almost unintelligible growl.

Beck cursed when he felt his arms and legs snap to his sides and he fell into the dirt, unable to move. It had been a disastrous error to believe his opponent a simple animal when in fact it, too, had the gift of sorcery. It was too late to issue the counterspell, and Beck could only lie there helpless while the bull thundered across the field toward him.

*Demon's breath!* A bead of sweat trickled down his face.

In no time, the animal skidded to a stop in front of him, lowered its head and flipped Beck onto his stomach with one horn. Then, with a violent thrust, the bull speared him through the back and lifted him into the air.

Beck screamed out in pain. The beast shook its head victoriously and Beck, impaled on the tip of one horn, felt his back break. His body went completely numb below the waist.

He almost blacked out from the agony, but fought to retain consciousness as his vision began to fade. His arms still pinned to his sides, he found that he could move his hands and stretched them toward the large head beneath him. His fingers were just long enough to grab onto the bony protrusions over the bull's eyes. The beast must have known what Beck intended, because it let out a desperate howl and tried to shake Beck loose.

It was too late.

"*Morbendi.*"

The bull-like animal fell to the ground dead.

Beck gritted his teeth in misery when he hit the ground alongside the fallen animal. The binding spell now released, he used the strength in his forearms to drag his body off the horn embedded in his back. Panting from the exertion, he pulled himself free with a nauseating sucking sound. None of the instructors in the arena rushed to his aid, and he knew they wouldn't. He was on his own.

Reaching out with his healing sorcery, he probed his back for the injury. Fortunately, the spinal cord was unharmed, but two vertebrae had become dislocated from the stress of the bull's gouging maneuver. Forcing the pain away, he went to work realigning the vertebrae and knitting together the ligaments and sinew that held the bones in place.

When he finally finished, he was soaked in sweat, but the pain was gone.

Beck flinched when he heard the grate open again.

He turned around and sat up.

A tiny, blonde-haired girl in a short tunic walked toward him.

He got to his feet quickly and tested his injury. It felt completely healed. Yet, he felt unsure what to do. What kind of threat could this little slip of a girl cause to him?

She continued to approach and bounced a ball in the palm of one hand. He waited. If the instructors expected him to simply kill a small girl out of hand, he would have to disappoint them.

By the time Beck realized that the ball in the girl's hand was actually an orb of fire, she had already launched it at him. He sidestepped out of the way but, just like his earthen missile at Odawa, the ball circled around behind him and struck him in the back. His shirt immediately caught on fire. Instinct had him falling to the ground and rolling instead of using a spell to put out the fire, but it worked equally as well.

The little girl was upon him now and looking down at him with large blue eyes. She smiled innocently, and he hesitated with the spell that was on the tip of his tongue. In that brief pause, the girl's face transformed into the visage of a demon and she opened her mouth wide in a hideous scream, unleashing a stream of lethal fire that blazed out of the opening.

Beck shrieked as the fire engulfed his face. He kicked the girl with his powerful legs and sent her sprawling to the ground. His face still aflame, he crawled on hands and knees over to where she lay. The demon countenance now gone, she smiled at him again and blinked her eyes adoringly.

Beck did not use the killing curse. This little girl would serve as a reminder to him to never again hesitate in the face of evil. Reaching out, he encircled her tiny neck in his hands and twisted, killing her.

He fell back down on the dirt once again and issued a spell this time to put out the fire. His face felt like it was sloughing off his skull in shredded, smoldering pieces.

As he went to work to heal his injuries, a single tear fell from his eye and rolled down his blackened cheek. He didn't cry from the pain or for the death of the girl or in anticipation of the next fight. He cried because the training was taking too long. He cried for a different little girl that he loved desperately, but feared he would never see again.

# CHAPTER 28

## An Oath of the Mage

For Beck, the fighting arena became endless days of brutal contests of will and strength. After defeating the bull and the girl and healing his atrocious burns, he faced an array of deadly threats—vicious creatures, simulated natural disasters, and even the disease of his own body. His instructors expected him to defeat them all.

And, he did.

But, amid the success in the arena and always in the forefront of his mind were thoughts of his incredible failure as a parent. *Oh, how Kiernan must despise me!* She had been right the entire time and instead of listening to his wife, he abandoned her, forcing her to go after Kenley and face Avalon Ravener on her own. No amount of victory in the ring could assuage the self-loathing he felt.

When the last challenge ended, the instructors in the stands commended his efforts with thunderous applause, and Arias walked out to greet him.

"You did well, Beck," the Mage commented with a smile. "Your healing skills are remarkable. The best I have ever seen in an apprentice."

Beck looked up at the silver-haired Mage. "But, I hesitated with the little girl."

"Yes, but one time only and you learned from your mistake. Do you know that many apprentices stay in the arena for hours suffering burn after burn because they cannot bring themselves to harm a child? Evil comes in all guises and you knew not to be fooled by an innocuous cloak. You have the heart of a warrior, Beck. I am not suggesting that you enjoyed killing the girl, but you are seasoned in battle and are intelligent enough to know not doing so would only have painfully prolonged the inevitable."

His tall guide pointed to a teepee that had somehow materialized behind him. "You are ready for the journey of observation. Go to your death bravely, apprentice."

What did that mean? Beck shook his head and scrambled into the second tent, the impatience of a man still within him. Inside, he noticed the same circle of stones and tin cup as the first teepee. Sitting, he drank the potion and fell into a deep sleep.

****

When Beck awoke and exited the tent, he was surprised to find that he was standing in the city of Iserport. He had not been to the city in many years, but recognized the buildings from his previous visits with Kiernan. A woman passed by and he smiled at her in greeting, but she looked right through him.

Arias Sarphia glided up to him and answered his unspoken question. "No, the people cannot see you. This journey is for observation only."

Together, mentor and apprentice walked the streets, unnoticed, and Arias pointed out the things he wished for Beck to see. They studied the behaviors of men and women in countless settings and circumstances. The strengths and weaknesses of humankind were laid bare for him to observe—greed, envy, apathy, hatred, racism, and jealousy mixed with altruism, love, compassion, resilience, curiosity, and intelligence.

The strongest motivators for the actions of people Beck observed were the most primal—basic desire for love and family and freedom. Conversely, he witnessed the devastating effects when these desires were not fulfilled.

He walked at Arias' side for leagues over the land of Massa as his Mage guide imparted all of the wisdom he had gained over the centuries. Beck learned of man's ethical responsibility toward the earth. He discovered what the destruction of the island's natural resources did to the quality of the air and the ability to sustain life. He glimpsed the possibility of futuristic technologies for harnessing the wind and sun to create power.

Through observation, he studied the languages of all the different races—including the Malakai. He learned of the existence of other islands in the Arounda Ocean, some three times the size of Massa, and the people that populated them.

For days and days, he walked beside his educator and witnessed the effects of disease and how it spreads among unsuspecting people. They traveled to the rural areas of the island and Beck observed the results of poverty, famine and drought.

At the end of the journey, he understood human existence on an intellectual level that far surpassed his previous awareness and even commented on this to his guide.

The man held up a finger. "Yes, to learn and observe is critical to personal growth. However, you must also be able to feel what others feel. True power is the miraculous by-product of our experiences." With that statement, the third teepee came into view and Arias uttered the now familiar, but still bewildering, phrase. "Go to your death bravely, apprentice."

Beck entered the tent numb with heartache. The parallels were not lost on him. For all of his achievements here, he was a disappointment in his own world. For all the power he gained, he would be unable to use it to save his family. Too much time had passed. Weeks now. Far too long for anyone to be in the presence of evil, but especially a little girl.

There was always the chance that Kiernan, Rogan, and Airron had found a way to save Kenley. He clung to that hope, but still tears of helplessness fell from his eyes as he lifted the third cup to his lips with shaking hands and drank.

\*\*\*\*

When Beck came to, Arias waited for him outside of the tent. This time, he walked the earth at the side of his guide not as himself, but as the personas of others.

He was a woman giving birth for the first time and suffered through the excruciating pain of labor followed by the poignant wonderment of bringing a new human being into the world. He cried in pain when a child of his own body died in his arms, and cried with joy when another child was brought back from the brink of death with the healing arts.

He was a middle-aged man gravely ill with sickness and filled with worry of how his family would survive without him as chronic, debilitating pain pulsated through his body.

He was a young boy and experienced how it affected the human spirit to be ridiculed and bullied.

He was a Cyman warrior, oppressed to the point of listless stagnation from having fundamental freedoms stripped from his life.

The months passed.

Then, the years.

Beck's beard, sprinkled now with gray, reached to his chest. In all that time, he never once forgot Kiernan or his children. Were they all still alive? Were his boys strong strapping men now? It may even be that Kiernan had remarried by this time.

In the end, he had been unable to save Kenley but did not regret his decision. It took a very long time to acknowledge, but he now understood that he made the only choice available to him under the circumstances. It is the responsibility of a parent to protect their young, and he never could have lived with himself or looked Kiernan in the eye again had he not tried everything in his power to try and save his daughter.

When the last teepee came into view, he almost turned away from it. His education was at long last at an end, but what did his old world hold for him? Did he still have a family to return to? How would people view him now? Would they even recognize him?

He finally understood the phrase that Odawa and Arias Sarphia said to him repeatedly.

He *had* experienced death.

At every phase of his journey, old beliefs and assumptions were discarded for new awareness. What he had been had died, but what he was now had been born.

He was Mage.

\*\*\*\*

"Deliver the oath."

Beck knelt before Arias Sarphia, took his hand and, even though he had never been taught the words, they rolled off his tongue. "I vow to employ the teachings of the Mage for the greater good of humanity. I vow that all actions will be conducted in good faith and without deceit. I vow never to use the arts to cause harm to the innocent, and I vow to destroy evil utterly and without remorse. I am now and forevermore, Mage."

Arias nodded and placed a hand on his shoulder. "You are a young Mage and still have much to learn, observe and experience, but I am very proud of you. You did well."

Beck bowed his head in deep respect. "My sincere gratitude to you, Mage Arias."

"Please stand." The centuries-old Mage looked directly in his eyes when he stood before him. "Use your power wisely, Beck. With the exception of the Oracle, you now have insights and knowledge that none in your world possess. Your understanding of life's truths is integral to your ability to serve the people of Massa. You are expected to be patient and compassionate, a teacher, and a protector. You are a master of all, Mage Beck."

"I will do my best." He paused. "You mention an Oracle. Who is the Oracle?"

"A woman who lives on the island, although she does not stay in one place for long. She has the unique ability to see events in every dimension. In her mind, she can travel all of the worlds and this capacity bestows on her divine power and acumen. Seek her out if you ever need a patron."

Beck raised his eyebrows. "I think I did meet her in the village of the Malakai, but didn't get the impression that she was very friendly."

"She is your friend, Mage. On that you can depend." Arias handed Beck a black cloak similar to the one that Galen Starr wore when Beck last saw him in Nysa.

"Black?" Beck questioned.

"You have not yet earned the white," he said with a wink. "And, let us hope that it is a very long time until you do. Farewell, Mage." Arias Sarphia turned from him then and was gone.

Overwhelmed with unexpected emotion, Beck entered the tent. It had been many years since he last had done so, but he remembered what to do. Sitting down on the floor, he picked up the tin cup and drank for the last time.

****

Beck's eyes fluttered open, and he felt exhausted and hungry, all of his human needs clamoring to be met for the first time in a very long time. Exiting the tent, he found that he was back in the village of Torg where he started his journey, but it was empty. The tents and huts and villagers were all gone.

A bundle on the ground caught his notice, and he looked down. Digby's old backpack laid in the same place he left it long ago. It still sat there, untouched. How odd. He thought for sure someone would have taken it by now and used its contents. Shrugging, he picked up the pack and threw his new black cloak around his shoulders. He turned for one last look behind him and noted with amusement that the teepee was gone now also.

Picking his way through the village that was no more, he suddenly stopped when his Mage senses detected another person nearby. He scanned the area carefully. "You there, by the tree, you may come out now."

An old woman walked out from behind the tree.

*Ah, the mysterious Oracle.*

"I see that a Mage walks the earth again," she observed in a gravelly voice.

Beck nodded. "Do you need help? Is there anything I can do for you?"

She shook her gray head and smiled. "No, but there is much I can do for you. The Oracle will be your eyes when the time comes."

"When will I need you and where can I find you?"

She nodded in satisfaction. "Now, you ask the right questions."

"What have you seen, Oracle?"

"A beast comes."

"How do I defeat it?"

"You will not defeat it. I see six others who will battle the beast."

"When?"

"Not for a very long time, but do not concern yourself, Mage. When the time comes, I will find you." The old woman gave him a wide, toothless grin, and shuffled off behind the tree again and disappeared.

Her enigmatic message did not disturb him as it once surely would have. What will be, will be, he thought. If a threat surfaced, he would rise up to meet it. Until then, he would put it out of his mind.

He resumed his walk out of the village, but took a different route this time. After so many years of traveling the land with Arias, he now knew a far shorter way than the one he had taken previously.

He hoped Aquataine still operated waterway transportation and that a boat would be available. If not, he would have to walk. He didn't have any coin to purchase a horse.

As he traveled through Haventhal, he tried not to think about a reunion with his family—wasn't sure he wanted to experience the pain of what he may find. But, thoughts of them continued to creep into his consciousness. Especially, his wife. A love like the one he shared with Kiernan was impossible to forget. Extraordinary in every way, her beauty, her compassion and her strength never failed to move him. Best friend, partner, lover. She was all these things and so much more. But, he loved her most for the way she loved him. He was a better man by virtue of having Kiernan Everard Atlan in his life.

Did he still?

The answer to that question was the one he dreaded the most.

When he finally arrived at the Aquataine grate, he was pleased to discover that it had been kept clear of overgrowth. a good sign that the watershifters were still allowing passage.

An Elven Gardien appeared, but he simply nodded at Beck and then melted back into the forest as quietly as he came. Fortunately, the Elf must have recognized him somehow, even though the Gardien looked far too young to remember him.

Beck climbed through the grate and descended the limestone steps into the caves of the watershifters. The little water port village was deserted as it was late at night here, but he felt relief at sight of the boat anchored at the dock. Oddly, it looked very similar to the one Digby owned.

Beck continued forward, but then stopped in his tracks when Digby appeared on the boat's deck. He waved his arms and his tall body jumped in the air to get his attention. "Prince Beck! You made it!"

The watershifter knelt as Beck neared.

"Dear Highworld, Digby, I'm surprised to find you still here."

The watershifter shrugged his thin shoulders. "I promised you I would wait, Your Grace."

"But, all this time? I'm not sure what to say or how to thank you."

Digby's face registered confusion. "You are actually back much sooner than I expected, Your Grace."

"Sooner than you expected?"

"Yes."

Beck's heart skipped a beat. "Digby, just how long *have* I been gone?"

The watershifter scrunched up his face in thought. "Oh, nine or ten hours."

Beck's hand flew to his face. The beard was gone. "But…that means that I've only been gone from Nysa for a little over three days." His legs threatened to buckle when he realized what that meant.

He still had a family to go home to. There was still hope for Kenley.

Digby nodded, but Beck didn't see it. He was already stepping onto the boat. "Please rise, Digby and get me to the Kondor grate as fast as you can. There is no time to waste."

"Still impatient I see," remarked the watershifter with a wry grin.

"You are wrong, my friend. Impatience does not drive me this day. It is love."

Digby looked at him, tilting his head in consideration. "There is something very different about you, Your Grace."

"Yes, Digby, there is," Beck agreed.

# CHAPTER 29

## Into the Jaws

Airron walked beside Rogan across the undulating stone terrain, his soft leather boots kicking up wisps of dust with each step. The sun was making its crawl into the western horizon, but intense heat still hung over the land. Airron wiped at the sweat beading on his forehead.

"Don't worry, my friend, I will be guarding your back," Rogan assured him.

"It's my front that I am worried about."

"Unless Avalon Ravener has developed immunity to fire, she doesn't stand a chance against the two of us."

Airron wished he could feel as confident. He would have died both times he had gone up against the witch had help not intervened. Besides, it wasn't Rogan who would be fighting this day. At least not initially. The Dwarf's role was to find and remove Kenley from harm. With no spell casting or combat experience to offer, Diamond remained at the camp to care for Kenley once she was freed.

That left Kiernan and Sapphire to help him battle Avalon.

"Do you think it will work?" Rogan asked.

Airron snorted. "Oh, yes, the prospect of my death will draw the witch out. Just the sight of me sends her into a screeching tantrum every time. Trust me, it's not pretty."

Rogan turned around. "I don't see the others."

"You're not supposed to. It is called an invisibility spell for a very important reason."

"I didn't realize how cheeky you get when you are nervous."

"I'm not nervous. I am resigned."

Airron wiped the sweat again with the back of his hand, but it wouldn't be long now. He could see the cave entrance now and the large, one-eyed figures standing on the ledge in front. Movement caused him to squint in the glare. Below the ledge, five of the Cymans were making their way down the mountain and one carried a child in his arms. "Demon's breath, what is she up to?"

"She's bringing Kenley to us? Something is not right."

"I know, but be ready," he warned Rogan. "Whatever happens, take Kenley and run."

Rogan's only reply was a grunt. A grunt of defiance or acknowledgement? He hoped the latter, and his friend didn't attempt any heroics where he was concerned. Kenley was the important one, not him.

The silence was deafening as they drew closer to the witch's sorcerous jaws.

The Cymans had reached the valley floor, but Airron's eyes were again drawn upward when Avalon appeared at the cave entrance using the body of the young girl she murdered at the mining settlement east of here.

She watched him come and when he was within shouting distance, she yelled down to him. "Approach no further, Elf! You are in perfect killing range right where you are."

"I am here for the girl!"

"Of course, you are."

"Give me the girl and I will turn myself over to you to do with as you wish."

Avalon snickered. "How noble. But, why would I want a dried up, marked bodyshifter like you when I have a young pureblood on my hands?"

The comment gave him pause, as it was his first inkling into Avalon's motives. "Because you want me dead and you know it."

"I can have both."

"I might have something to say about that."

"Where is the earthshifter?"

"Busy."

He could see her shrug. "My plans will work with any *Savitar* body. Ready to give up yours?"

"Actually, I have grown pretty fond of it."

The Cymans stopped and stood fifty paces away, Kenley struggling in the arms of the soldier holding her. Airron felt a sudden shift in the air, and a slight breeze brushed past him. It must have been the women. The time was now. He needed to goad Avalon off her perch so that Sapphire and Kiernan could do their part.

"Remember," he said to Rogan. "Grab Kenley."

"Three down and two to go," Avalon trilled in a singsong, confident voice.

Airron shook his head in confusion. "Riddles again, Avalon?"

"Purebloods, Elf!  This is about salvaging what the shifters have squandered away. Massa will be a land where the strong rule the weak, not the other way around!  My brother was right, but I will admit that his methods were flawed. I don't need a Demon Army to help me succeed. Not when I will have pliable purebloods under my control. Together, we will be invincible!"

As if rehearsed, one of the Cymans stepped forward and turned the child around, lifting her up.

"Noooo!"  A heartbreaking wail pierced the air and suddenly Janin became visible as she sprinted out of the circle of invisibility and toward the Cymans.

Airron cursed when he realized that it wasn't Kenley Atlan that the Cyman was holding, but Jala Radek.

"Maman!" cried the girl when she saw her mother, little hands reaching for Janin.

Rogan yelled for his wife and sprinted after her.

"Damn it!  Rogan!  It's a trap!" Airron growled after him.

Rogan didn't get far, and neither did Janin. In midstride, Janin smashed face first into an unseen barrier and was thrown back onto the stone floor. The force of the impact rendered her unconscious. Rogan reached his wife just as the five Cymans turned around and started back toward the steps cut into the mountain.

Airron couldn't see Sapphire, but heard her voice. "Rogan!  I cut a hole in the shield!  Go through now before it collapses."

With a worried glance at his wife, Rogan shot to his feet and raced toward Sapphire's voice.

"Now!" she screamed.

Rogan leapt into the air at her command, summoned fire, and hurled a fiery spear at the Cyman furthest away from his daughter. The Cyman tried to dodge the flaming projectile, but he was too slow. The soldier roared as his clothes caught fire and the flames licked rapidly over his body. He crashed to the ground and writhed in pain as he tried unsuccessfully to douse the blaze.

Rogan kept running.

Avalon stepped further out onto the ledge, threw her arm out, and a large fragment of loose rock at the base of the mountain pitched toward the unsuspecting Dwarf.

"Watch out, Rogan!" Airron yelled, running now, too.

Rogan ducked just in time, the stone missile missing him by mere inches.

The Cymans almost made it back to the mountain with Jala when another scream filled the air and another Cyman went down.

Avalon threw her arm out again, and the invisibility cloak was ripped away.

Kiernan, visible now, had reached the fleeing Cymans and was trying to wrench Jala out of the arms of the soldier carrying her. From behind, another Cyman grabbed Kiernan around the neck, lifting her off her feet. As she dangled in the air, she kicked out and thrashed violently in an attempt to free herself from the man's grip around her throat.

Sapphire, dark hair flowing behind her as she ran, pointed and screamed at Kiernan's attacker.

"*Bindeno!*"

The soldier let go of Kiernan and dropped to the ground like a felled tree with his arms and legs glued tight to his sides.

Rogan summoned a club of fire and stalked toward the Cyman holding Jala.

Seeing his opening, Airron shifted into his eagle form and took flight. In just a few flaps of his powerful wings, he cleared the distance to his target. Diving toward the fighters on the ground, he reached out with his curved talons and snatched the little girl out of the one-eyed creature's arms. With his burden struggling beneath him, he wheeled away from the group. Flying low to the ground, he pulled up when he saw the blonde sorceress rushing forward. He set the girl down gently and it was at that moment that a crushing blast struck him from behind and sent him flying end over end through the air.

The last thing he remembered was the sound his skull made when it hit the stone ground.

****

As soon as Airron plucked Jala to safety, Kiernan unsheathed her sword and pointed it at the towering Cyman's throat. "Where is Kenley Atlan? Tell me now!"

Before he could respond, Sapphire jumped onto his back and grabbed his head in her hands. "*Morbendi.*"

"Sapphire!"

She shrugged as she jumped free of the falling giant. "That's one less enemy we have to fight later. We have Jala, let's go."

With a growl, Kiernan called Rogan off his chase of the last Cyman and the three of them sprinted back toward camp.

Kiernan risked a cautious look back, but Avalon was no longer standing in the cave entrance.

When they reached Janin, Rogan bent down, lifted his wife into his arms, and continued running. Kiernan sucked in her breath when they came across Airron with an anxious Diamond, holding Jala, standing over him.

Sapphire cast a hover spell and Airron rose off the ground. She guided his lifeless body through the air with her hand around his wrist.

At the campsite, Rogan set Janin down tenderly on one of the bedrolls, and then reached for his daughter. "Are you all right?" he asked her, wiping her hair out of her face.

"Daddy! Reilly!" the little girl squealed, pointing back toward the cave.

He pressed her face into his shoulder. "I know, baby, and we're going to get him out. I promise."

Kiernan looked back toward the mountain. Three Cymans were dead, one fled, and another still lay incapacitated by Sapphire's binding spell. Avalon Ravener would not make another appearance now and that left her with no other choice. She had to go in after the children.

Diamond crouched next to Airron where a frightening amount of blood matted the hair on the back of his head. "I need bandages!"

Rogan hurried to his pack and retrieved them for the sorceress. She accepted them, but looked up at Kiernan with concern in her eyes. "I wish I could do more, but I'm not a healer."

Kiernan grimaced at Airron's ashen pallor. He looked close to death. "I know. Keep pressure on the wound and watch over him until I get back. He will be all right. He has to be."

Rogan, who had been tending to a waking Janin, glanced up at her with a question in his eyes.

"Yes. I am going in," she answered.

He nodded. "I expected as much. Diamond, will you stay and look after Airron and my two girls?"

"Of course."

"I am coming, as well," declared Sapphire.

Kiernan nodded and the trio took off back toward the mountain once again.

"Should I set an invisibility spell?" asked Sapphire.

"Don't bother," Kiernan replied. "She knows we're coming. Just remember the plan. Bind her so I can mindshift her. Rogan, the Cymans will be up to you."

"Hope they like heat," he growled.

It didn't take long to make it back and after passing the Cyman on the ground, Kiernan started up the stairs that led to the cave entrance. She raced upward, slowing only when she neared the top ledge. Holding her hand in the air to stop the others, she listened carefully for sounds inside, but didn't hear anything.

Cautiously, she scaled the remaining few steps and crouched on the lip of the shelf. She peered into the cave. It was empty. She motioned for the others to follow, and they hugged the left wall as they walked further into Avalon's lair.

It surprised Kiernan to find the chamber decorated with tapestries, heavy furniture pieces, and lit braziers that cast large dancing shadows on the walls. Then, again, Avalon had been living here for quite a few years.

She stopped and glanced up at the wall on her left. Two sets of iron shackles were set into the stone at just the right height to hold a man's outstretched arms and legs.

This was where Avalon held Beck.

Filled with fury at the sight, she almost screamed out a challenge to the witch, anxious to meet her face-to-face. With effort, restraint prevailed, and she turned her head away in revulsion.

Advancing forward silently, she exited the main chamber and entered another just as large and that held several blanketed pallets for sleeping. She was wondering just how many rooms this hideaway held when she saw three passageways branching off at the back of the room. She looked back at her companions. "We're going to have to split up."

Rogan nodded. "I don't like it, but it seems we have no choice."

"Be careful," she warned her friends. "Remember, if you find either of the children, just pick them up and run. Don't stop for anything or anyone else."

Kiernan walked to the passage on the left, Sapphire took the center, and Rogan, the far right.

Stepping into the dark and narrow tunnel, Kiernan wished she had a torch to light the way. In pitch blackness, she held her hands out against the walls to guide her way forward. After a few paces and a slight bend in the corridor, a faint glow came into view ahead.

Inching forward slowly, her hand suddenly lost contact with the wall to her left, and she realized there was another passageway or alcove off the corridor she was in.

Unfortunately, the realization came too late, and she didn't even have a chance to scream when an enormous hand snaked out and clamped over her mouth, dragging her into the dark depths of the recess.

# CHAPTER 30

## Betrayal

Rogan called light to his palm and the narrow corridor lit up in a soft yellow glow. He scowled at sight at the dark alcoves lining the walls, any of which could be hiding Avalon or her minions. Walking forward slowly, he looked into each recess warily as he passed, but all were empty. With the exception of his footsteps that rang with a hollow echo through the tomb-like tunnel, it was quiet.

Around a slight bend, the muted glow of another chamber appeared ahead. Moving faster now, he made his way through the passageway and strode out onto the shelf of a cliff face overlooking a depthless black canyon. He glanced to the left and saw Sapphire step clear of the center corridor, but Kiernan had yet to appear.

Straight ahead, directly across the way, stood another sheer cliff and the two were joined together by a long stone bridge that spanned the chasm between them.

On the cliff on the other side of the bridge stood Avalon, five Cyman soldiers, Reilly and Kenley. Alarmingly, both of the children had leather collars around their necks. A Cyman soldier held the leash attached to the collar on Reilly and Avalon held Kenley's leash.

Avalon Ravener didn't know it, but with that despicable act, she just purchased his silent vow that she would die that day. No quarter given. No mercy shown. Nothing short of the end of her existence in this world would satisfy him. It didn't matter at whose hand, as long as it came to pass.

"Sapphire, what a pleasant surprise," remarked Avalon. "Since you have so conveniently delivered the *Savitars* to me, I assume that you thought about our conversation. Does this mean you are you with me?"

"Yes, Avalon, I'm with you."

"Did you have to kill my Cymans on your way in?"

"They're your pets, and I don't trust them."

Rogan went cold inside.

Slowly, he stepped back into a crouch and faced Sapphire, summoning a ball of fire.

"Don't even think about it, shifter," she hissed. "Any fire you throw at me will be directed right back at you by my shield."

He shook his head at her in disgust and let the fire go. "After all you know of Avalon Ravener, how can you possibly ally yourself with her? Demon's breath, Sapphire, she killed your own mother and admitted as much to Beck."

Sapphire turned a hostile glare back toward Avalon. "So, it was you. I had my suspicions, but didn't want to believe it."

"What is that firebrand saying?" Avalon demanded.

"You killed my mother, Avalon?"

"Your mother?"

"Gemini Starr! Do not play dumb!"

Avalon shrugged her shoulders without even a pretense of remorse in the action. "I had no idea that Gemini Starr was your mother. Her death was payback for Adrian and that was all!"

The dark-haired sorceress clenched her fists.

"Sapphire! The world is ours for the taking! We will have five purebloods under our control. Don't grow soft on me now, girl! My rule will have no place in it for cowards!"

Sapphire continued to glower silently.

"Think of the power that will be yours, Sapphire! Together, we will rebuild the coven with you as the High Priestess. Every sorceress on the island will be under your thumb, and every Lord and Sovereign will bow to you!"

"I thought you were made of more than that, Sapphire," Rogan commented bitterly. "I never would have believed the promise of power would turn you to the side of evil."

"This isn't about power for me," Sapphire told him. "Massa is an island of magic, Rogan, and should be governed by magic users. I have always felt that way. We're stymied by the ridiculous laws of people far beneath us. Think about it! To this day, magic users remain in exile. Only their place of confinement has moved from Pyraan to Bardot. Do you see magic performed anywhere other than Bardot? No. There are thousands of shifters on the island, probably far more than anyone suspects, but they don't come forward because of the stigma attached. This cannot continue! Magic is too valuable to throw away. Whether through sorcery or shifting, as a people we need to explore the depths of magic's possibilities. With free rein, the strides we can make to create a more advanced society are limitless!" She shook her head. "My mother never understood this."

"And, neither do I! No decent human being would suggest the subjugation of others to achieve their goals. There are other, better ways."

"It is the law of nature, fireshifter. Those eliminated in the struggle for survival are trivial. Only the strong shall prevail."

Avalon clapped her hands. "Well said, Sapphire! I will ask again. Are you with me or against me?"

Sapphire sighed audibly. "It must be done. I am still with you."

"Wonderful! Now…wait, where is the bodyshifter?" Avalon asked.

"As good as dead," Sapphire told her.

"No, not as good as dead! Until, I see his corpse, he still lives to cause me trouble. I will see all of the *Savitars* dead once and for all, here today at Farout Falls!"

A scuffling commotion broke out at the far end of the shelf. Two Cyman soldiers held a struggling Kiernan between them. "Ah…here is the Princess now."

"Maman!" Kenley cried and tried to wrestle away from Avalon, but the leash around her neck pulled her up tight. Kenley's hands flew to her throat in an attempt to relieve the pressure Avalon was exerting.

"Stop! You're killing her!" Kiernan screamed and renewed her fight to break free from her captors.

Sapphire ignored the fuss and shouted over to Avalon. "What do you want me to do?"

"Don't harm the Princess yet! I will need her body to get the two boys out of Bardot." She looked across the chasm at Rogan. "Kill the fireshifter."

Rogan crouched again and faced Sapphire just as a furious roar resounded through the cavern. Rogan whipped his head around in time to witness a sinewy white ball of fury leap onto Avalon's back. She shrieked in surprise, but before Baya could tear into the sorceress' neck, she disappeared to the ground, although what shape she took Rogan could not see.

Kenley, the length of her leash now on the ground, turned toward Reilly and began to unbuckle his collar. For some reason, the Cyman holding Reilly stood by passively while Kenley tried to free his son.

Sapphire saw none of this as she had already turned to him with a menacing growl. Rogan searched wildly for a way past the sorceress to the bridge, but there was only the cliff wall to his left and an unfathomable drop to the right.

"*Reversi!*"

The spell caused Rogan's body to jerk upright from his crouch and to his horror, his feet began to shuffle backward toward the abyss. His arms floundered as he tried to stop his body from moving closer to a fatal plummet.

"Reilly! Kenley! Run!" The children would never be able to get away from the giant Cymans, but he had to try. He looked over his shoulder. One more step and he would be over.

"Baya! Lead the children to safety!" he cried in desperation.

If Kenley and Reilly could just manage to escape this chamber, they might have a chance. Maybe Airron had recovered. He could very well be on his way into the cavern now and would arrive in time to save Kiernan and the children.

The Elf did like his theatrics.

Rogan's heels hung over the ledge and stones and dirt dropped away, disappearing into the black hole. His life with Janin flashed before his eyes, and he actually managed a small smile despite regret at the pain his death would cause her.

Sapphire raised her hand to sweep him from the ledge at the same time that a thick fist lashed out and struck her in the side of her face.

It was one of the Cymans.

Sapphire collapsed to the shelf floor. Without hesitating, the soldier reached down, picked her up over his head and threw her into the chasm.

Rogan looked over his shoulder in shock and…fell.

He tried to grab the edge on his way past, but couldn't gain purchase on the loose dirt and gravel on the sharp precipice. For a heart-stopping moment, he was airborne, and then his body jerked to a sudden stop. The Cyman who killed Sapphire had Rogan's forearm grasped in an enormously strong hand. Rogan dangled from the soldier's grip and then the giant hoisted him back up onto the cliff ledge.

Panting from the flow of terror-induced adrenaline, Rogan looked up at the Cyman with confusion on his face, and then Kiernan was there, peeking around his body. "They are with us. Come on."

Rogan's heart still beat violently, but he got to his feet. Reilly, Kenley, Baya and the five Cymans on the other side of the chasm were running across the bridge.

Avalon was nowhere to be seen.

Kiernan sprinted out to meet the children and ushered them toward the ledge with Baya and the Cymans following quickly behind.

Finally recovered from his near death experience, Rogan met them as they stepped off the bridge. He picked up Reilly and ran toward the center tunnel. "Follow me!" Not bothering with light, he sprinted through the dark passageway with the others racing after him.

A now familiar, but just as horrifying, high-pitched scream ricocheted throughout the cavern, and the frenzied flap of beating wings pursued their retreat. Bursting through the narrow corridor, Rogan ran through the chamber with the wooden pallets.

"Hurry!" he heard Kiernan shout and the sound of pursuit grew louder and more threatening. "We're not going to make it!"

His lungs threatening to burst, Rogan ran faster with his burden. He made it to the main chamber and then skidded to a stop at the exit to look back. Kiernan was running in the middle of the Cymans and holding Kenley's hand.

Rogan's eyes widened in horror when the creature that was once Avalon Ravener exploded out of the center passageway and dove at Kenley, her clawed hands reaching to snap her up.

Kiernan bent down over Kenley, and pulled her close to her chest into a protective ball and rolled to the floor.

Avalon screeched in anger that her prey got away and wheeled around for another attempt.

Rogan set Reilly on the floor and summoned fire, but the confined space made it difficult to unleash for fear of harming those he was trying to save.

Avalon flew low over the heads of the beleaguered group and one of the Cymans jumped up and seized her leg. She squealed and beat her wings furiously around the Cyman's head in an attempt to untangle herself from the snare. The Cyman held on, and ripped her from the air, swinging her in a circle before sending her sailing toward the cave wall.

Before her body hit, she bodyshifted again and disappeared from sight.

Kiernan immediately got to her feet, picked up Kenley and ran. She waved at Rogan, "Go!"

He grabbed Reilly and started down the stairs on the outside of the mountain. He couldn't move as fast on the treacherous descent and the others quickly caught up to him.

When Rogan finally made it down to the valley floor, he hit the ground running. He did notice that two of the Cymans took the time to pick up their comrade who had been cursed with a binding spell and had been lying unmoving on the ground.

A few moments into their frantic escape, he heard the most horrific gurgling sound, a scream, and then a bestial yelp. Turning back, he saw Avalon, shifting once again into the female body she used in the cave, grip Kenley's leash in a vicious yank that sent the little girl crashing to the ground. Kiernan and Baya were lying still on the stone.

Three of the Cymans worked together to gather up Kiernan and the Draca Cat and ran to where Rogan stood waiting.

Dazedly, Kiernan came to and struggled with the Cyman holding her. "Kenley! What is happening to Kenley?"

Avalon waved her free hand and Kenley twitched upright to her feet and started walking toward them.

"Do as I command, girl!" Avalon yelled at her.

With a trembling arm, Kenley pointed and the air around them began to swirl in a strengthening wind. She moved her hand in a circular motion and a maelstrom of dirt and pebbles peppered the space between them. Tears created dirty tracks down Kenley's face as she was forced to airshift against her will, and the magic surged from her in an uncontrolled torrent.

One of the Cymans who had stopped to stare, realized his mistake and turned to run to avoid the advancing tornado.

A cry wrenched from Kenley's throat as she turned the growing vortex directly at the running Cyman, and the strength of the wind sucked him up into the center of the funnel, spun him around, and spit him out again to soar through the air and crash into the ground.

"Kenley! Rogan, what's happening?" Kiernan screamed when the air became so thick with debris that her daughter disappeared behind the gray mist of the whirlwind.

Rogan bent over Reilly to protect him with his body. "I can't see anything!"

A scuffle broke out beside him. One of the Cymans grabbed the arm of another.

"Let go, Cyrus!" the soldier yelled trying to jerk himself free.

"Arlen, you can't go out there!"

"The witch will 'urt 'er, Cyrus! I just can't stand by and let that 'appen to a little girl!"

"But, you will be killed!"

Arlen suddenly bellowed a laugh that to Rogan's ears, bordered on madness. "Don't you see, Cyrus? I am makin' this choice!" he yelled over the wind. "For the first time in my life, I am doin' what *I* want to do! Not a choice the dark Mage forces on me or the witch or even Captain Lucin. I am finally free, Cyrus! I am free and I am goin' to save that little girl!"

"Arlen, no!"

"I'm comin', Kenley!" With that declaration, Arlen ran into the mist and the whirlwind swallowed him whole.

Cyrus cried out for his friend several more times, and then his voice became muffled in the fog that surrounded them all. Gale-force winds battered at them furiously, and Rogan was finding it difficult to remain on his feet. Kiernan reached out to him and threaded her arm through his to help keep her balance.

"We have to get away from here!" she shouted over the din.

The cyclone continued to grow in diameter, and Rogan lost all sense of direction. Grasping Reilly tight with one hand and Kiernan with the other, he felt the terrifying pull of the vortex. Kiernan was right, but which way to run? If he chose wrong, he could lead them directly into the eye of the storm.

"Rogan!" Kiernan's legs were swept out from under her, and his grip on her arm was the only thing that prevented her from flying free. Her body hovered over the ground as he fought to pluck her from the power of the tornado.

"Don't let go!" he shouted and struggled to move against the buffeting tempest. Muscles straining, teeth gritted, he refused to let go of either Reilly or Kiernan, but the potent pull of the raging twister hammered at his grip on both.

Suddenly, the wind lessened around them, and Kiernan fell to the ground. She scrambled back upright and Rogan felt her stiffen beside him. "It can't be," she whispered. "He's dead."

He followed her gaze and peered through the mist.

The silhouette of a lone man walked toward them. Dressed in black, a long cloak billowed out behind him as he strode undaunted through the wreckage of the night.

# CHAPTER 31

## Utterly and Without Remorse

Somehow, the air remained clear around the imposing figure, and he took on recognizable features as he strode to the Cyman, Cyrus, and settled a large hand on his shoulder. "Your friend is at peace with his decision. Do not belittle or underestimate the power of choice."

The Cyman nodded almost hypnotically, and Kiernan fell to her knees in disbelief at the mirage before her.

It was Beck.

Standing tall and resolute before her in his black cloak, he reminded her nothing so much as his grandfather, Galen Starr.

He turned his gaze to look down at her, kneeling on the ground. "Hello, my love."

All she could do was stare at him, afraid that if she said a word, he would wink out of existence.

Beck wasn't supposed to come home.

"Have you forgotten your husband so soon?"

She shook her head, ashamed that she had not believed in him.

"Do you remember how desperately he loves you?"

Her body trembled and she could hardly see him through her tears. "Remind me," she whispered.

Giving her that dimpled smile that was so achingly familiar, he reached down and lifted her into his strong arms. Hair whipping around her face, she wrapped her arms and legs around him and buried her head into his chest. He stroked her back tenderly. "For a time, I thought that I had lost you," he told her huskily. "You can never know what that did to me. To have you here in my arms, to smell the sweetness of your skin, to feel your heart beating against mine, is almost more than I can handle. You are all that is beautiful in my life, Kiernan Atlan. I live for you and I would die for you. Do you remember now?"

Head still buried in his shoulder, she said, "It's a good start."

He chuckled.

She lifted her head to look into his face. "You came home," she stated, surprised to see tears of his own trickling down his face.

"I promised you I would."

"I know, and I wanted to believe you...it's just that—"

He reached his hand up to place a finger on her lips. "You don't have to explain. I understand. Are you all right now?"

Kiernan nodded and he set her on the ground. "Beck, Avalon has Kenley!"

"I guess I'll just have to get her back then."

His confidence and strength infused her like a palliative cure, but outside of his arms, she felt cold and alone. She wanted nothing more than to cling to him and lose herself within the safety of his embrace, but she resisted the urge. Kenley needed him.

Beck turned and reached out to pat Reilly Radek on the head and then traded enthusiastic grips with Rogan with the deep affection of long-time friends.

Seeing Baya lying on the ground, Beck dropped to his knees and placed his hands on the cat's body. After a few seconds of Beck's focused attention, the Draca Cat stirred and then sat up onto her haunches dazedly.

Without another word, Beck turned directly into the whirling mass of the tornado and disappeared within its depths.

The sight panicked her, and she felt like she was losing him again. "Beck!"

As if in response to her shout, the roar of the wind came to an abrupt halt and the swirling air slowed. Kiernan covered her head for protection as the debris-filled murk fell to the ground with a relentless pattering on the stone.

Then, there was silence.

The space around them cleared and Kiernan saw Arlen and the other Cyman who had been caught up in the cyclone, lying on the ground.

Beck stood directly in front of Avalon and Kenley. Their daughter, still leashed, covered her face as tears still poured from her eyes.

"How did you do that?" she heard Avalon demand of Beck.

He held a palm up in front of her. "Before you think for a single second more that you can use my daughter as a tool for evil, let me explain the truth of your situation. You stand before a Mage."

Even from the distance, Kiernan could hear Avalon suck in her breath. It mirrored Kiernan's own. Beck was a Mage? In such a short time?

"Kiernan, come here, please." He didn't turn around when he said it, but she heard him clearly. She hurried over to his side. "Take Kenley back to your camp. I will be along in a moment." As soon as the words were out of his mouth, the leash fell from Avalon's hand.

Kenley, freed from her constraint, ran to Beck and threw her small arms around his legs. He smiled and wrapped an arm around her. "I didn't want to hurt anyone, Daddy. I could not stop what I was doing!"

"I know, baby. This is not your fault. Please go with Maman now."

Kenley peered around Beck's legs at the Cyman called Arlen lying on the ground and began to cry. "I killed him!"

"No, Ken, you did not kill him. He still lives, and I will heal him in a few moments. I promise. Can you be a big girl and run along with Maman now?"

She nodded and reluctantly let go of Beck's legs to take Kiernan's hand.

Kiernan looked askance at Avalon. She stood rigid with her mouth open wide as though an invisible wad of cloth had been stuffed into it. And, while everything else looked frozen in place, her eyes spun wildly.

"You…you will be along in a moment?" Kiernan questioned Beck.

He nodded, but still had not taken his eyes off Avalon.

As Kiernan led Kenley away, she heard him say, "You have committed your last act of violence on this island, Avalon Ravener."

**\*\*\*\***

In the now clear and calm twilight, Beck stared at the woman who had caused such devastation on the island and to his family and yet he hesitated, his two oaths at war inside him. As a shifter, it was difficult to take a human life—any life—but as a Mage he had vowed to defeat evil utterly and without remorse. Killing an enemy in battle was one thing, but to stand here and kill a woman in cold blood was quite another.

He knew that Arias Sarphia would not approve, but he lifted his hand and released the ball of air inserted in her mouth, and let the invisible ropes around her body slip away.

Avalon instantly sucked in a deep breath and rubbed her arms. "A Mage you may be, but a very inexperienced one."

He tipped his head in agreement. He knew he still had much to learn.

"Looking back on this very moment, you will remember that it was your hesitation to kill me that proved fatal. You never should have released me from my bonds." Avalon disappeared, seemingly into thin air.

Beck cursed and spun around searching for the sorceress. With a shake of his head, he remembered the little girl he killed during Mage training. His blood oath and compassion for humanity had led him to make the same mistake twice, but he now realized the error in his thinking. Avalon Ravener was not human. What humanity she may have once held had been destroyed long ago when she invited evil into her heart, and she deserved neither his charity nor his mercy. The words of his Mage oath flashed in his mind.

*Destroy evil utterly and without remorse.*

His unequivocal acceptance of that phrase came to him at the same time that Avalon's spell slammed into his back. His body flew through the air, but he now had his own spell to use.

"*Pilloni.*"

A pillow of air caught and cradled him inches before he would have slammed into the hard sandstone floor of the valley. He jumped to his feet, but Avalon must have cast an invisibility spell because he couldn't see her. The landscape was so flat that even in the growing darkness, he could see the profiles of Kiernan, Rogan, Reilly and the Cymans walking to their camp, but Avalon was gone.

"I am here, Mage!"

Avalon stood on the ledge of the cave entrance.

He uttered the hover spell, and his arms windmilled through the air as his body zoomed toward the cave. He would definitely need more practice with this spell.

Avalon laughed and disappeared inside.

Beck made the ascent at a high rate of speed and landed hard, skidding across the floor and crashing into Avalon's mahogany table in the center of the chamber.

When his body came to a rest, he looked up and caught a glimpse of Avalon's black robe disappearing into the next chamber. He chased after her.

Chained to the wall in the main chamber for the duration of his last visit, he had never ventured this far into the cave. Pallets for sleeping lay scattered throughout the room and at the back wall three more passageways. He picked the corridor on the left and sprinted through, casting out with a detection spell for the presence of life. It was empty, so he didn't slow until he saw the light of the opening up ahead.

At the exit, he stepped out of the tunnel and found himself in a cavernous chamber split by an unfathomable, dark chasm. A stone bridge spanned the gap between the ledge he was on and another, much wider ledge on the other side.

He looked to the right and noticed a woman on the ground. He ran to her and turned her head.

It was Sapphire.

He ran his fingers over her body in a healing probe and found that the only recent injury was a very hard blow to the head.

"Sapphire! Wake up."

The sorceress stirred. When her eyes focused on him, she scrambled away as if afraid of him.

Beck held out his hands to calm her. "It's just me, Sapphire. Relax."

"What happened?" she asked, looking around at her surroundings.

He shrugged. "I just came in here and found you like this. You don't remember?"

She shook her head. "Where are the others?"

"Back at their camp, but why would they leave you in here?" He reached out a hand to help her to her feet.

"I don't know. I really can't remember anything."

"Well, you did take quite a wallop. Do you think you can walk?"

A guttural laugh cut through the cavern. Across the abyss, Avalon appeared from behind a boulder.

Beck pushed Sapphire back behind him with one arm and moved to stand in front of her.

Avalon shook her head. "And, you call yourself a Mage? Let's see," she said holding up her fingers to count. "Your sorcery is rudimentary and pathetic. You let me go when you should have killed me. And, you have committed your second fatal mistake of the evening."

"Such as?"

"You turned your back to a sorceress."

"Thank you for the save, Avalon," Beck heard Sapphire say right before a powerful kick sent him sailing over the ledge and out into the air. Stunned over the fact that his friend had been conspiring with Avalon Ravener, it took him a moment to recover. He fell over thirty feet before casting a spell to stop his descent, and he shot back upward through the air.

He landed smoothly this time, in the middle of the stone bridge with Avalon on one end and Sapphire on the other. Standing sideways, he held one hand, palm out, to each sorceress and took a deep breath.

Time slowed as he drew on the power of his magic to calm his mind and body, and every minute detail of the cavern came into sharp focus. The faded detail etched into the stone balustrade, the tiny cracks that scattered the surface of the bridge, and even a larger fault line that ran deep under the mountain floor.

He would not hesitate again.

There was a lesson in every failure, and every lesson would make him a better man, a better Mage.

Lowering his head, he sought the power of the earth, harnessed its strength and brought it forward, drawing it in. He directed his magic at the fault line deep within the core of the rock and struck at it with every bit of power he held.

The mountain trembled.

The cracks in the surface of the bridge fractured and spread with ominous snapping sounds as the fault began to quake and widen.

Beck looked up and time slammed back into place. Although it felt longer, the span of one heartbeat occurred since he landed on the bridge from his fall.

With a strenuous scream, he pushed out with his palms and both women sailed back through the air. The bigger threat was Avalon so he turned and sprinted toward her first. Hand out, he pinned her to the ground in a sorcerous grip of steel.

The reluctance was gone.

He approached the woman who had killed Bajan, Gemini Starr, Citrine, the dark-haired girl whose young face stared back at him now, and the countless other nameless souls just for the use of their bodies. He couldn't forget that the woman also tried to kill him, his wife and his daughter.

*Destroy evil utterly and without remorse.*

Leaning down, he took her head into his hands and she screamed in denial. In the end, he did show some mercy. Avalon deserved much worse. She deserved to suffer.

"*Morbendi.*"

Her head rolled to the side, lifeless eyes wide, and her mouth still open in a soundless scream.

Turning, he sprinted back onto the bridge, now swaying dangerously from the threatening grumble of the mountain. He felt one end collapse and had to jump in a running leap to the other ledge as the surface of the bridge disappeared beneath his feet.

He landed in a crouch and scanned the cliff.

Sapphire was gone, but she would not get far.

He ran through the center, narrow passageway and came out into the room with the pallets just as the sorceress erupted out of the corridor on the left.

She skidded to a stop when she saw him and held up her hands when he walked toward her. "Please, Beck. Don't do this."

*Destroy evil utterly and without remorse.*

 "Beck, please."

He kept walking.

"I ask for your forgiveness! You are a shifter, Beck Atlan! Remember that! Remember your blood oath to serve and protect!"

"You forfeited the right to ask for forgiveness when you sided with evil."

As she lowered her head and cried, Beck cast the killing curse for the second time.

# CHAPTER 32

# Home

Diamond had just finished tying a fresh bandage around Airron Falewir's head when a massive explosion rocked the world. On instinct, she leaned over the Elf with her body as stone fragments from the mountain blasted into the air like balls of iron shot from a cannon. A gray cloud billowed outward from the mountain in a rippling, seething mass too far away to reach them.

Kiernan had been sitting down on a bedroll with Kenley, but now lurched to her feet. "Beck!"

Diamond covered her mouth with a fist and choked back a sob. Beck could never have survived such a destructive blast! *Dear Highworld, how much more can Kiernan take? How much loss and heartbreak is one woman expected to endure in a lifetime?*

"Uh, I can't breathe under here."

"Oh, sorry," she said and slid off Airron.

"What happened?" he asked.

"I'm not sure." Diamond stood and stared. Where a mountain once stood was now a smoldering pile of rubble and the vast blue of the Arounda Ocean glittering in the distance.

A huge boulder rolled free from the ruins. Rotating across the sandstone at considerable speed, the stone grew smaller as it covered the distance and soon arms and legs became visible sticking out of the rock. When the boulder made its last revolution, the stone broke apart and fell away.

A man stood.

It was Beck, and he was covered in what Diamond recognized from the Academy as an earthen coat of armor.

Kiernan began to laugh hysterically, wrenched back from a momentary spiral into darkness.

Airron, standing now, patted Rogan on the back as they exchanged grateful smiles that their friend was alive. The three children and Cymans whooped joyously.

Thoughtfully, Diamond watched Beck approach.

She didn't think the others could see it yet, but he wore his power and strength now like a second skin. As he should. He was Mage and virtually indestructible. With the command of sorcery and shifting, not to mention his political influence as a member of royalty, there wasn't a person on the island who could stand against him.

All of that power in the hands of one man would be terrifying to Diamond if not for one detail. Formidable beyond measure, he was also pure of heart. There wasn't an ounce of evil in Beck Atlan.

He smiled a crooked smile at his wife, and she picked up the sides of her dress and ran to him.

For all his might, she just hoped it would be enough.

Squatting down, she retrieved her diamond from her pack and stroked it anxiously. After Kiernan told her that Sapphire had turned against them, she realized it was the Spell Casting sorceress who had clouded her ability. Just before the explosion, she read her stone and discovered a frightening image.

The scene was hazy and indistinct, which meant that it would not happen for some time yet—many years perhaps. But, it *would* happen. Of that, she had no doubt.

A beast was headed for the shores of Massa. An implacable, sinister presence that would stop at nothing to achieve its goals. What those goals were or what shape the beast would come in, she didn't know, but it would come.

She took one more hard look at Beck Atlan—at his strength and kindness and newly acquired wisdom. The sight soothed her fears.

The Island of Massa was in very capable hands.

\*\*\*\*

"Give me one more, Baya." Airron leaned his head down so that his mouth lined up with the Draca Cat's muzzle. Baya exhaled the Healing Breath directly into his lungs, and he immediately felt the magic work its way through his body, mending his injuries. The pain, the aches, and the exhaustion melted away from his body like the molting of new skin.

When the last vaporous trail disappeared into his mouth, he stood and bowed to the cat. "Thank you, my friend."

Baya tilted her head in acknowledgement.

Airron removed the bandage around his head and watched his friends revel in spirited conversation.

It was over.

Avalon Ravener was dead, and they were still alive. He wished he could stay to celebrate with his friends, but he had somewhere to be.

Grabbing his pack from the ground, he walked over to join them. "Despite a delightful afternoon," he said, interrupting several conversations, "I must leave you now."

Kiernan bristled. "What? Where are you going?"

"Haventhal."

"At least travel with us to Elloree and take the waterways to Sarphia."

He shook his head and threw his pack at her. She caught it by the strap. "I can travel faster over land. You'll take care of my pack and clothes for me?"

"Of course." She gave him a hug. "Be careful."

Beck stepped forward, a layer of dirt still covering his hair and clothes. "It will take some time for me to escort the Cymans to Northfort, but we still need to have that talk. Will you return to Bardot soon?"

"With two nephews to help raise? Of course. Besides, I think Kane is going to be a master bodyshifter one day, and somebody has to teach the kid."

Beck threw his head back in a hearty laugh and after all they had been through, it sounded so innocent and so pure. He grabbed Airron in an embrace. "I hope you find what you seek. Come back to us soon."

"I will."

Beck released him and Rogan planted his feet in front of him with his arms crossed. "The only thing he is seeking is another girl to kiss. What has it been? Over a week now?"

"Fourteen days to be exact."

"When will I see you again?" Rogan asked.

"Are you going to cry?"

"Of course not, you blasted Elf! Just stay safe, all right."

Airron promised with a laugh and after a broad farewell to the rest of his companions, he walked behind one of the horses, undressed and shifted into his black Grayan wolf. The horse screamed and rolled his eyes in terror when he saw the large wolf appear at his side.

Slinking from behind the terrified animal, the wolf poised his muscular body to run, but suddenly stopped and turned, giving one last grin to the humans before loping off east toward Haventhal.

The wolf ran the entire day and night without stopping. The next morning, he crossed streams of water at the shallows and once on the other side, took time for a brief rest before pushing on.

He sensed other animals in the area, but they avoided him.

The wolf preferred the fertile forests of his homeland over the bleak landscape he now traveled, but didn't put too much thought into it. Soon, he would enter another forest, this one wetter and more humid.

He stopped one more time during the night for sleep and at last, footsore and exhausted, the wolf slithered into the city with the bright lights at dusk, careful to avoid notice.

At the back of a small stable, the air shimmered and Airron Falewir stood and opened the side door to the building and slipped inside.

Breathing in the familiar scent of his horses, a warm feeling came over him. He walked into the tack room and retrieved the spare tunic and leggings he kept there for this very purpose. Once dressed, he walked outside into the early evening. He only employed two servants at his home, a housekeeper and a groomsman, but they only came during the day and would be gone by now.

Airron didn't go into the house, there was no time. Instead, he strode through the grounds to the gate in front, yanked it open and walked out onto the streets of Sarphia. People waved to him in greeting and he acknowledged them all with a smile and tilt of his head.

This Elven city was truly one of beauty, and he felt like he was seeing it through new eyes this night. Shining lights in every tree brilliantly complemented the star-filled sky. White domed palaces and slender spires inlaid with gold captured the lights in radiant reflections. Manicured pathways, lily ponds, and vibrant flowers decorated every estate in a multitude of colors.

He wondered how he overlooked it before. How could he not have appreciated what seemed so undeniable now?

Suddenly feeling anxious, he increased his pace and even began to run, hopping over hedges and low stone walls like a blacktail deer. He was sprinting by the time the house came into sight.

A guard stood at the gates, but recognized him and let him in without question.

Airron hurried up the steps and knocked on the door impatiently. The sound of music drifted to him from the open windows.

A silver-haired butler in servant's livery answered the door and when he saw Airron, wrinkled his nose as if he smelled something unpleasant. "Ah, Master Falewir. What can I do for you?"

"Let me in, Quincy," Airron said and took a step forward.

The man wasn't very big, but he moved in front of Airron and blocked his way. "The Lady is busy with a recital and is not receiving guests at this time. If you will come back—"

"Move."

"Master Falewir, you cannot—"

Airron shoved the man into the marble foyer. Ignoring the butler's protests, Airron strode to the sitting room where he heard the music and pushed open the doors with a bang. The music broke off abruptly and every female violet eye in the room turned his way.

Melania sat before her harp and several Elven ladies dressed in fine attire sipped tea while they watched her play.

Airron only had eyes for the girl at the front of the room. He had never seen a lovelier sight in his life. She was dressed in a blue silk gown, and her silver hair hung loose in soft ringlets around her face. Her hands were still poised on the strings as she stared at him.

Quincy was still mumbling discontentedly behind him, but one of the women—it sounded like Melania's mother—told the butler to quiet down.

Airron started forward up the through the aisle of chairs.

"What are you doing here, Airron Falewir?" Melania finally demanded.

"I choose you."

A gasp rippled through the room.

"You asked me to choose you above all else, and I am doing that now."

"You could not do so before," she pointed out.

"I was a damn bloody fool."

Melania's proud eyes narrowed. "It's too late."

"Like hell it is." Without waiting for another rebuttal, he strode to her side, reached down and lifted her into his arms.

"Put me down!" She struggled against him with her fists, but he held her too tight. He was never letting go of her again.

The women tittered behind their gloved hands, and Melania's mother spoke up. "Oh, darling, stop fussing so! You know you love him!"

The struggles stopped, and she peered up at him from underneath her eyelashes. "I do love him," she confessed, "but the question is, does he really love me?"

"Yes! I was miserable after you left. I nearly got myself killed because thoughts of you filled my head. I do love you, Melania, and I realized the truth of it the moment you walked out of my life."

"Are you sure?"

"I have never been more sure of anything."

She laughed and threw her arms around his neck. "You have much to learn about women, my husband."

"Teach me. I'm a fast learner."

"That is not what Rogan says."

"Dwarves lie."

Amid the snickers of the ladies and the grumbling of the butler, Airron carried his wife from the sitting room and out into the evening air.

"Welcome home, Airron Falewir."

He smiled. "I am home."

# RULING NOBILITY OF MASSA

## ISERLOHN
King Maximus Everard
*House Colors - Black & Scarlet, Sigil - Golden Lions*
Princess Kiernan Everard Atlan
Prince Beck Atlan
Princess Kenley Grace Atlan

### MEN AT ARMS
Darin Morel - Captain, Royal Guard, Personal Guard to King Maximus
Kirby Nash - Captain, Royal Guard, Personal Guard to Kiernan Atlan
Roman Traynor - Captain, Royal Guard, Personal Guard to Beck Atlan
Bo Franck - Captain, Iserlohn Army
Hugo Bassus - Commander, Second, Iserlohn Army

### COURT MEMBERS
Lord Davad Etin
*House Colors - Red & Blue; Sigil - Flying Eagles*
Lord Abram Winslow
*House Colors - White & Gray; Sigil - Crouching Wolves*
Lady Ava Conry
*House Colors - Brown & Black; Sigil - Savage Badgers*
Lady Lillian Knapp
*House Colors - Gray & Purple; Sigil - Shadow Panthers*
Lord Gage Gregaros
*House Colors - Black & White; Sigil - White Tigers*
Lord Johan Hamilton
*House Colors - Red & Yellow; Sigil - Red Dragons*

# RULING NOBILITY OF MASSA

### DEEPSTONE
King Erik Rojin
*House Colors - Blue & Maroon; No Sigil*
Kal Rogan Radek
Kali Janin Radek
Reilly Radek
Jala Radek

#### MEN AT ARMS
Klay Arsten - General, Iron Fists, Personal Guard to King Erik

### HAVENTHAL
King Jerund J'El
*House Colors - Brown & Green; Sigil - Ficus Tree*
Thorn J'El
Airron Falewir

#### MEN AT ARMS
Raine Aubry - First Gladewatcher, Personal Guard to King Jerund
Loren Faolin - Gladewatcher
Leif Oliver - Gardien

# ABOUT THE AUTHOR

Valerie Zambito lives in upstate New York. A great love of world building, character creation and all things magic, led to the publication of her first novel in the epic fantasy series, Island Shifters in 2011 and the Angels of the Knights paranormal series the following year. Please visit **www.valeriezambito.com** for more information.

Book One:  Island Shifters - An Oath of the Blood
Book Two:  Island Shifters - An Oath of the Mage
Book Three:  Island Shifters - An Oath of the Children
Book Four:  Island Shifters - An Oath of the Kings
Angels of the Knights - Fallon
Angels of the Knights - Blane
Angels of the Knights - Nikki